NECROMANIAC

BRYAN CASSIDAY

Bryan Cassiday
Los Angeles
ISBN 9798988189534
Published in the United States of America
First Edition: October 22, 2024

BOOKS BY BRYAN CASSIDAY

Scream of Silence (Demons Book 1)
Burn Hot Burn Long (Apocalypse City Book 2)
Hotbed (Apocalypse City Book 1)
Zombie Apocalypse: The Chad Halverson Series 1–7
Cutthroat Express (Zombie Apocalypse: The Chad Halverson
Series Book 7)
Knot of Fear (Scott Brody Thriller 5)
Threads (Scott Brody Thriller 4)
Electric Green Mambas (Scott Brody Thriller 3)
Horde (Zombie Apocalypse: Chad Halverson Series Book 6)
Ice in the Blood
Crime Blotter USA
Murder LLC (Scott Brody Thriller 2)
Bolt (Scott Brody Thriller 1)
Riptide of Fear
The Payout
Force of Impact (Ethan Carr Thriller 3)
Dying to Breathe (Ethan Carr Thriller 2)
Countdown to Death (Ethan Carr Thriller 1)
The Bus Stops Here—and Other Zombie Tales
Two Moons Rising
Alien Assault
Comes a Chopper
Zombie Apocalypse: The Chad Halverson Series 1–5
Helter Skelter
The Anaconda Complex
The Kill Option
Blood Moon: Thrillers and Tales of Terror
Fete of Death

Chapter 1

Men in animal masks were trying to kill him.

Hog Head was wearing a black silk cassock. In one hand he gripped a pistol, in the other a knife with a foot-long blade. He was climbing up the ladder that led to the trapdoor in the attic floor.

Unable to breathe, terrified, Brady lay paralyzed on his back on the attic floor, watching Hog Head thrust his head through the trapdoor opening. Brady knew he couldn't escape. Hog Head was going to kidnap him and take him to a satanic cult, where the cultists would assault him and sacrifice him to Satan.

A SIG P365 his father had given him was lying on the floor three-odd inches from Brady's hand. He tried to move his hand to grasp the pistol. Nothing doing. His hand wouldn't move.

Hog Head stared at Brady.

Brady's face broke into a sweat as he struggled to reach the pistol just beyond his grasp. His hand wouldn't move. He felt powerless. His eyes popped with fear.

The cult was going to torture him and kill him. He had to defend himself. Yet he couldn't move.

Hog Head trained his pistol on Brady. "Come with me, kid. The supreme leader wants you."

Why couldn't he move?

Hog Head climbed into the attic and towered above Brady.

"Get up and go down the ladder," said Hog Head.

Unable to speak, Brady stared at him.

"Are you listening, kid? Move."

Hog Head used his foot to nudge Brady in the rib cage.

"Get the lead out," said Hog Head.

Brady glanced at the pistol that lay on the floor and tried to reach it with his frozen arm. His arm didn't budge.

Nevertheless, Hog Head kicked the handgun away, noticing that Brady was eying it. It skidded across the hardwood floor and crashed into a suitcase.

Brady tried to scream. He didn't want the cultists to abuse him and kill him in order to sacrifice him to Satan.

Hog Head brandished his knife in front of Brady's terrified face.

"Want me to cut you?" snarled Hog Head. "I'll cut you good. Think I won't? The leader doesn't care if I leave a scar on your face with my knife. As long as you're alive, is all he cares about. We're gonna strip you naked and pass you around the campfire to every member of our cult before we sacrifice you to the Great One." A sinister laugh escaped his lips. "Get the picture? We like 'em young. A ripe ten-year-old like you. Now get your sorry ass up off the floor," he said, motioning with his Glock.

Brady strained every muscle in his body to move, but nothing happened.

Hog Head brought his knife close to Brady's face, a little over an inch from Brady's eyeball.

"I'll cut out one of your eyes," said Hog Head. "How's that sound? I ain't kidding, kid. Get up and go down the ladder."

Brady saw the point of the knife edging closer to his eyeball, the blade flashing in the wash of a single naked light bulb mounted in the ceiling. He could see part of his horrified face staring back at him, reflected off the polished carbon steel blade zeroing in on his eye.

In a cold sweat, Brady jackknifed awake in bed, his eyes bugging out.

Just a dream. He scoped out his bedroom, not seeing anyone in it. He had been remembering events that had taken place eight years ago when he was ten years old.

He had escaped the cult, thanks to his Dad, who had killed the kidnapers and died in the act. However, Brady had not escaped justice.

He was tried for murdering his mother.

The jury didn't buy his explanation that he wasn't the one who had killed his mother, that it was the demon that possessed him who had done the deed. They believed Brady was mad. They found him not guilty by reason of insanity. The judge sentenced him to the Rosehill Asylum for the Criminally Insane, a depressing brick affair with narrow windows even though he was only ten years old at the time of the murder.

Eight years later, when he was legally an adult at the age of eighteen, the authorities at the insane asylum decided to release him, thinking they had cured him of his delusion of being possessed by a bloodthirsty demon named Theresa who had ordered him to shoot his mother to avenge her own murder at the hands of *her* mother, the psychotic and suicidal actor Deirdre Turner.

Brady Carney didn't think he was cured, because he didn't think he was insane in the first place. No matter what the doctors at the insane asylum told him, he knew for certain that Theresa had possessed him at his family's house, previously owned by Deirdre Turner, in the Hollywood Hills and had forced him to kill his mother.

Not that anyone gave a damn about the truth. They were all just doing their jobs.

He remembered his final session with his psychiatrist at Rosehill.

Chapter 2

"Do you admit you murdered your mother, Brady?" asked Dr. Coleman, a middle-aged, goateed man wearing a red cardigan sweater and a black necktie.

His voice displayed little emotion. It sounded almost soothing.

His lumpy face looked like it was molded out of clay. His cheeks hung down past his jawline. He was sitting next to his patient couch, tapping his ballpoint against a yellow legal pad clipped to a Masonite clipboard that lay on his lap.

Brady lay on his back on the couch, listening to the soft clicking of the pen nib against the legal pad that reminded him of a crow pecking at bread crumbs scattered on a concrete sidewalk.

"Yes," he lied.

He knew if he kept telling Coleman the truth that the demon Theresa had possessed him and forced him to fire the gun in his hand to kill Karen in their rental car, the shrink would never agree to release him from the institute for the criminally insane.

"It is vital that you admit your guilt in the murder of Karen," said Coleman. "Otherwise, you are in denial, and you will be imprisoned here until you admit the truth."

"I understand."

"Do you?" said Coleman, scrutinizing Brady's face with suspicious eyes that peered out behind horn-rimmed spectacles. "Being in denial means you remain uncured of your delusions."

"I am not in denial," said Brady.

"If you continue to insist that some demon named Theresa killed your mother, you are in denial. In other words, you are not sane, and I can't approve of your release from this institution."

"OK."

"Be honest with me. Did you or did you not kill Karen, your mother?"

"I killed her," Brady lied.

Coleman stopped tapping his pen nib. His eyes bored into Brady's.

"I must know the truth," said Coleman.

"'What is truth?' said jesting Pilate."

"I don't want to play semantic games with you. When I speak of the truth, do you understand what I mean?"

"I know what happened the night of the murder if that's what you're asking me."

"I want you to be honest. That's what I want from you. Honesty. If you're honest with yourself, you'll be honest with me. Does that make sense?"

"I'm telling you the truth."

"Then you admit you killed your mother?"

Brady didn't answer right away. He wondered if Coleman could somehow tell Brady was lying when he said that he killed his mother. But how could Coleman tell? How could anyone tell for sure when another person was lying?

"Yes, I admit it," said Brady.

"Do you confess you killed her?"

Why did Coleman insist on harping on the subject?

"How many times do I have to answer this?" said Brady.

"Until I'm convinced you believe the truth—that you murdered your own mother in cold blood."

"I fired the bullet that killed her."

"You must see the truth before I can clear you as cured of your delusions and then release you from the institution."

"I understand."

"Let me be clear. Do you understand that you are guilty of murder when you say you fired the shot that killed your mother?"

"Even if Theresa ordered me to fire the shot?"

"Who is Theresa? There is no Theresa. She is a figment you created to take the blame for your commission of murder."

Brady said nothing.

"By creating the figment of Theresa you are demonstrating that you continue to be in denial."

"I didn't create anyone."

"Theresa is a figment your mind conjured to release you from feelings of guilt for your homicidal action. Believing in this imaginary figment proves you're in denial."

"I don't believe in any figments," said Brady, eager to be released from the suffocating confines of the insane asylum.

Theresa wasn't human, he knew. She was a demon that had possessed him the night of his mother's murder.

"Do you know the difference between right and wrong?" said Coleman.

"Yeah."

"Is it right to commit murder?"

"No. Unless I'm a soldier fighting a war. It's all right to kill the enemy in a war. The more enemies I kill, the better."

"We're not talking about war. Do you deny you murdered your mother?"

"I was the one who fired the gun that killed her."

Coleman leaned toward Brady. "Do you feel guilt for murdering her?"

Brady could feel Coleman's warm breath blowing against his cheek. The guy must have eaten garlic and pickles for lunch. Brady disapproved of Coleman's choice of foods.

I didn't kill her. Theresa possessed my body and killed her. I feel no guilt for a murder committed by a demon.

However, Brady knew if he told the truth, Coleman wouldn't release him from Rosehill. Brady couldn't stand this place. He had to get out.

"Do you feel guilt for murdering your mother?" persisted Coleman.

"Yeah," lied Brady, hoping his facial expressions didn't reveal his true feelings.

"Do you admit you were in denial when you claimed that it was the demon, not you, who had murdered your mother?"

Brady nodded yes.

"I want you to speak your answer aloud," said Coleman.

"Yeah," lied Brady.

It was the demon Theresa who had murdered Karen, but he would never be permitted to walk out of here a free man until he lied about Theresa's existence.

Coleman studied Brady's impassive expression, trying to ascertain the veracity of Brady's words.

Brady thought of nothing. No one could read minds, especially if the mind was blank. Or maybe he should build a wall in his mind like George Sanders did in the movie *Village of the Damned* in order to prevent the evil Midwich children from reading his thoughts.

His gaze riveted on Brady, Coleman adjusted his spectacles as if he could increase his visual acuity with a flick of his wrist. He cleared his throat noisily, perhaps trying to convince Brady he had read Brady's mind.

Brady didn't react.

If Brady remained calm, he was convinced Coleman would release him from this dungeon for psychos. Spending too much time among gibbering lunatics could drive you nuts. Brady feared for his sanity if he was forced to stay at Rosehill much longer. Living in the real world was bad enough, but living with homicidal maniacs was worse. One wrong word or expression could result in an enraged inmate beating your face to a pulp or slitting your throat with a cafeteria plastic knife.

Chapter 3

To Brady's chagrin Coleman wasn't done with his interrogation.

"Why were you sitting in the car with your murdered mother when the police arrived at your house?" he said.

"I don't understand your question," said Brady.

"Why didn't you run away and try to escape after you killed her? The police said you had plenty of time to escape, but instead you sat in your car with her dead body."

Because I didn't kill her. Theresa did.

Brady realized he couldn't tell Coleman the truth without ruining his chances for release from the asylum. He had to come up with a plausible answer.

"I was too stunned by what I had done to do anything," he said.

"Why did you kill her?"

"Because . . ."

"Yes?" said Coleman, all ears, cocking his head toward Brady.

"Because she threatened to kill me."

Coleman nodded. "The police have a record of you filing a report about her threatening to kill you. Is that what you're referring to?"

"Yeah."

He hadn't told the cops the rest of the story. That his mother was possessed by a demon and wasn't acting like herself. He didn't think this was the right time to bring up her possession to Coleman, who didn't believe in demons. Brady's only route of escape from the asylum lay in not bringing up demonic possession and instead taking full responsibility for the murder of his mother.

"You felt in danger of losing your life at your mother's hands," said Coleman. "Is that correct?"

"It is."

"Do you believe your fear of her gave you the right to murder her?"

"Uh . . ."

Brady didn't know how to answer. Coleman wanted him to take full responsibility for Karen's murder. If Brady claimed self-defense, wasn't that tantamount to refusing to take responsibility for his actions, i.e., blaming them on someone else?

"Uh . . . I believe I have the right to defend myself from somebody trying to kill me," he said at last.

"Was Karen trying to kill you when you shot her?"

"No," he said, which was true.

"Then you had no right to kill her."

"Correct."

"And you are guilty of murder. Yes or no?"

"Yeah," lied Brady.

"Because you were of sound mind when you pulled the trigger. You were not possessed by a so-called demon called Theresa."

Brady nodded yes even though what Coleman had said was untrue.

"You didn't try to run away after you had killed your mother because you were overwhelmed by crippling guilt. Is that not so?"

"Yeah."

"You, not some demon called Theresa, murdered your mother in cold blood."

"Yeah," muttered Brady.

Coleman leaned back in his chair. "If you have seen the error of your ways, you are not in denial, in which case I can get you released from here because you were only ten at the time you committed matricide and you've already served eight years."

Music to Brady's ears. He hoped Coleman was leveling with him.

"Let's be clear on this," said Coleman. "You confess to killing your mother."

"She wasn't my mother," Brady heard himself say, though he hadn't intended to say it.

He knew the truth, that his mother had been possessed by a demon when they had lived in the cursed house in the Hollywood Hills. But if he wanted to get out of the bughouse, he couldn't reveal that she had been possessed.

"What?" said Coleman, widening his eyes in disbelief. "The police took her fingerprints. There can be no question as to her identity. She was Karen Carney, your mother."

Brady rubbed his forehead, trying to think up a plausible explanation for his statement.

"I mean, she wasn't acting like herself when we were living at that house," he said.

"Hmm," said Coleman, stroking his goatee.

His pulse accelerating, Brady couldn't tell if Coleman had bought his explanation. Brady didn't know what he would do if he had to spend another day in this madhouse. He was already crawling up the walls. He might tie some sheets together and hang himself from a lamp fixture in the ceiling.

Leaning forward, Coleman drummed a tattoo on his desktop, studying Brady's face. "I see. But do you admit that she was your mother, that you did indeed murder her?"

"It was me. I fired the bullet that killed her."

Coleman stopped drumming his fingers and straightened in his chair.

"Do you feel remorse for your actions?" he said.

"I feel sorry for killing her."

Coleman nodded with satisfaction.

To get released from this rat's nest, Brady had to play the shrink's game. The purpose of the game was to get Brady to confess to murder even though it wasn't true. The truth was Brady had been possessed by the demon Theresa at the time of the murder and therefore could not be held responsible for matricide. Such an explanation was unacceptable to Coleman, who required him to accept guilt for committing murder before Coleman freed him.

"If you are released, how do you plan on atoning for your crime?" asked Coleman.

"I—I—don't know."

"Have you given it any thought?"

"I—I'm not sure when I'm gonna be allowed to go free. I haven't thought about what I'm gonna do afterwards."

Staring at Brady, Coleman inserted his pen in his mouth and clamped his teeth on it like a dog worrying a drumstick.

Brady couldn't figure out what Coleman's gesture meant. Was Coleman not satisfied with Brady's answer about his future plans?

What was he supposed to answer? Was he supposed to say he would go to church every day and pray for forgiveness even though he wasn't religious? He had no idea what kind of answer Coleman was expecting. The hell with it. Brady couldn't figure out a lie that would satisfy Coleman's question. He said nothing, watching Coleman gnaw the pen in his mouth.

"I see," said Coleman, whipping his saliva-coated pen out of his mouth and letting loose a disarming yawn. "You're not telling me what you think I want you to say to get released, are you?"

"No."

"Good. Because that doesn't work with me. I can tell if you're lying."

"Right."

"It's all about knowing the difference between right and wrong and taking responsibility for your action. That's what sanity is. When I deem you sane, I will order your release."

"I understand."

"You also should feel guilt for committing murder. If you don't, you're a sociopath and shouldn't be released from here."

"I feel guilt."

"Your creation of the figment Theresa landed you in hot water," said Coleman. "However, I understand that you were under duress after committing the murder, and it was traumatizing your psyche. Which is why the judge committed you to an asylum where you could recover."

"I have recovered," said Brady, determined to get his walking papers.

"I don't want you to have a relapse if we release you."

"That won't happen."

"Excellent. Now I need to know what you're going to do in the outside world if you're released."

Brady thought about it. "I want to find out why evil exists in the world."

"Interesting. What if there is no why?"

"There must be a reason. Everything has a reason."

"Philosophers have been debating the subject since the beginning of time, and none of them agree on a reason. Don't become disillusioned if you can't find the answer. Good luck."

Chapter 4

Brady couldn't believe he was free.

Even though he knew he didn't belong in the bedlam called Rosehill that he had called home for eight years, he had thought he would never get out. The screams of lunatics in padded cells resonating through the corridors of the asylum would forever be with him in his dreams and in his memories.

He wasn't on easy street by any means. Now that he was discharged from the asylum, he had to find a way to support himself.

He hadn't learned a trade in the bughouse. The staff was too busy injecting him with drugs to control his "psychosis" to teach him a trade. The truth was they didn't teach vocations at Rosehill for the simple fact that it wasn't a vocational school. They had their hands full controlling their patients with drugs.

How could he earn a living?

He was walking down Sunset Boulevard in West Hollywood when he passed a shop advertising a medium. He paused in front of the picture window, where a sign stenciled on the glass in white cursive letters explained that the medium was in touch with the spirit world and could contact deceased relatives for customers. Which gave Brady pause.

Why couldn't he contact the deceased? He had already had contact with the spirit of Deirdre Turner's daughter Theresa. If he was receptive to Theresa, why wouldn't he be receptive to other spirits of the deceased? He had the gift to communicate with the dead. Why not make a living at it like the ill-fated occultist Dr. Rudolph Armitage, who had worked for Brady's mother.

Brady knew the drill for exorcising a possessed house, having witnessed it firsthand at his former house in the Hollywood Hills. All you had to do was smudge it with sage to free it from a demon. True, it didn't work at his house which was possessed by a uniquely powerful demon, but it should work for most houses, according to Armitage. If the sage didn't work, Brady could always hold a séance to exorcise a haunted house. He was convinced he had the gift to contact spirits of the dead, as evidenced by his contact with Theresa's spirit.

Wearing a bright cadmium yellow and fluorescent lime aloha shirt unbuttoned to reveal his grizzled chest hair, a five-eight middle-aged man with a white beard and a nicotine-stained white mustache exited the shop and approached Brady.

"Can I help you?" said the man, unleashing a toothy grin, "Are you in need of contacting an ancestral spirit? I am Manfred the Medium at your service."

"Are you a professional medium?"

"I am indeed," said Manfred, reeking of patchouli.

Brady cleared his throat. "Ah, do you know the occultist Rudolph Armitage?"

"I did, actually. The poor bastard. His life was a tragedy. The world is a horrible place for some people. An endless chain of calamities that never cease. Armitage was one of those people who can't buy a break for love or money."

"Doesn't he have an office around here?" said Brady, scoping the neighborhood.

"He used to. He was murdered eight years ago. A cult member slit the poor bastard's throat. It was horrific. It was in all the papers. How could you miss it?"

"I've been away for the last eight years. Was he a good medium?" said Brady, eager to change the subject from himself.

"He was, but I'm better. Not that I'm bragging, but honesty goes a long way in this business." Manfred leaned closer to Brady and whispered, "There's a lot of fraud in the world of mediums, since they deal with the supernatural, which most people can't understand or see."

Brady nodded yes. "Do mediums have a lot of competition?"

"It's dog eat dog. Especially in this location. We're in great demand by the movie people. They're all tuned into the spirit world and the great beyond. They're in the know, and they want to make contact. The folks here are more spiritual than elsewhere. Maybe it's because of all the horror movies they make. I dunno." Manfred grinned. "What I do know is they have shitloads of money and they're glad to part with it."

"I hear ya."

Manfred squinted at Brady's face. "Don't I know you? Do you live around here? You look familiar."

"No," said Brady hurriedly and strode away.

He didn't want to be recognized as the kid who had shot his mother. He wasn't sure anyone could recognize him now that he had aged eight years since the murder. He was much taller and ganglier than he used to be, and his face had become more masculine. It used to be rounder and fleshier when he was an innocent kid. Now it had angles to it which made it appear gaunt with a knobby Adam's apple beneath it.

He would need to change his name when he went into business for himself as a psychic.

He stopped in his tracks on the sidewalk in front of a clothing boutique, lost in his thoughts.

Or maybe not. Would it help his career if prospective clients knew he had been involved in the cult assault on a haunted house? But they would also know he had been charged with murdering his mother and had done time for it in a loony bin. Would people forgive him since he had been punished for his crime? Maybe. But probably more people might want him to be incarcerated for life and would stay away from his business in droves.

If he advertised himself as the person who was possessed by a demon who told him to murder his mother, the Rosehill authorities might throw him back in the bughouse, realizing he had lied to them about his so-called cure. Or did they have the power to commit him again after they had released him? He wasn't sure of the law, but he didn't think they could recommit him if they thought he had lied to them to get released. He wasn't going to worry about the loony bin screws anymore. To avoid any problem with the Rosehill authorities he would use a phony name when he put out his shingle as a psychic.

Still, he figured clients would shy away from him if they knew he had killed his mother even if he was possessed at the time. Hiring a matricide would rub them the wrong way. He would leave out the murder when he advertised himself.

He resumed walking down Sunset, turning over his options.

If he billed himself as someone who had been possessed, would-be clients would believe he could contact spirits and therefore be persuaded to hire him instead of, say, Manfred the

Medium. It was the only sales gimmick Brady could think of. He had nothing else he could use for self-promotion as a medium. He didn't have a PhD in parapsychology like Professor Armitage. Yet Brady knew he could get in touch with the spirit world, because Theresa had possessed him when he was ten.

All Brady needed now was a name for himself.

Brady the Psychic didn't have much of a ring to it, nor did Brady the Medium, nor Brady the Exorcist. He settled on Brady the Believer, a spiritualist who specialized in exorcisms. After all, he was a believer in demons after having been possessed by one named Theresa.

Chapter 5

Because of her dreadful experiences in life Libby had taken refuge in a crematorium, the Elysian Fields Forever Crematorium to be exact. She supposed it was a rule of thumb that such people as herself who led wretched lives gravitated toward nunneries. But Libby wasn't a believer. She didn't believe in a deity that was making sure goodness prevailed in the end and all was right with the world. Her experience in life had taught her otherwise.

She chose a crematorium as a refuge because nobody visited them except morticians and others in the death business who delivered her corpses to be fed to the cremation chamber.

They wanted nothing from her besides leaving their cadavers at her door. It suited her fine. The less she saw of people, the better.

She was thirty-three. She had started this job three years ago after her life had taken a turn for the worse and she had realized people were more corrupt than she could have imagined and were to be avoided. She shortened her at-the-time long brunette hair to a pageboy cut and set up shop at the crematorium.

She was five seven and kept herself in good shape. She kept a set of weights in the office and adhered to a daily regimen of lifting every morning. In point of fact, she didn't do a lot of lifting in her job. The workers from the funeral parlors offloaded the corpses from their hearses in makeshift wooden coffins designed to burn easily and placed them in position on the cart that she used to transport them to the conveyor belt in front of the oven.

Seymour Hemlock, the erstwhile manager of the crematorium, was an aging hunchback with a cast to his eye who abhorred people and took malicious joy in feeding their corpses to the furnace in revenge for the way people had treated him in life. Maybe he had let her manage the business because he saw a kindred spirit in her. However, he was wrong about her. She didn't hate people like he did. She distrusted them, because she had been burned too many times. She didn't yearn to fry everybody alive like Hemlock. She just wanted to be left alone.

He had hired her as a bookkeeper, because she was a college graduate. She didn't have any accounting experience, but he figured that she, as a college grad, could handle a desk job.

Libby didn't know for sure why he had hired her. He never hit on her. The only interest he showed in women was in their corpses. She had worked for him as his assistant for a little over a year when he had told her he was going to retire and let her manage the business. Libby didn't have to think twice before voicing her acceptance of his offer.

She had no life outside the crematorium. In her leisure time she read horror novels and watched horror movies on TV. Some days she felt like she was missing something in life, such as the companionship of a good friend. But she knew good friends were hard to come by in the corrupt world she had experienced when she had made the social circuit. In the end, she couldn't trust anyone. There were just too many scammers and other criminals in California, and for some unknown reason they seemed to gravitate toward her.

She granted there was the possibility she was paranoid. At least, other people might think she was, but they hadn't suffered the way she had at the hands of others. Or was she imagining that other people had it better than she had? If it was true they were getting burned like her, why did they continue to gravitate toward each other, unless it was like moths to a flame? She had to figure they had it better than her when it came to socializing.

On reflection it didn't matter. What mattered was she came to the realization she wasn't going to advance up the social ladder. She couldn't explain why that was the case. But the fact was, people kept torpedoing her life. The only way she could prevent them from doing so was to stay away from them.

So be it.

The less people she saw the better. Her relationships with people caused nothing but trouble. Here in the crematorium she could sit by herself and wait for the delivery of the next cadaver to be incinerated. And she could make a living doing it.

Not that she was rich. Far from it. She didn't have a Lamborghini parked in her carport. But she could pay her rent on time and buy groceries at the supermarket. And after a day at work she could afford subscribing to a couple of streaming services like Shudder and Screambox, which both showed horror movies.

True, it was a thankless job with no future, but so what? She wasn't a ruthless social climber who enjoyed trampling over people to get to the top rung of the ladder.

Incinerating cadavers wasn't a job a lot of people would like, but it suited her fine. Most people wanted to forget the fact that their futures included death, whereas she was reminded of it every day at work. It didn't faze her.

To Libby it was a kind of comfort to know her days were numbered. She wouldn't have to suffer at the hands of other people bent on her demise after she shuffled off this mortal coil.

Being around corpses unnerved most people. But not Libby. Not a day went by when she wasn't around at least one stiff. On busy days she dealt with scores of dead meat. They didn't scare her. They were dead. It was the living who scared her. They were the ones who could, and did, wreak havoc on her life.

Busy days had their drawbacks.

On days when business was booming, she could smell the stench of burning flesh, because she had to keep opening and closing the furnace to keep feeding corpses into it. Frequently opening the furnace allowed the stench of burning flesh to percolate into the crematorium despite the presence of an industrial-sized fan placed strategically in the building.

Most days, however, she didn't notice the stench, as it exited through the chimney into the sky like it was supposed to, and the fan wasn't needed, which she saved for hot days when fetid odors lingered in the warm summer air.

Today business was on the slow side. It gave her time to think about her dreadful life in the so-called real world, where she had learned there was no justice. No such thing as karma. For her, life was all bad luck and grief. The law was a joke, and perpetrators of evil rarely got their just desserts. She had found out the truth the hard way.

She felt safe in the crematorium, because nobody wanted to be reminded of death. Hence, nobody visited crematoriums. She had the place all to herself.

She was sitting behind her desk in her small office watching *Night of the Living Dead* on a seven-inch portable TV that sat on her desktop when she heard knocking coming from the furnace. She started.

She bolted out of her chair to the furnace door.

It could be the heating elements in the furnace that were making the racket. When they heated or cooled off they sometimes caused a din. But she hadn't burned a single corpse in the furnace today. It didn't make sense that the elements would be clanking this morning.

She heard the clanking again. It was definitely coming from the furnace.

A horrifying thought struck her.

Was a corpse in the furnace? A corpse that hadn't died even though the mortician had assured her that the corpses he supplied her with were dead? Could he have been mistaken about one of his stiffs? Had he come by before she had arrived at work and loaded a cadaver into the furnace without her knowledge? But how could he get through the locked door?

The poor victim could be suffocating even now as they lay on the retort slab waiting in horror to be incinerated. They could be signaling somebody to free them.

Her heartbeat racing, Libby pelted to the computer and pressed the button to open the furnace door.

As the ceramic and steel door hummed open, she peered into the oven lined with silicon carbide heat-resistant bricks. Nervously expecting to see a person suffocating on the slab, she inspected the interior.

She saw no one.

The oven was empty.

She sighed with relief. False alarm. It was a nightmare she had often—that one of the cadavers she had loaded into the furnace was still alive when she initiated the incineration. Not today. She breathed easier now.

Then what was that noise she had heard emanating from the furnace earlier? Maybe she had imagined it. But she didn't think so. Could the noise she had heard have been issuing from the zombie movie she had been watching? Again she didn't think so. She was convinced the noise's source had been the furnace.

Shaking her head in confusion, using the computer, she powered shut the furnace door.

She retreated to her office and froze in her tracks. She heard the knocking again. She wheeled around and eyeballed the furnace door. The sound was issuing from the furnace. She couldn't get her head around it. The furnace was empty. She had just inspected it. Nobody could be trapped inside it.

Maybe there was something wrong with the equipment. It shouldn't be clanking, especially when it wasn't in use. It hadn't been used once today.

The clanking stopped.

She would have to have the machine inspected. It must be broken.

It was strange, though, and, she had to admit, unnerving that it was clanking. She had never heard the furnace make that sound before. She hoped the furnace wasn't getting ready to explode.

Well, nothing lasted forever. Machines broke down sooner or later.

She returned to her desk, sat behind it, and resumed watching the zombie movie.

The clanking recommenced.

She stiffened in her seat. The noise was definitely not coming from the movie. She launched herself out of her seat to the furnace.

The noise was coming from inside the empty furnace.

She produced her cell phone and called the furnace repairman. There was no way she was going to listen to that clanking all day long. She would pay him extra to get him to arrive as soon as possible.

It sounded for all the world like someone trapped inside the furnace was hammering one of the silicon carbide brick walls with some sort of iron tool like a wrench.

She wasn't going to open the furnace again. She already knew it was empty. Nobody was trapped inside it.

She wished the noise would stop, though. It was getting on her nerves.

She heard the doorbell ringing.

She hoped it was the furnace repairman.

24

Chapter 6

Libby opened the front door.

"We got a delivery from the Westland Funeral Parlor," said a fortysomething guy in a grey uniform.

Beginning to lose his hair with a receding hairline, he compensated for it with thick whiskers on his round face. Cauliflower ears bracketed his head. A uniformed Hispanic guy some ten years younger with a hatchet face stood behind him looking bored. Libby could see his shaved head over the first guy's broad shoulder.

"I wasn't expecting a delivery from Westland today," said Libby, noticing their black hearse parked in the driveway with its tailgate open, exposing the casket inside.

"They don't tell me anything. My name's Bellini. I just follow orders."

"OK."

"Do you have a cart to transport the casket?"

"At the side door. I'll open it for you."

Both of the men were wearing purple industrial nitrile gloves. She had never seen either of the men before. She hadn't received a delivery from Westland for quite a while.

Libby reentered the crematorium. Tandy the tabby cat came bounding toward her, meowing. He rubbed against her leg, looking expectant.

"I can't feed you now, Tandy. You have to wait."

Libby retrieved the cart that was standing next to the furnace and wheeled it toward the side entrance. The cart had a series of steel rollers on top of it which made it easier to load and offload coffins.

She opened the side door, where the workmen were waiting for her.

They wheeled the cart to the hearse and loaded the wooden casket containing the corpse onto it. Bellini withdrew a tan pressboard clipboard from the back of the hearse and laid it on top of the casket. He and his assistant rolled the cart back to the side entrance.

Bellini handed Libby the clipboard that secured several papers under its clip. "Could you fill out these forms, affirming you received the delivery of the package?"

"Sure," said Libby, fishing out a pen from her purse.

She flinched when she heard the clanking commotion in the furnace start up behind her.

"Do either of you know how to fix a furnace?" she said.

"No way, José," said Bellini. "They don't pay me enough to handle two jobs. Hell, they don't even pay me enough for one job," he said, a crooked smile cracking his face.

Nodding, she set to filling out forms on the clipboard.

"Did you drop the corpse off at the other building for inspection so they could remove all steel from the body?" she said.

"They removed the rings and stuff," said Bellini.

He peered through the side door into the crematorium at the furnace.

"Looks spooky in there," he said. "Doesn't it creep you out being locked inside this mausoleum all the time?"

"No," said Libby, signing a form.

"Don't you have any help?"

"I can manage."

"Cooped up inside this dreary place with a bunch of stiffs. I dunno. Most people wouldn't like your job."

"I'm not most people," she said, signing another form on the clipboard.

The furnace clanked louder.

"What's that noise?" said Bellini.

"The furnace."

"I'd have it looked at before using it again."

"The last cadaver I had in there weighed over three hundred pounds. Maybe he broke the furnace."

"Could be," said Bellini, nodding, his face doleful. "How did you get him into the furnace by yourself?"

"I rolled the cart to the furnace door. No problem."

"Let the machines do the work. That's what I always say."

"He was a serial killer shanked in the throat by a fellow inmate who took an instant dislike to him."

"A con killed the Milwaukee Cannibal in the joint too," said Bellini's cohort, nodding. "Live by the sword, die by the sword."

Bellini stared at Libby. "You get convicts shipped here?"

"We get all kinds," said Libby, skimming another form on the clipboard.

Bellini shook his head. "You couldn't pay me to do your job."

"Why not? He was dead."

"Ghosts, lady."

She looked up from the clipboard at him. "You believe in ghosts?"

Bellini laughed. "I was pulling your leg." He paused. "But still I don't know how you sleep at night, doing what you do day in and day out. Just looking at that brick furnace bums me out. Reminds me of Hitler's gas chambers. And you're here looking at it day after day. Don't you have nightmares?"

"I don't believe in ghosts. I sleep like a baby."

"She has cojones," said the other deliverer.

"How would *you* know, Alejandro?" said Bellini, his face smug.

"You couldn't get me to spend even one day in this place," said Alejandro, nodding at the crematorium. "Probably rats in there and everything else."

"Tandy takes care of the rats," said Libby.

She saw Tandy scamper away from the side door into the interior of the crematorium when he spotted the two deliverers. He didn't like strangers.

"I bet you don't sleep here at night," said Alejandro.

"Actually, I do," said Libby.

"No, no," said Alejandro, worry creasing his brow.

Bellini laughed. "He scares easy. He won't even watch horror movies. He's never seen *Nightmare on Elm Street* or *The Texas Chainsaw Massacre*."

"It's not true that I haven't seen a horror movie. I saw *The Crawling Eye* on TV."

Bellini chuckled.

"How does he deal with transporting stiffs for a living?" said Libby.

"I *deliver* them," said Alejandro. "I don't *look* at them. They're in sealed coffins by the time I get them."

Libby signed another form and kept it for herself.

"Everything looks in order," she said, handing the clipboard back to Bellini.

"Mr. Deng is officially in your custody now," said Bellini. "Whatever happens to him now is on you."

Bellini and Alejandro returned to their hearse, shut its tailgate, and drove out of the driveway, blasting AC/DC's "Highway to Hell" on the radio.

Chapter 7

Libby eyed the casket. It was much smaller than the serial killer's. The furnace should be able to handle it without incident.

The question was, was the furnace out of order? Just because it was clanking didn't necessarily mean it wasn't working. The heating elements could be cooling off. Perhaps they had become overheated due to the enormous size of the previous cadaver of the serial killer which had crammed the retort.

She had no idea when the repairman would arrive.

She rolled the cart containing the casket to the oven door.

She didn't like the idea of sitting around waiting with the corpse in the room for the repairman. The corpse would start to stink up the place.

Seeing that the deliverers had left, Tandy darted to Libby's leg and fell to rubbing against it, yowling for food.

"Hold your horses," said Libby, gazing down at Tandy, who was looking up at her with crystalline lime eyes.

Libby thought she could smell the cadaver already. It was a noxious odor. She wasn't sure where it was coming from. It smelled worse than rotting garbage. She felt like throwing up. It must have been coming from the stiff because she hadn't smelled it before the deliverers had arrived. She screwed up her face on account of the stench.

If the mephitic odor was emanating from the corpse, the obvious solution to eradicating it was disposing of the corpse.

Libby decided to start the cremation process. She opened the oven with the computer.

She lined up the cart to feed the coffin onto the conveyor belt that led into the furnace.

Libby donned flamingo pink nitrile gloves. She wasn't planning on removing the cadaver from the casket, but you could never be too careful when handling dead people.

She raised one end of the cart with the press of a red plastic button on the right side of the cart, making it easier for her to push the coffin down the steel rollers onto the conveyor belt that fed the oven.

The casket was made of combustible wood and had no other function than to contain the corpse and burn easily along with its contents.

She loaded the casket into the oven and closed the retort door. She initiated the cremation process with the flick of a button on the computer console. The retort roared to life. It seemed to be operating fine despite the clanking it had made earlier.

She didn't hear Tandy. Where had he gone? She cast around the crematorium for him.

Her heart stopped.

She hadn't enclosed Tandy inside the oven with the cadaver by accident, had she? Had he somehow crawled inside the oven without her seeing him. She wanted to scream.

"Tandy," she cried.

Should she turn off the oven? It was too late now. The retort would already be hot enough to kill a cat.

"Tandy," she cried again. "Come here."

Tandy darted out of the kitchenette and bundled toward her, expecting food.

Grasping her chest, Libby fetched a sigh of relief.

"Where were you? You almost gave me a heart attack." She lifted Tandy and pressed him against her chest. "Don't scare me like that again."

Libby eyed the retort. Everything seemed to be functioning without a hitch. The cremation process would take about two hours.

She put Tandy down, and they made a beeline for the kitchenette.

"Is that all you think about? Food?"

Chapter 8

Not only did she have an office here, she had a kitchenette, a bathroom, and a bedroom. The bedroom had a TV and a bookcase stuffed with books, mostly thrillers and horror novels. In the main room—she could hardly call it a "living room" in a crematorium—she had placed an antique grandfather clock, a gift from her mother.

Standing against the wall in its imposing grandeur, the clock nevertheless added an appealing cozy charm to an otherwise dreary brick-walled chamber. It also reminded her that her time on earth was running out, no matter how young she was. Her future was a rocky road that would inevitably lead back here to the oven no matter how long it took to return. It was only a matter of time before she became just another product of the cremation chamber, a pile of ashes to be poured into an urn.

She took it in stride. Death was part of life. She accepted death and kept on living.

The crematorium was her home. She couldn't afford the rent in this part of town anyway. She had everything she needed here. Why did she need an apartment?

It wasn't like she was doing a lot of entertaining. She wasn't doing any. The only way to avoid the omnipresent corruption in the world was to seek isolation. Here she was isolated save for the deliveries of cadavers that needed burning.

Who in their right mind would want to pay a social visit to a crematorium? Nobody. And that was the way Libby liked it. The corrupt world wanted nothing to do with her as long as she stayed in the crematorium.

She owned a laptop with an Internet connection. For the most part she didn't use the Internet because it was rife with scammers who swamped cyberspace with their pernicious ads that enticed the unwary with toxic lies, ripping off customers or worse. What could you expect? The Internet was created to separate people from their money or to make it easier to do so. Its expertise was marketing. Most sellers were more or less honest. But, as they did everywhere, predators ruled. She didn't use to be so cynical until Ed Grainger had turned her life upside down.

Grainger was an evil genius at using the Internet's Dark Web to enable him to perpetrate his crimes, investing in Mexican cartels that peddled narcotics and engaged in human trafficking. He was a monster that a corrupt society had let loose on the world.

Libby cleared her mind of the cancerous memory of Grainger. Dwelling on the creep accomplished nothing. It only served to infuriate her. What infuriated her even more was her inability to do anything about him, to get anything resembling justice.

She hoped she would live long enough to see the day justice was doled out to him, but her hope was fading. She was feeling more and more certain Grainger had gotten away with murder and would never pay for his crimes.

She opened a can of cat food for the bright-eyed Tandy and spooned it onto his ceramic plate that lay on the Formica countertop. Libby lowered the plate to Tandy. Watching her eagerly, Tandy yowled and rose on his hind paws to swipe a paw at Libby's hand that held the dish.

"Is this what you want?" she said.

Tandy meowed.

Libby placed the dish on the kitchenette linoleum floor.

Purring like an idling Porsche 911, Tandy scarfed down the fish-scented food.

Libby watched him, smiling. Until she heard the clanking of the furnace.

Tensing, she bolted to the retort and surveyed it, making sure there was nothing untoward about the machine. Everything looked OK. She scoped out the furnace's computer monitor. No error messages.

She sniffed that noisome odor again. It was sickening. It wasn't burning flesh. While the furnace was operating, its door had an airtight seal. The stench was coming from elsewhere.

The machine clanked two more times and became silent except for the humming it made as its flames consumed the cadaver inside its belly.

Shaking her head in puzzlement at the cause of the clanking, Libby returned to the kitchenette. When she set eyes on Tandy, who was scarfing down her food, Libby felt the sudden urge to reach for the carving knife inserted in the knife block on the counter and chop off Tandy's head.

She cut across the floor and snatched the knife from the block. Knife in hand, she approached Tandy, who was absorbed in the gobbling of his meal. She glared at him and reached toward him with the knife, fixing to slice off his head with the ten-inch blade.

She caught herself at the last minute and backed away from him in shock. What the hell was she doing? Feeling nauseous she inserted the knife back into the knife block on the counter.

Tandy finished his meal and moseyed out of the kitchenette, licking his chops.

Libby couldn't believe what she had almost done. She hurriedly washed her hands off, as if she could clear her mind of evil thoughts by cleaning her hands.

The furnace clanked again.

"Oh, shut up," she yelled at it, out of sorts.

She needed to get a hold of herself. She would never do anything to harm Tandy. She loved animals. How could she even think of killing Tandy? The thought of harming Tandy caused her to shiver with dread.

What was wrong with her? Was she coming down with Covid or something? She felt her forehead with the back of her wrist. She didn't feel like she had a fever.

Maybe she was spending too much time alone. Could she be having these horrible thoughts because she didn't socialize? But why would she want to take it out on her cat? It made no sense. She was acting out of character. Until now she had never in her life dreamed of harming an animal, especially her own pet.

Maybe she needed a shrink. Not that she could afford one. But her head must be messed up.

She had to stop thinking of Ed Grainger. She had started harboring evil thoughts when she had remembered him and his vile criminal act. Thinking of him never failed to inflame her.

She took a deep breath to calm herself down and eyeballed the furnace as it did its job. Other than its occasional uncharacteristic clanking, it was operating as normal.

Sometimes she felt like she was walking a tightrope over a chasm of bedlam. At times like these, she wondered what kept her going. Somehow she soldiered on by looking forward to a sunnier day in the future. She wasn't a Pollyanna by any means. But you couldn't walk with a dark cloud over your head forever. You would go nuts or blow your brains out.

Stinking thinking never solved anything.

She was sick of thinking.

Arms akimbo, she stood in front of the furnace and listened to it doing its job.

She consoled herself with the idea that she was doing something important—aiding grieving relatives by cremating their deceased loved ones. Nobody could accuse her of being a scammer like most everybody else. For her it was an honest day's work for an honest day's pay, meager though it was.

But who wanted to be rich? Everybody, of course, including her. But the problem with being rich was it attracted every scammer in the book. Scammers preyed on the rich, smothering them and sucking their blood like mosquitoes.

She could do without the scammers, thank you. As long as she didn't go bonkers being alone with corpses all the time.

As a matter of fact, she could already be in the process of going bonkers, thinking about slicing Tandy's head off. What was that all about? She shivered with anxiety.

Chapter 9

Libby walked after Tandy with the intent of calming him down. Strangers always stressed him out.

The better part of six feet away from him she noticed with a start that it was freezing in this section of the crematorium. It was so cold she could see her breath vaporizing when she exhaled.

She continued walking. The temperature returned to normal.

She backtracked to the cold spot and figured it measured two square feet.

How bizarre. She had never noticed it before. Did it have something to do with the clanking furnace? How could it? She didn't see the connection. It was in the seventies outside. It shouldn't be anywhere near this cold inside the crematorium, especially with the furnace in operation.

Maybe the furnace repairman could figure it out.

The overhead lights flashed on and off.

"Uh-oh," she said, looking up at the lights.

Had she overloaded a fuse when she had turned on the furnace? The furnace had never blown a fuse before. Why now? Everything seemed to be going haywire at the same time. *Furnace guy, where are you?*

She returned to her office to file the forms she had received from the deliverers.

On her way to the office she heard the doorbell ring.

She halted, turned around, and made for the front door, expecting to see the furnace repairman.

She opened the door.

It wasn't the repairman.

It was her friend Jackie, or should she say her *only* friend Jackie? Jackie was the only one who didn't think Libby was strange for working at a crematorium.

Chapter 10

At five ten Jackie de Matteo was tall for a woman. She never felt comfortable about her height. Towering over most women made her feel self-conscious. She didn't have the looks to be a fashion model, nor did she have the stately bearing of one. Instead she felt awkward. In her midthirties she was tall enough to play guard on a women's basketball team, but she didn't have the coordination to excel in sports.

"Hello," she said, wearing distressed jeans and a short-sleeved, baggy coral sweatshirt.

"Hi, Jackie," said Libby. "What brings you here?"

"I was in the neighborhood. I thought I'd drop by. Are you busy?"

"I'm cremating a corpse," said Libby, glancing behind her at the humming furnace.

"Sounds like fun," said Jackie, looking ill.

"All in a day's work."

"I'll come back another time if you want," said Jackie, turning to leave.

"Come in. The machine is doing all the work."

"Well, OK. I won't stay long."

Jackie entered the crematorium and looked around.

"Don't you get bummed out, working here every day?" she said, her spirits dampened by the gloomy environs. "A little warm in here."

"It's the furnace. But it's not warm everywhere."

"What do you mean?"

"Follow me."

Libby led her to the cold spot in the crematorium.

"Where are we going?" said Jackie.

"Stand here," said Libby, pointing to the area where she had felt like she was freezing.

Puzzled, Jackie did so.

"Brrr," she said, rubbing her arms in front of her chest. "It feels like an icebox. Is the A/C on over here?"

"This building doesn't have an A/C."

Jackie exhaled a cone of grey mist. "Then why's it so cold?"

"Beats me. I'm glad you can feel it. I thought I might be imagining it."

"Is this the first time you noticed it?" said Jackie, stepping away from the cold zone.

"Yep."

"I wonder how it got there."

"I dunno, but I wish it would go away. It's creepy."

"You need to get out of this place more often. Dealing with dead bodies every day. Jeez. I don't know how you handle it. Isn't it bummer city?"

"I don't mind. I'm making a living. That's the important thing. And I'm pretty much my own boss. That's important too."

Jackie nodded. "Bosses are a pain, namely, my editor. Half of my headlines he throws out."

Libby didn't have a living room to entertain guests. Instead she led Jackie to the kitchenette, modestly appointed with a small butcher block table and two cane chairs.

"Let's sit down," said Libby. "Want a cup of coffee?"

"Sure. I came over because I was wondering if you wanted to see a movie with me."

Libby poured two cups of coffee, set them on the table, and sat down opposite Jackie.

"What movie?" said Libby.

"It's the restored uncut print for the British horror movie *The Wicker Man*. They're showing it at the Nuart."

"The one with Edward Woodward and Christopher Lee?"

"Yeah."

"I saw it once on cable. But I don't know if it was cut or not."

"It's batshit good. The uncut version is supposed to be the best."

"You already saw it?"

"A long time ago, but it was the cut version on TV. I'll never forget the ending."

The furnace started clanking even louder than before.

Jackie jumped in her seat. "What's that?"

Libby glared out of the kitchenette at the furnace. "It's that damn furnace."

Chapter 11

"Does the furnace always do that when it's on?" asked Jackie.

"It never makes any noise besides humming," answered Libby. "I don't know what's wrong with it."

"Maybe you should turn it off," said Jackie, looking worried. "It might be getting ready to explode."

"It was clanking before I loaded a corpse into it."

"You mean, when it was off?"

"Yeah."

"I don't know anything about machines. But that doesn't sound good."

"I called the repairman."

"Why don't you turn off the machine till he comes?"

"I don't like turning it off in the middle of a job. The part of the body that's intact will start stinking if I don't finish the cremation."

Jackie grimaced and set down her coffee cup. "I'm losing my appetite."

"No worries. Everything will be fine if I let the machine finish its job."

"I'm glad you know what you're doing."

Libby got the impression Jackie was being sarcastic. Libby felt angry. Her gaze fell on the carving knife jutting out of the knife block on the counter. She felt a mad urge to grab the knife and cut off Jackie's hand that was lying on the tabletop next to her full ceramic coffee cup.

"Of course, I know what I'm doing," cried Libby, shooting to her feet, startling Jackie.

"That's what I just said," said Jackie, trying to placate her.

"You accused me of not knowing what I'm doing," said Libby, fit to be tied.

"No, I didn't. I said you *know* what you're doing."

"But you meant the opposite."

"That's not true."

Libby searched Jackie's face, determining if Jackie was being sarcastic.

Libby could reach the knife, withdraw it from the block, and plunge the ten-inch blade into Jackie's throat in less than a minute.

"Are you OK?" said Jackie.

Libby pulled herself together. She wasn't herself. She didn't lose her temper at the drop of a hat. She rubbed her forehead. Maybe she was coming down with a bug. Why did she even think about killing Jackie? She needed to see a shrink. It was the second time today that she had wanted to kill.

She sat down. "I'm all right."

"I never seen you so mad. Your face was red as a beet."

"I think I'm running a fever, is all."

Libby hoped Jackie would buy her excuse.

"Maybe you have Covid," said Jackie. "You don't want to mess around with that stuff."

"It's not Covid. My sense of smell is fine. I can smell the stink in here."

"Yeah. What is *that*?"

"I dunno. It never smells this bad in here."

"Too bad you don't have any windows. I got an idea," said Jackie, snapping her fingers. "Buy some Glade air freshener. That might help with that virus you picked up."

"It's a twenty-four hour bug. It's nothing."

"I wish your furnace would stop making so much noise," said Jackie, listening to the clanking. "It's getting on my nerves."

"We could step outside if you want."

"No, that's all right." Jackie stood up. "Maybe I should go. You need to rest to recover from your bug."

"I'd like to see *The Wicker Man* with you."

"Great. Let's go Friday."

Libby smiled. "Let's."

"You get some rest."

"I feel fine. Just a slight fever."

"I insist. That Puritan work ethic of yours is gonna kill you. Lie down for a little while. Take a break."

Libby felt herself becoming angry again. She resented people telling her what to do. It was *her* life. She was going to live it as she pleased. She liked keeping busy. Sitting around doing nothing didn't agree with her.

She glanced again at the carving knife handle protruding from the knife block.

"Are you all right?" said Jackie, sensing something was wrong, eying Libby with concern.

"I'm fine. You're starting to sound like my mother."

"Your face is getting red again."

Libby heard an androgynous voice in her head.

She's a pain in the neck. Kill her. Take the knife and cut her throat.

"No," muttered Libby, fighting the voice.

"No what?" said Jackie, bemused.

Libby whipped the carving knife out of the block. She realized she had the knife in her hand.

Do it now. Kill her.

Libby resisted the voice.

"What are you doing?" said Jackie.

"I'm gonna prepare dinner," said Libby.

"It's kind of early for that, isn't it?"

"I eat early. Is that all right with you?" said Libby testily.

Embarrassed, Jackie apologized. "I get the message. I'll leave."

She turned to depart.

Libby tossed the knife on the counter in disgust. What was she thinking?

Jackie stalked toward the front door.

Feeling sorry for hurting Jackie's feelings, Libby followed her.

"I really want to go to the movie with you, Jackie. I'm sure I'll feel better Friday."

Jackie halted and slewed around with a smile on her face.

"I'll be here at eight," she said.

"Eight it is," said Libby, returning Jackie's smile. "I love a good horror movie."

"That's why I asked you. You're the only one of my friends who does."

Jackie headed out the door to her gold VW Bug parked in the driveway.

Libby stood in the doorway and watched her.

Now she was hearing voices. Maybe it was the fever. But she didn't have a fever. She had made it up for Jackie's sake. Then why was she hearing voices? Maybe she was just talking to herself. No harm in that. But it sounded like somebody else's voice that she was hearing.

Smiling, she waved good-bye to Jackie as the VW backed out of the driveway. Jackie returned the wave.

Fine. You can slice her throat on Friday and make her pay for what she said to you.

The Bug drove away.

Screwing up her face, Libby clutched her head between her hands, trying to get the dreadful voice in her head to shut up.

The furnace clanked three more times.

"Shut up," cried Libby.

What was happening to her? She couldn't control her outbursts. And she was hearing voices. Insanity didn't run in her family. She was just tired. She was putting in too many hours at work like Jackie had told her. She needed to relax.

She made for her bedroom, sat on her moth-eaten recliner, and watched TV. They were showing the original version of *The Amityville Horror* on one of the cable channels. James Brolin was in the process of being possessed in his haunted house and being driven to murderous rages.

Sounded familiar. Maybe she was being possessed. She laughed at the thought. She didn't believe in that superstitious nonsense.

She had to admit she loved a good horror movie, but as for believing them that was another story.

Her cell phone chimed.

Chapter 12

It was the owner of the crematorium, Herbert Stringfellow.

Libby had met him only once in person. Their means of communication was their cell phones. Libby knew what he wanted, what he always wanted.

"You need to increase your processing of corpses," said Stringfellow in his ragged voice.

He always sounded like he was talking on a static-filled walkie-talkie even though there wasn't any static on the cell line. His scratchy voice was the static. Maybe he smoked too many cigars and had cancer of the throat.

The cremation furnace clanked twice, annoying her.

"Where am I supposed to get them?" she said. "Do you want me to kill someone?"

"Don't take that sarcastic tone with me."

What was wrong with her? She never talked back to the boss. She was always respectful. She knew he could fire her on a moment's notice.

"I'm sorry," she said.

"I'm losing money."

"What do you want me to do?"

"I just told you," he said, cheesed off. "Can't you hear?"

Libby winced at the sound of his yelling. She was trying to be respectful, but he was crossing the line with his meanness.

The furnace clanked three more times.

"You want me to murder a bunch of people so I can cremate them?" she retorted. "How 'bout what's left of my family?"

Nonplussed by her angry shouting, he said nothing.

It was out of character for her to chew him out. After all, he was the owner of the business. What right did she have to jump down his throat? She figured her job was hanging by a thread. What had gotten into her? She didn't want to lose her job. Apprehensive, she broke a sweat. Losing her temper with her boss was insane. She told herself to calm down..

"I'm sorry," she said. "I'm having a bad day."

"What's wrong with you?"

"Uh—the furnace is acting up. It's making weird noises."

"That's no call for you to get snappy with me."

"Of course not."

"You need to process more cadavers. Do you understand?"

"I'm doing my best. I can't help it if business is slow—"

"People are dropping dead every second. There's no shortage of stiffs. I don't understand what the problem is."

"You need to spend more money on advertising."

"Don't tell me what to do. I'm paying your salary."

"If nobody knows our crematorium exists, why should anyone use our services?"

"Let me remind you you're not in the ad department. Your business is to dispose of corpses. That's it."

"And that's what I'm doing."

"But you're not doing enough of it. Get cracking. Step up the pace."

In white heat, she could imagine her fingers wrapped around his scrawny throat like anacondas, throttling the cantankerous seventy-year-old codger.

"I want that furnace cranking out stiffs day and night," he went on. "Do you hear me?"

"I hear you."

He slammed his handset down in rage.

She may have run the crematorium, but Stringfellow ran her. It was *his* business. She just managed it. In other words, she did all the work while he got all the income, a small percentage of which he shared with her.

She glared at her cell phone. "I'm gonna kill you one of these days, slave driver."

There she was issuing threats again. It wasn't her nature. She didn't go around looking for fights. What was happening to her? The change in her personality was getting out of hand.

She tossed her cell phone on the bed and returned to watching *The Amityville Horror*.

If people would stop pestering her, maybe she could get some rest and be herself again, a person who minded their own business and didn't make waves. She was an easygoing sort, not a rabble-rouser. She went out of her way to avoid fights with people. She took it on the chin and muddled through life. She didn't froth at the mouth at every perceived slight.

This new angry version of herself scared her. How could she banish it if she didn't know where it had come from? She couldn't let it take over.

She watched the movie.

The Amityville horror was possessing James Brolin and forcing him to try to kill his family. Could it be that an evil entity was possessing her in the same manner and trying to turn her into a murderer? No. That type of thing happened only in movies.

But what other explanation was there for the change in her personality? A raging, aggressive Libby full of murderous menace was supplanting the long-suffering, withdrawing one. The only other explanation she could come up with was madness. She was becoming a full-fledged paranoid schizophrenic with multiple identities.

She refused to accept the idea that she was going insane. Was she becoming possessed like Brolin?

Maybe a psychic could help her find out the truth.

She headed to her desk, sat down, and awoke her laptop from Sleep mode. She searched the Internet for nearby psychics.

She came across Brady Carmody's name. Because a malignant demon had possessed him when he was a child and had tried to get him to kill his mother, he knew how to get in touch with the spirit world. It sounded something like what she was going through. Though she hadn't tried to kill anybody yet, she had felt like killing her friend Jackie and then Stringfellow when he had read her the riot act over the phone.

She looked up from her computer monitor.

On second thought, did she really want to go through with this and hire a psychic to tell her if she was possessed? If she *was* possessed, he might know how to exorcise the evil entity from her.

She believed her destiny was suffering, because it had been her lot in life. She suffered in silence. She accepted her destiny and endured. She had never believed she was supposed to kill people. Though she had good reason to kill Ed Grainger, she had never planned to do so. She had let the authorities take care of him. But they had failed, because there was no justice in the world. The scales of justice were tipped by money.

She had never entertained the idea of seeking vengeance and killing him.

Today she had thought about killing her cat Tandy, her boss Stringfellow, and her only friend Jackie for barely any reason at all.

She had to find out what was going on with her before it was too late to do anything about it. She would call Brady Carmody for a free consultation. Nothing like this had ever happened to her before, and she needed to know what was going on.

She produced her cell phone and called Carmody's number that was posted on his website.

Chapter 13

"Brady Carney here—uh—I mean, Brady Carmody."

"Hi," said Libby, wondering why he had told her the wrong last name. "This is Libby Genet. I saw your website. I would like a free consultation with you."

"Fine. My—uh—office is being repaired. Where would you like to meet?"

"We could meet here at the crematorium."

"Crematorium?" said Brady uncertainly.

Libby chuckled. "Don't be concerned. It's where I work."

"Oh. No problem. I would like to ask you a couple of questions first to make sure I'm the right person you're looking for."

"I'm listening"

"Are you experiencing a problem that you suspect might be supernatural in origin?"

"Yeah."

"Are you living in a haunted house?"

"It's not a house, but it might be haunted."

"Do you suspect you're being possessed?"

Libby nodded, her cell phone beside her ear. "I think it's possible, but I have to be honest with you. I don't believe in that mumbo jumbo."

"That's OK. I didn't either until it happened to me. When do you want me to come over?"

"As soon as possible."

"Give me your address and I'm on my way."

Libby gave him the address of the crematorium and terminated the call.

She watched the furnace do its job. Not that she could see anything other than its closed door. But everything sounded normal except for the occasional clanking, which also happened when the furnace was off, indicating to her that it wasn't affecting the operation of the machine.

Where was the repairman?

She heard a vehicle pull into the driveway.

Maybe that was him now.

She opened the front door, eager to speak to the repairman about the furnace.

A young lanky guy with dark hair and blue eyes clambered out of the driver's seat of a metallic carmine Jeep Gladiator. His eyes had a dreamlike quality to them. Clad in a pair of jeans and a faded polo, both of which had seen better days, he approached her.

It wasn't the repairman.

"Can I help you?" she said from the doorway.

"I'm here to see Libby Genet."

"That's me."

He approached her. "I'm Brady Carmody, the occultist. We spoke on the phone."

She hadn't realized he was so young. He looked like a college student. Was she his first customer? Maybe it wasn't such a good idea to hire him, but she had never hired a psychic and didn't know what to look for when searching for one.

"Come in," she said tentatively.

As he entered he tensed and stopped.

"What's wrong?" said Libby.

"I feel the presence of an entity."

Probably his standard opening line. Was this guy on the level? He couldn't have much experience at his job. He couldn't have been older than twenty at the most. Maybe he was one of those fake-it-till-you-make-it Silicon Valley types.

"How can you tell?" she said.

"I was possessed by an evil entity when I was very young. It forced me to do its evil bidding."

"OK," she said, not convinced he knew what he was talking about.

"I need to ask you some questions before we proceed."

"Fire away."

"Do you hear strange noises in your crematorium?"

"Definitely. The furnace clanks for no reason. It never used to."

"What about hot or cold spots? Do you have any inexplicable changes in the temperature in this building?"

Libby reacted with surprise. "How did you know?"

She led him to the cold spot in question.

"It's so cold I can see my breath over here," she said, sticking out her hand and feeling the frigid air.

Brady felt the coldness and watched his breath vaporize in front of him.

"I don't see an A/C here," he said, scoping out the area.

"No A/C."

"Doesn't it get hot in here when you run that furnace?"

"It's running now. The rest of the building gets a little warmer but not much. It's not comfortable in the summer, but whenever I ask my boss for an air conditioner, he says we can't afford one."

"My next question is very important."

"Do you want to go into the kitchen and have a cup of coffee first?"

"I drink only out of secure containers at houses I believe to be haunted. I'll take a can of soda if you have one."

What a weird thing to say. The guy acted paranoid. What kind of spooky customers did he get in his line of work? Well, she wasn't one of them.

"I don't have any poison in my kitchenette if that's what you're thinking," said Libby, offended at his insinuation.

"It's not you I'm worried about. I didn't mean to offend you. If you have an evil entity here, it will try to get rid of me when it knows I can sense it."

"It will poison you?"

"It will do anything it can to get rid of me."

"Wow. I don't know anything about evil entities. That's why I need help in trying to find out what's going on here."

Chapter 14

She led him to the kitchenette, thinking the guy was strange as well as paranoid.

He followed her, sensing the air and taking in the surroundings.

Libby opened the refrigerator, looking for minicans of ginger ale standing on the plastic shelf on the interior side of the door.

"Is ginger ale OK?" she said.

"Fine," he said.

"That's good, because it's all I have."

"The next question I have for you is very important. Do you find yourself acting out of character?"

Libby started when she heard his question. "How did you know?"

"It's what happens when you're possessed by an entity. It takes over your personality."

"Yes," she said, removing two cans of ginger ale from the refrigerator.

She handed him one of the green soda cans as the refrigerator door closed behind her.

"Unopened," she said, glancing at the can she handed to him.

"We have to be careful if you have an evil entity in the crematorium," he said, accepting the can.

"Have a seat. Do you think the entity will try to poison me?"

They sat down opposite each other at the small table. His knees touched hers. She flinched.

"Sorry," he said, shifting in his seat.

"No problem. You were saying you think the entity will try to poison me."

"Not you," he said. "If it killed you, it wouldn't have anywhere to go. The people you feel like killing are the ones it might try to poison."

"I've felt like killing a lot of people lately."

"It wants you to be its cat's-paw for committing evil if indeed there is an entity haunting this crematorium."

"Can't you tell if there is?"

"I sense a presence, but I can't be certain yet. From what you've told me, it sounds like you are in the process of being possessed." Brady paused and took a pull on his ginger ale. "Let me ask you another question. Do you hear voices in your head?"

"Uh—no."

She decided not to tell him about the voice in her head. She thought revealing it would make her appear to be going mad. After all, inmates in insane asylums heard voices in their heads.

"How long have you worked here?" said Brady.

"About three years."

"Did you ever have mood swings before—like you can't control yourself and want to kill someone?"

"No. That's what's so weird. I don't understand why it's starting now."

Brady thought about it. "An unclean, unsettled spirit must have entered your building recently."

"How could it have entered? I thought unsettled spirits who haunted houses were the previous owners of the house. My boss has owned this building for many years and still does."

"Let's see. You cremate dead bodies here. The unsettled spirit must have come from one of the cadavers you incinerated."

"Is that possible?"

"Anything is possible when it comes to the spirit world. Wherever there are dead bodies there are spirits."

"Why would they target me?"

"Because you're here, and they're here." Brady paused a beat. "Have you noticed insect infestations in this building?"

"Hmm. No. You mean, like ants?"

"Any insects. Usually but not always flies. How about weird odors?"

"Yeah. I figured it was a stiff, but they're usually treated so they don't smell when I get them. A really bad stink."

Libby tossed back her ginger ale.

Kill him. He's asking too many questions. He's too nosy.

That weird voice again.

"What is your assessment?" she said.

Plunge the carving knife through his heart. Or sever his jugular.

Libby glanced at the knife in the knife block on the counter.

Brady tilted his head as if listening to a sound barely perceptible in the distance.

"From what you have told me I believe an entity is in the process of possessing you," he said.

"Can you help me?"

"If you employ me, yes. My usual rates would apply."

He's a phony crook trying to fleece you. Don't fall for his scam. Kill him or he'll keep coming back for more money.

"How does this work?" she said.

"First, we have to find out who is trying to possess you. Usually it's the previous owner of a haunted house that is trying to possess the new owner."

"You mean, the person who had my job before me? But that was three years ago. Why would it take so long for him to try to possess me? And doesn't he have to be dead?"

She didn't know if Seymour Hemlock had died. The last she heard he was still alive and kicking.

"It shouldn't take three years," said Brady. "Your case is different. It must be the spirit of one of the cadavers you incinerated that's haunting you. That's the only thing that makes sense. We need to identify the spirit before I can do anything to help you."

Don't believe a word he says. It's a scam. Grab the knife and take him out.

"This is crazy," she said. "I don't believe in ghosts."

"I didn't either till one possessed me."

He's a fraud. Cut his heart out and cut it in half.

"Am I in any danger?" she asked, wishing the voice in her head would shut up.

"You are," answered Brady. "Do you want to retain my services?"

Get the knife.

"I have to think about it," said Libby.

Brady knocked back the rest of his ginger ale and stood up. "Fine."

Libby jumped to her feet, pirouetted, and whipped the carving knife out of its block. Gritting her teeth she wheeled around to face Brady, her knife at the ready.

Brady was already on his way to the front door, his back to her.

Chase him and kill him. Or he's gonna scam you.

Grimacing, Libby fought her urge to spill blood. She watched Brady exit the building. She stared at the knife in her hand.

"No," she cried, and flung the knife to the floor.

It skidded across the linoleum and thudded against the baseboard.

The light in the overhead ceiling of the kitchenette blinked on and off several times.

She eyeballed the light. Why did everything fall apart at once? A faulty circuit in the light. And a clanking furnace. What next?

She didn't believe in ghosts.

She remembered Occam's razor from one of her philosophy courses from college, which stated the simplest explanation was usually the correct explanation.

The simplest explanation for hearing voices was she was going nuts. The question was, when would she start obeying them? She shivered at the thought. *Kill, kill, kill,* the voice kept telling her.

She would pay a visit to her shrink.

Her shrink was more expensive than the so-called occultist, but her money would be better spent on the shrink. She couldn't bring herself to believe in ghosts.

Chapter 15

When Libby told her psychiatrist Melanie Hermosa over the phone that she feared she would kill someone, Hermosa told her to come right over for a session.

Libby put a Closed sign on the front door of the crematorium, locked up the business, and drove her gracefully aging pea green Fiat to Hermosa's office in Brentwood. She hoped her boss wouldn't mind, for, after all, this was an emergency. Not that he cared about her mental health. She wasn't going to tell him anything about the crematorium closure unless he found out about it.

He should be thankful she was going to be examined. Otherwise, he could end up being one of her murder victims.

Libby took a seat on Hermosa's leather recliner for patients. Hermosa's chair stood a couple feet from it.

At five six with shoulder-length brunette hair, Hermosa always seemed relaxed. Which helped relax Libby during her appointments. Sporting black butterfly-shaped glasses Hermosa pulled up her chair next to Libby. Hermosa wore a mustard yellow blouse with ruffled short sleeves and a scarlet skirt.

She took notes in her spiral notebook with a ballpoint pen.

"I'm hearing voices," said Libby, trying to relax. "It's stressing me out."

"Is it one voice or many voices?" asked Hermosa.

"One. It's a creepy voice. I'm not even sure it's human."

"What else could it be?"

"I dunno. There's something otherworldly about it."

"Why do you think you're gonna kill someone?"

"It keeps telling me to kill."

"Why?"

"It says people are plotting against me and scamming me or dissing me. Then it tells me to kill them. It even wanted me to kill my cat."

"When did you start hearing this voice?"

"It started today."

"Are you under a lot of stress lately?"

Libby chewed it over. "The same as usual. Nothing out of the ordinary. Am I going crazy?"

Hermosa didn't answer. "We call hearing voices 'auditory hallucinations' in my line of work."

"How do I get it to stop?"

"Why do you feel you might do what it tells you? Can't you resist it?"

"I've resisted it so far. But it's very insistent. I feel compelled to do what it tells me."

"It's OK to listen to voices in your head. Just don't do what they tell you. Think for yourself and use your own judgments before you act."

Libby knotted her face. "I'm finding it difficult to resist the voice. What it says makes sense to me."

"Committing murder never makes sense. It's wrong, and it's illegal. I'm sure you know better."

"I do. I dunno. It's hard to explain. If you heard the voice, you would understand."

Hermosa searched Libby's face. "I think you're OK. When you realize you have a problem, it means you're healthy. When you think it's OK to kill like the voice tells you, then you're mentally ill and need help."

"The voice is becoming more insistent. It's like it's trying to take over my body. Can you give me some kind of pill to fight off the voice?"

"I could prescribe you a sedative if you think it would help."

"I don't know what to do. That's why I came here."

"I could write you a prescription for Valium. It will calm you down."

"Will it get rid of the voice in my head?"

"If your condition is being caused by stress—and I think it is—I believe the Valium will help you."

Libby massaged her brow. "I don't want to go crazy."

"I don't believe you're going crazy. Put that out of your head."

"Do you believe in ghosts?"

Hermosa chuckled. "Not at all. My abuela used to. She used to tell me ghost stories when I was young. She insisted they were true, and I believed her back then, because I didn't know any better."

"Then you don't believe in possession either."

"Like in *The Exorcist*?" Hermosa shook her head no. "That supernatural stuff is for movies. In the real world what you see is what you get. You can't see ghosts, so they don't exist."

"What about evil entities? Do you believe in them?"

"You mean, like demons?"

"Yeah."

"No demons. People have to take responsibility for their actions. Blaming their miserable lives on demons and ghosts is a cop out."

"I used to think like that until this voice got into my head."

"I'm pretty sure that in your case the voice is a product of stress." Hermosa adjusted her glasses on her aquiline nose. "You need to be able to stand up to the voice. I believe you can do it."

Looking uncertain, Libby shut her eyes. "It's getting more forceful."

"Now it's my turn to ask you. Do you believe in ghosts?"

"I'm not sure. I didn't until I started hearing the voice urging me to kill people."

"Ask yourself, why would a ghost want anything to do with you?"

"I have no idea."

"Do you hear the voice now?"

"I hear it when I'm in the crematorium. Nowhere else." Libby paused. "So far anyway."

"Why would a ghost in the crematorium want to haunt you? Did you cremate any relatives recently?"

"I don't know any of the people I've cremated. And that's the way I like it."

Hermosa scribbled notes in her notebook.

"Then why would any of them want to haunt you?" she said, pressing the top of her pen against her chin.

Libby sat up on the recliner. "You're right. It doesn't make sense. The voice must be stress related like you said."

"Have you heard the voice while you've been here?"

"Not a peep."

Hermosa tapped her pen against her chin. "Your job must be causing your stress. Don't let your job get to you. Try Valium."

She wrote out a prescription for Libby.

Libby took it. "Did your abuela tell you what the ghosts wanted from the people they haunted?"

"Each ghost is different. Their souls can't rest in peace for different reasons. But she told me stories that were passed down to her by her ancestors. People were more superstitious in the old days. They used to believe in that stuff."

"*Espero que no creas en fantasmas y demonios.*"

"I don't. They don't exist." Hermosa did a double take. "I didn't know you spoke Spanish."

"I don't."

Hermosa's face registered surprise. "You just spoke Spanish to me."

"That's weird. What did I say?"

"You said, 'I hope you don't believe in ghosts and demons.'"

"How can I speak Spanish if I don't know Spanish?"

"Maybe you heard it on a TV show." Hermosa pouted. "On the other hand, what you said isn't a common phrase. I don't know where you would've heard it."

Confused, Libby stood up. "I'm not myself lately. That's why I came to you." She angled toward the door, holding up her prescription. "I'll pick up this prescription at CVS."

She exited the office. She knew a couple of words in Spanish, but she didn't know how to make sentences. How could she have spoken Spanish? Maybe Hermosa had misheard her. Which seemed unlikely.

What was going on inside her head?

Chapter 16

When Libby got back to the crematorium, she realized with a start that she had left the furnace running. Normally she wouldn't leave the building if the furnace was in operation. It was a safety measure to prevent the building from burning down in case the cremation chamber malfunctioned and caught fire.

Everything seemed to be in order, she noticed, casting around the crematorium.

The oven wheezed to a halt. It had finished cremating Mr. Deng.

The repairman must not have arrived, because Libby hadn't seen a note taped to the front door stating that he had been there while she was at her shrink. All the better for her. If word got back to Stringfellow that she had deserted her post, she would never hear the end of it.

Tandy loped across the floor, meowed, and rubbed his head against her leg.

"Are you happy to see me or do you just want to eat?" said Libby.

Tandy looked up at her with his green jewel eyes and meowed.

Libby figured she knew the answer.

"Don't you ever get tired of eating?" she said, making her way to the kitchen.

She had taken a Valium and was feeling better. Maybe Hermosa had been right that she just needed to relax. Maybe she was driving herself too hard.

You need to kill Tandy. He's getting in your way.

Not again. Why wasn't the Valium working? She was hearing the voice in her head again. She was sick of it.

As if on cue the furnace fell to clanking.

Of course. Why shouldn't it clank? Nobody had fixed it yet. Where was the repairman?

She entered the kitchenette and used the electric can opener to open a can of cat food for Tandy. She scooped the contents onto Tandy's plate on the counter and set the plate on the floor.

Kill Tandy. He's monopolizing your time.

Libby eyed Tandy, who was gorging on his fish-stinking food.

"No," said Libby, backing away from Tandy, afraid she might lose control of herself and attack him.

She felt the overpowering urge to latch onto the carving knife and lop off Tandy's head. Why wasn't the Valium thwarting her violent urges?

Grimacing, she grabbed her right hand as it reached for the knife handle. She needed to prevent her hand from clutching the knife and beheading Tandy. Her right hand had a mind of its own, struggling to reach the knife stored in the knife block on the counter. Gnashing her teeth, Libby resisted her unruly hand by attempting to yank it away from the knife. The hand would not be denied. It kept fighting her.

"Get out of here, Tandy," she cried, worried she wouldn't be able to prevent her hand from seizing the carving knife.

Tandy glanced up from his food at her, wondering why she was yelling at him. He returned to devouring his food.

"You need to go, Tandy. I can't control my hand. I don't want to hurt you."

But some of her *did* want to hurt him. She felt like somebody else was trying to take over her body.

Maybe the occultist Brady was right about an entity trying to possess her. Hermosa's prescription of Valium wasn't working. If anything, it was making her weaker and less able to resist the violent urges overwhelming her.

Kill the cat. Kill the damn cat. All it does is eat and take up space. Kill it.

Libby snagged the knife and advanced on Tandy. Tandy yowled and scampered away.

Hearing knocking on the front door, Libby approached it, knife in hand. She cracked the door.

It was the furnace repairman.

Fortysomething, sporting a crew cut, he was wearing a grey uniform with his name Bill written in red cursive letters over the left breast pocket of his button-down shirt.

"I got a call to check out the retort," he said with a thin-lipped mouth with tiny teeth that looked like white corn kernels.

"Come in," said Libby, hiding the knife behind her back and opening the door. "I've been waiting for you."

He smelled like stale cigarette smoke. She was glad he didn't light up in here.

"I can't believe the traffic today," he said.

"LA. I know."

"What seems to be the problem?"

"The retort keeps clanking for no reason."

"While it's operating or at rest?"

"It doesn't matter. It clanks when the oven's on or off."

Bill nodded. "When was the last time you had it inspected?"

"I can't recall. Did you bring the right equipment?"

"I have all the equipment I need in my van. I always come prepared."

Bill neared the oven in his leather work boots. "It feels warm. Have you been using it lately?"

"You're smart."

He looked at her, picking up on her sarcasm. "Look, I know my job, is all. OK? No reason to get snarky with me."

"You're touchy, aren't you, Bill?"

"Lady, I didn't come here for a social visit. Let me put it to you this way. I didn't come here to make friends. I came here to make money. Understand?"

He's insulting you. He doesn't like your company. Kill him.

The voice was right. She felt her hand tighten on the knife handle behind her back. She found herself clenching her teeth again.

"You're a repairman for Chrissake, not the president," she said.

"What did you say?" said Bill, taken aback.

"You act like you're the president. Can't you do your job instead of giving me lessons in civility?"

"I don't have to take this," said Bill, smoldering. "Fix your damn furnace yourself if you're so smart."

"Your boss is gonna tan your hide for leaving a job."

Shaking his head Bill stalked toward the front door.

"Some people," he muttered.

Libby ran after him.

"Are you gonna apologize?" she demanded behind his back.

"For what?" he said over his shoulder. "You're the one who insulted *me*."

She stabbed him in the backbone with her knife.

Arching his back he groaned and reached behind him, feeling for the knife. Libby yanked out the blade and plunged it home again into his spine.

"Argh," said Bill.

Good work. Stab the creep again. He dissed you. He deserves to die.

Libby withdrew the knife and punctured Bill's left lung with a forceful jab, yelping with delight.

Bill made a sound in his throat like he was gargling.

"How dare you get uppity with me?" said Libby, glowering at him.

Coughing bright red blood from his pierced lung, Bill crumpled to his knees like he was begging forgiveness, but instead of words blood poured from his mouth.

"Too late to beg for your life, buddy," said Libby. "You should've been nicer to me. Didn't your boss ever teach you the customer is always right?"

Bill made another gargling sound.

"This is what I think of wiseasses," said Libby before ripping his throat with the blood-soaked carving knife. "This is what I think of repair guys who think they're the president."

Blood erupted from Bill's severed artery. His eyes starting out of their sockets, he fell forward and smashed his face against the floor, breaking his two kernel-like front teeth. He wasn't surprised it didn't hurt. Nothing would ever surprise him again.

Chapter 17

Libby gasped at the bloody corpse at her feet. She dropped her knife.

What had she done? *Ohmigod.* What was happening to her? What was she supposed to do? Call the cops and confess? She didn't want to go to jail for the rest of her life.

What had got into her? She had to control her temper. She had never done anything like this in her entire life. Her shrink's Valium hadn't done a bit of good.

Maybe she wasn't going crazy. *Maybe she already was crazy.* Maybe that was why the Valium hadn't worked.

Either that or . . . the occultist was right. An evil entity was in the process of possessing her. The voice . . . It had egged her on, goading her into killing Bill. Poor Bill.

It was too late to help him.

She wanted to scream. What was she supposed to do? She had killed a guy in cold blood.

Get rid of the stiff.

It was the voice filling her head again.

She pulled a face.

Put the stiff in the oven. Without a corpus delicti there is no murder. Burn it. You have your very own disposal unit.

She eyed the cart, whose height was adjustable. She would have to lower it if she had any hope of lifting Bill's corpse onto it. He was much heavier than her. She wished she had somebody to help her lift the body.

She could call Jackie. Jackie was big and pretty strong. What was she going to tell her? *Jackie, I just killed someone. Can you help me cremate him?*

Somehow Libby didn't think Jackie would like the idea. Jackie might even call the cops.

Libby hammered the front door with her fist in frustration.

She didn't have time to throw a fit. She had to do something before another customer arrived.

Blood had pooled under the corpse. Libby would have to clean the floor after disposing of the body. She had a lot of work ahead of her.

She realized this was the perfect place to kill someone, because it would be easy to eliminate the murder victim without leaving a trace so that nobody was the wiser. The furnace would incinerate all evidence of murder.

She put on her nitrile gloves, rolled the cart to Bill, adjusted its height to a lower setting, and attempted to lift the bloody cadaver onto it by latching onto the two arms. She groaned under the weight. This was going to be harder than she had thought.

She let go of the corpse, stood up, and stretched her back, massaging her lower back muscles.

She had no choice. She needed to get the stiff onto the cart and roll it to the furnace. She had no time to spare.

She bent over, lifted Bill's arms, and tried to hoist him up onto the cart, which was about a foot high, since that was the lowest height she could adjust it to. The cart kept sliding away, preventing her from loading the body onto it even though she had locked its wheels, which scraped across the hardwood floor without gaining purchase.

Cursing, she continued struggling to load Bill onto the cart.

She froze when she heard someone knocking at the front door. *Another delivery*, she thought in horror.

She couldn't remember if she had locked the door after she had let Bill in.

The blood drained from her face when she heard the click of a key twisting inside a lock and saw the brass doorknob revolve.

Chapter 18

The door swung open.

Her heart in her mouth, she couldn't believe her eyes. Stringfellow entered through the doorway. He never visited her here. He was the only other person who had the key. What rotten luck.

Rooted to the spot, Bill's arms in her hands, she locked her gaze on Stringfellow like a guilty crook caught in the act.

Appalled, Stringfellow stared at her.

"Good God," he said. "What happened?"

Libby had to think fast. She had to come up with a plausible explanation.

"Uh—uh . . . ," she trailed off.

Stringfellow gaped at her.

Think of an answer, she told herself.

"They just delivered this body," she said. "It fell off the cart. I'm trying to get it back on."

"But the blood. Why's there blood all over the floor? He must still be alive," said Stringfellow, his voice fraught.

Libby had to come up with an answer.

"This is how they brought him," she said. "He—uh—was shot during a bank robbery and died on the sidewalk in front of the bank. The cops brought him straight here."

"Cops?"

"Yeah. Cops delivered him."

"Don't they know they're supposed to take him to the morgue first?"

"Yeah, well—rookies."

"He looks like he's still bleeding."

"No. He's dead."

"Why's he on the floor?"

"Uh—he slid off the cart because of all the slippery blood."

"This is a health hazard. He could have a blood-borne disease."

"That's why I'm wearing gloves," said Libby, holding up one of her hands with a blood-streaked glove on it.

"Cops. Doesn't anybody do their job right these days? Look at the mess," said Stringfellow, surveying with disdain the blood pooled on the floor. "Wait a minute," he said, his eyes flinty.

"What?" said Libby, fearing he didn't believe her.

"I saw a repair van in the driveway. Where's the repairman?"

Christ. She hadn't thought of the van. She had to conjure an explanation.

"Uh—uh—"

"Uh, what? What's going on here?"

Her palms sweaty, Libby felt her heartbeat accelerating. At least she had one thing in her favor. There was so much blood on the corpse's uniform that it covered the company name and Bill's ID tag over his breast pocket.

"He'll be back in an hour," said Libby. "He's on his lunch break."

"Why didn't he take his truck?" said Stringfellow suspiciously.

"He—he walked to the restaurant in the strip mall near here. He said his doctor told him he needed to get more exercise."

Stringfellow harrumphed. "Strange." He paused. "I guess it's a good thing he wasn't here when the stupid cops showed up. Wait. Why did you call the repairman? Is the furnace broken?"

"It's not broken. It works, but it's making a weird clanking sound. I thought it was best to get it checked out."

Stringfellow shrugged. "All right."

"Why are you here?" said Libby.

She couldn't get over his presence at the crematorium. She hadn't seen him here in years. He had once told her the place bummed him out.

He leveled a death stare at her. "I called you earlier, and nobody answered. I couldn't understand why you weren't answering your phone."

"Uh—I had to step out for a moment."

She chewed herself out for having left her cell phone in the crematorium office when she had visited her shrink.

"You're never supposed to leave this building when you're on the job," he said. "You know that."

"It was an emergency."

"Nothing is more important than your job. Nothing takes priority over it. Understand?"

"It won't happen again."

"I came here because I thought something had happened to you."

"I'm OK."

"I should fire you for deserting your post."

Put a knife through his scrawny wattle.

She rejected the voice's demand.

"This isn't the army," she told Stringfellow.

She wasn't going to let the voice pressure her into committing another murder.

"It's more important than the army," said Stringfellow. "It's more important than your life. It's your job."

"My bad. Could you help me load this body onto the cart?"

Stringfellow heaved a loud sigh. "I'm not a spring chicken anymore in case you haven't noticed. I have arthritis in my knees."

"It's too heavy. I can't do it by myself."

"I'm paying *you* to do this stuff."

"Those cops didn't help me load the stiff onto the cart. They just dumped the body on the floor and took off."

"I thought you said the body slipped off the cart because of the blood."

"You—uh—must have misheard me. It was a dump and run," said Libby, becoming entangled in her lies.

She couldn't remember what she had told him.

"It's unbelievable the bums the city hires these days," he said.

"I hope they never come here again."

"As long as the city pays us. That's the important thing. This ain't a free garbage dump for scumbag criminals."

"I won't let those cops in the door next time."

Disgust contorting his face, Stringfellow approached her, careful not to step in the blood smearing the floor.

"Jesus Christ, what a mess," he said. "The cops who did this should be shitcanned."

Chapter 19

"I'll take his arms, and you take his legs," said Libby, getting ahold of Bill's arms.

"I can't believe we're doing this. I better not get a heart attack. Heavy lifting is a good way to trigger a heart attack in someone like me. I already have a herniated disc in my back. I don't want another one."

"We can't leave the body in the middle of the floor. It's unsanitary."

"It'll scare away customers too," grumbled Stringfellow. "Lazy cops. That's the trouble with people these days. They want a Ferrari in their garage, but they don't want to put in the years of hard work it takes to buy it. They want everything handed to them just because they were born. It's like we owe them for their being born."

"On the count of three, lift," said Libby. She counted.

Stringfellow stooped, gripped Bill's ankles, and, grunting, lifted.

Libby lifted Bill's arms. Walking backward, she guided the corpse toward the cart behind her, her back hurting. With Stringfellow's help she managed to place the corpse onto the cart.

"Never again," said Stringfellow, hunched over, blowing out his cheeks, his eyes popping.

"Thanks."

Straightening up, Stringfellow breathed heavily and felt his heart. "It's ticking like crazy."

"I don't know what I would have done without you."

"I better not have a heart attack."

"You look fine."

In any case, he looked better than Bill.

"You need to report those cops," said Stringfellow. "Their behavior was unprofessional. You don't dump a body at a crematorium and run. Did they fill out all the papers at least?"

"Uh—no."

"Sons of bitches. Why didn't you get them to fill out the papers?"

"They pulled a 'dump and run.' After they dropped the body, they hightailed it. What could I do?"

"You should never have let them in the building in the first place."

"They were *cops*. I couldn't say no to cops."

She hoped he was believing her tissue of lies.

"We need to report them to the LAPD," said Stringfellow.

"I didn't get their badge numbers."

"Argh. You can't let this happen again. If they try to dump another gunshot victim covered with fresh blood in the crematorium, be sure to get their badge numbers. They won't dare leave a cadaver here if you can ID them and file a complaint."

"Right."

"And don't ever leave the office again when you're on the clock. We lose business when you go AWOL. What if a client called and wanted to make a delivery while you were out?"

You can't let him talk down to you like you're a naughty child. Kill him.

There was the voice again. She felt resentment against Stringfellow building inside her, the voice acting as a bellows stoking the flames of ire. However, she refused to kill another person. She felt horrible about killing Bill. She would carry her grief to the grave.

"What's taking you so long?" he said.

"What?"

"Why aren't you putting the corpse inside the oven?"

"I just finished cremating another corpse. I haven't had time to clean the ashes out and put them into the cremulator."

"Well, you don't want to mix up the ashes of the two bodies, that's for sure. Just because the cops do a lousy job doesn't mean it's OK for *us* to cut corners. Like my late and lamented dad used to say, there's no point in doing a job if you don't do it right."

She wished he would leave. She found herself becoming furious with him. She was getting sick of his staticky voice lecturing her.

Stringfellow eyeballed the corpse and narrowed his eyes. "How did you say the deceased died?"

"The cops—uh—said they shot him when he attempted an armed robbery of a bank," said Libby, trying to remember what she had told him earlier.

"They lied."

"What?"

"Look at his throat. They slit it. Hmm. I didn't know cops used knives to subdue suspects."

"You're right," said Libby, glancing at Bill's ragged throat, becoming nervous. "I didn't notice."

"Yet another reason to report the pikers. Why are we paying such sky-high taxes and inflated cop salaries if they can't do their job right?"

"We don't have a choice in the matter," said Libby, commiserating with him.

"Can you do your job now or will I have to fire you?"

"I can manage," said Libby through gritted teeth, putting the kibosh on her urge to find her carving knife and slash Stringfellow's furrowed mug.

Stringfellow inspected the corpse. "The question is, why did the cops say they shot the guy when they actually cut his throat?"

"Like you said, they did sloppy work."

"This has got to be reported to police headquarters."

"The cops might start using a different crematorium if we cause a fuss," said Libby, thinking fast.

"This is highly irregular," said Stringfellow, his face stern.

"It's not our fault the cops are incompetent. As long as the city pays us, that's what matters."

Of course, the city wouldn't pay them, but Stringfellow didn't know that.

Stringfellow pursed his lips with displeasure. "Make sure you clean all of the blood off the floor. And do it fast. I don't want things to get backed up. You could get another delivery any minute. We need to be able to burn more bodies ASAP. The retort needs to be on fire every minute of the day for us to turn a profit. I don't want customers lined up outside, waiting."

"Of course not."

"They'll go to another crematorium if that happens. We can't afford to lose customers."

You need to kill the prune-faced geezer. Cut off his head and microwave it.

The voice was egging her on again.

"Get the blood off the floor first," said Stringfellow. "If customers see it, they'll think this place is a slaughterhouse and take off."

"All right," said Libby.

Stringfellow glanced at his wristwatch. "I need to go."

Finally.

"I want this place spotless when you're done," said Stringfellow, indicating the blood-drenched floor with a dismissive gesture.

Kill his sorry codger ass now.

"I'll get a mop," said Libby, looking for the carving knife she had used on Bill, goaded by the voice.

What had she done with the knife?

"Remember. Your job's hanging by a thread. You don't want to end up being a greeter at Walmart, do you?" said Sringfellow, turning to depart.

Libbie shook with anger. Everybody was getting on her nerves. If she had had the knife in her hand, she would have flung it into his back.

Stringfellow groaned. "I feel shortness of breath after lifting that corpse. I'm going straight to the hospital, and I'm gonna dock your paycheck for the medical bills I get as a result."

Frowning, he retreated to the front door on his rickety legs and left.

"I thought he'd never leave," she muttered.

Chapter 20

Something was seriously wrong with her. Hermosa had told her she wasn't going nuts. If she wasn't going nuts, then an entity must be in the act of possessing her like the medium Brady Carmody had told her.

The Valium Hermosa had prescribed for her hadn't prevented her from committing murder. She had no reason to kill the repairman Bill. She barely knew him. Yet there he lay dead on the cart.

Maybe she needed a new shrink who would diagnose her as psychotic. However, she didn't want to be locked away in an insane asylum. She wanted to stop committing murders.

She retrieved a mop and a galvanized steel bucket from the kitchen closet and set about cleaning the blood off the floor. She mopped up the blood and squeezed it into the bucket. She had to work fast. She couldn't allow anyone to see her mopping up blood. Not everyone would be as gullible as Stringfellow, who had gone away, believing the cops had killed Bill.

Tandy wandered into the room and sniffed the blood.

Libby shooed him away. She didn't want him to get infected from a possible blood-borne disease.

Emitting a brief meow of displeasure, Tandy scampered off. He sat in the corner of the room, licked the back of his paw, and began washing his face and whiskers with it.

When Libby finished mopping up the blood and squeezing it into the bucket, she carried the bucket and the mop to the bathroom and spilled the blood out of the bucket into the bathtub. She rinsed out the blood that remained in the bucket. She also rinsed the blood off the mop. Running cold water out of the bathtub faucet, she drained the blood out of the bathtub.

She left the bathroom and checked out the retort, which was now off, since it had completed burning Deng's corpse. But the cremation wasn't over. Now she had to transport the ash and bone fragments into the cremulator, which would grind the bones into ash. The cremulator took anywhere from one to three hours, depending on the number of bone fragments of the cadaver skeleton that remained.

Using a wire broom she pushed Deng's ashes and bone chunks out of the back of the retort onto an eight-foot square screen. The ash dropped through the screen while the bone chunks remained on top. Using the computer she lowered a large overhead magnet over the screen to attract any pieces of metal from medical devices that had been implanted in the body. After the metal adhered to the magnet, Libby punched a button on the computer that raised the magnet from the screen. Now only the bone chunks remained on the screen.

At the computer controls, Libby guided the screen into the cremulator, deposited the bone chunks into the machine, and reinstated the screen back to its original position behind the retort.

She turned on the cremulator to pulverize Deng's bone chunks.

Since the retort was empty she could reload it with Bill's stiff.

She wheeled the cart to the open furnace door and loaded the corpse onto the conveyor belt that led to the door. By this time Bill's body had ceased bleeding. She made a mental note that she would have to clean his blood off the cart and the conveyor belt. She switched on the conveyor belt and transported the body onto the slab of specially made masonry materials that resisted heat inside the furnace.

Now that Bill was inside the retort he could find out why it had been clanking. She caught herself laughing at her joke. What was wrong with her? She was cracking sick jokes and laughing at them. She had never done that before. She had knifed the guy in the back and slashed his throat, and she was joking about it.

This new cruel version of Libby horrified her. It had to be the work of the demonic entity that was taking over her body and displacing her. Brady had warned her about the evil entity. He had said he could help her. It was obvious her psychiatrist Hermosa could not. Hermosa's Valium had accomplished nothing. If anything, it had made things worse by relaxing her and lowering her defenses, facilitating the entity's bid to possess her.

Libby had difficulty believing in demonic possession, but it seemed like it was the only explanation for her aberrant behavior.

She started the fire in the cremation chamber to dispose of Bill's corpse.

Even though she felt guilty about killing Bill, she wasn't going to call the cops and confess to the murder. After all, she wasn't the one who had done the killing. It was the demon that possessed her, according to Brady the occultist. She had to take his word for it, because she knew nothing about supernatural demons. The question was, could he save her from the demon's possession? She didn't know.

What she did know was that she needed help. She couldn't go on like this. She would end up killing someone else at this rate.

Tandy loped up to her, froze, and arched his back, hissing.

"What's wrong, Tandy?" said Libby.

Tandy scurried away.

What was that all about? Tandy had never run away from her before. Maybe she had Bill's blood on her. She needed to take a shower and wash her clothes. She didn't know cats were afraid of blood. Maybe he had seen her murder Bill. Did cats run away from you if they saw you kill somebody?

She flinched when the retort began clanking again.

She shouldn't be surprised. Bill hadn't fixed it.

She scoped out the crematorium. She didn't see any more blood. Nobody would ever know she had just murdered someone here today, especially with the disappearance of the corpse, which would turn into unrecognizable ash when the retort and the cremulator were done with it.

Even if nobody ever suspected her of murder, she would know for the rest of her life that she had murdered Bill. It was something she would never forget. She would never live down the shame.

She couldn't go on like this. What if she killed someone else? The idea overwhelmed her, sending shivers down her spine. She needed help.

Going to doctors hadn't helped her. She had tried a psychiatrist. What about a different kind of doctor? Could there be something physiologically wrong with her? Could she have a brain tumor that was forcing her to lose her temper and commit murder? Was that even possible? She had never heard of such a thing. What kind of specialist would handle a brain tumor? A brain surgeon.

No way. She couldn't afford a brain surgeon with her paycheck. Her skimpy health insurance didn't cover the cost of brain surgery. She would probably have to get a CAT scan and an MRI as well. She remembered seeing a TV show on brain tumors that enumerated all the scans needed to detect one. There was something called a PET scan that she would also need.

She had never heard of a PET scan. She had had to look it up in a dictionary. It was an abbreviation for positron emission tomography, in which a radioactive tracer was injected into a vein. The tracer flowed through the blood and attached to brain tumor cells. When the tracer hit the tumor, the tracer appeared on a PET machine that revealed the tumor and whether it was dividing quickly, which would indicate cancer. She had remembered the description of the PET scan because the idea of radioactivity in her blood had turned her stomach. How could radioactivity in the blood be good for you?

Her insurance would drag their feet for months to avoid approving all these scans if the insurance did indeed approve them.

Then of course she would need a brain biopsy so the doctors could get a sample of the tumor and inspect it for cancer. To get a sample of her brain they would either cut out a piece of it or inject it with a needle that would remove brain tissue. After the biopsy, you might have complications, such as bleeding of the brain or damage to it. Just thinking of it repelled her.

And what if the doctors found nothing wrong with her? She might end up with a bleeding damaged brain all for nothing.

She was quickly talking herself out of going to a doctor to find out if she had a brain tumor. This was what she got for watching a TV show on brain surgery.

For sure her insurance wouldn't foot the bill for any kind of surgery. She had dealt with them before and knew how stingy they were. They would keep putting it off ad infinitum, waiting for her to die no doubt.

Anyway, if she had a brain tumor, wouldn't it be giving her headaches? She wasn't experiencing headaches. She was experiencing mood changes. *Violent mood changes that she couldn't control.*

She doubted a brain tumor was causing her to kill.

Which left possession as the only remaining explanation.

She called the psychic Brady Carmody and arranged a meet at the crematorium.

Chapter 21

Libby opened the front door to let in fresh air. The odor of blood lingered inside the building. She needed to clean the air for future customers.

She started when she saw Bill's repair van parked in the driveway. She had forgotten all about the van. She needed to get rid of it. Leaving it in the driveway would invite suspicion. Sooner or later, Bill's boss was going to come looking for him when he didn't report back to the office. Libby couldn't let the van be found here.

She retreated to her office desk, pulled open the bottom drawer, and removed the plastic bag that contained Bill's possessions that she had found in his trouser pockets before loading him into the cremation chamber. She needed to get rid of the possessions, because they could link her to Bill's murder. She would ditch them later. Maybe bury them somewhere or chuck them into a Dumpster at the strip mall.

For now she needed Bill's keys to his van.

She fished out the blood-stained keys from the plastic bag. Wincing at the feeling of coagulating blood on her fingers, she hurried toward the repair van in the driveway.

She climbed into the driver's seat and keyed the ignition.

Sitting behind the wheel she wondered where to abandon the van. She couldn't ditch it too far away because she wanted to be back at the crematorium when Brady arrived for their appointment.

She settled on the Von's supermarket.

She was glad Bill's van was an automatic. She couldn't drive a manual transmission.

She backed out of the driveway, drove to the Von's, which was a little farther away than the strip mall, and abandoned Bill's van in the parking lot. She locked the van and took the key with her. She would trash it with the rest of Bill's belongings.

She called an Uber and got a ride back to the crematorium.

When the Uber dropped her off in her driveway behind a red Jeep Gladiator, she saw Brady Carmody standing in front of the crematorium front door as if waiting for someone to open it. She dismissed the Uber driver and, approaching Brady, she picked up on traces of Bill's blood left on her hand by the van key. She hid her hand in her jeans pocket.

"I had to run an errand," she said.

"I haven't been here long," said Brady.

She unlocked the front door and let him inside the crematorium.

She wondered how much she could tell him. She doubted she could risk confessing she had killed Bill. Brady might report her to the cops.

She couldn't get over how young he looked. He couldn't have much experience in exorcising demons.

"How many possession cases have you handled?" asked Libby.

"Not many," answered Brady. "But I was possessed by a demon ten years ago. I have firsthand knowledge of the subject."

"How did you exorcise the demon?"

"The demon left me after it was finished using me."

"It left of its own free will?"

"More or less."

"Then you didn't exorcise it?"

"No, but I studied the occult under a professor with a degree in parapsychology. He taught me how to exorcise demons." Brady looked around the crematorium. "I'm getting vibrations that evil is present on the premises."

Throw this guy out.

Libby recognized the voice in her head and felt irritated. She wanted the voice gone.

This Brady guy's a scammer. He wants your money. He's gonna take you to the cleaner's.

She tried to ignore the voice.

"I went to a shrink, but she didn't help me one bit," said Libby. "In fact, she made things worse by getting me to take Valium to relax me."

"Sedatives make it easier for a demon to possess you."

"I found that out through experience."

"Shrinks can't protect you against possession."

"My psychiatrist doesn't believe in ghosts or demons."

"I know. I've dealt with shrinks. They believe ghosts exist only inside your head. I know otherwise from firsthand experience."

"Which is why I contacted you. Can you exorcise me?"

"There are ways to exorcise a person who is possessed."

"What ways?"

"First I have to ask you a few questions."

"Fire away."

"All right. Let's begin. Are you possessed, or is the demon in the act of trying to possess you?"

Libby screwed up her face with puzzlement. "How am I supposed to know?"

Kill him. He's a scammer who wants your money.

"Can you fight him off?" said Brady.

"I—I think so," said Libby. "On the other hand, I've noticed changes in my personality. I'm more vicious than I used to be."

Brady nodded. "Changes in personality indicate demonic possession. But if you're aware of changes in your personality, it indicates the demon has not completed his possession. You still have the ability to fight him off and escape."

"Are there any other signs I should know about?"

Brady paced around the room in thought. "Have you noticed yourself speaking languages you don't know?"

"Why, yes. I spoke Spanish to my psychiatrist. I don't know Spanish. How could I do that?"

"Speaking in tongues happens in cases of possession."

"I don't know how you can know all this. You're so young," said Libby, trying to come to grips with his youth.

"Like I said, I was possessed when I was ten, which gave me firsthand insight. I've made it a goal of mine to study possession and find out everything known about the matter. Possession is a terrifying experience, and I'll do everything I can to prevent it from happening to anyone."

Chapter 22

Brady didn't explain to Libby that he didn't defeat the demon child Theresa who had possessed him. Theresa had left him because she had used him to accomplish her purpose of wreaking revenge against her mother, who had murdered her in a bathtub.

Theresa had no more use of him after she had used him to kill his own mother, a symbolic act of vengeance against the demon's murderous mother who had committed suicide after murdering her two children.

Brady wasn't going to go into the specifics of his possession with Libby. He didn't think she would approve of his killing his mother. Why would Libby want to hire a matricide? Why would anybody? Which was why he didn't include that information on his website that advertised his services as an occultist. And it was why he didn't use his real last name. A potential customer might recognize it and decide to look elsewhere for an occultist.

"We must be certain you're possessed before we proceed," he said.

"You said earlier that you think I am."

"I do sense an evil entity here. It doesn't mean he has possessed you yet. I need to ask you a few more questions."

"Fine."

"Do you have blackouts?"

"I don't remember any."

Which didn't necessarily mean she didn't have them, decided Brady. She could be having blackouts and forgetting them.

"Do you find yourself becoming angry at people for no reason?" he said.

"I do."

Brady nodded. "Do you feel like you want to kill them?"

Her face turning ashen, Libby paused. "I—uh—I've thought about it."

"I know this is gonna sound crazy, and I'm not trying to accuse you of anything, but have you killed someone?"

"Of course not," she blurted, taken aback. "What kind of a question is that?"

She paced around the room irritably.

"I'm asking you things that indicate you are possessed," said Brady. "That's all. I'm not a cop."

"You sound like a cop. You're gonna ask me where I buried the body next."

Brady shook his head no. "The truth is that when people are possessed they are not only capable of committing murder they actually commit it. I didn't mean to offend you."

Worked up, Libby rubbed her face. "It sounds awful."

"When a demon possesses you, you become his agent of evil. Do you feel the urge to kill animals?"

"I'm not a monster. I don't kill animals. I have a pet cat."

"Have you felt the urge to kill your cat?"

"Absolutely not," said Libby, ticked off. "What do these questions have to do with being possessed?"

"A lot, unfortunately. It's a good sign you haven't felt any urges to kill. What about voices? Do you hear voices in your head?" he said, searching her face.

She stared back at him. "Yeah."

"When I asked you this question earlier, you said no."

She paused. "I—I thought you might think I was a psycho, so I lied before."

"For the record I don't think you're a psycho. What do the voices say?"

"It's just one voice. It tells me to hurt people."

Brady nodded, his young face doleful. He said nothing for a while.

"Well?" she said. "What do you think?"

"I believe you're in the initial stages of demonic possession. From what I can gather from your answers, the demon doesn't have complete control over you. Which means I can help you prevent it from possessing you."

"What happens if you can't help me?"

"You don't want to think about it."

"I need to know," she said, nervously clenching and unclenching her fist.

"You will kill people. Demons want to kill. Killing is the ultimate form of evil."

"How do we stop it?" said Libby, agitated.

"By preventing it from possessing you."

"Why does it want me to kill people?"

Brady thought about his possession by the demon child Theresa.

"They have a reason to vent their rage by killing," he said. "We need to find out that reason. Then we can identify the demon. We need to know whose sprit is unsettled before I can exorcise it. It's a spirit that can't rest in peace who is trying to possess you."

"I can't stand the idea of it," said Libby, throwing up her hands in anguish. "Just thinking about it makes my flesh crawl."

"That's a good sign. It means you can still fight off the demon."

Brady was ad-libbing. He didn't really know if what he had just said was true. Even the so-called experts didn't know anything for sure about the supernatural. It was open to interpretation. Incarcerated in the insane asylum, he had reads hundreds of books on the supernatural and on parapsychology in the asylum library, and no two experts agreed on anything. Nothing could be proved. If he had learned anything, it was that the supernatural was cloaked in a veil of darkness that nobody could penetrate. Some claimed they could, and nobody could prove them wrong. Anybody could claim anything on the subject without being categorically refuted. Which gave rise to a raft of fraudsters.

Brady didn't consider himself a fraud. He had actually been possessed. He knew of what he spoke. He could commiserate with people suffering the same ordeal. He hoped he could help Libby. He could certainly try.

"Can you help me?" said Libby.

"The problem here is that so many restless spirits could be haunting this building because it's a crematorium, where many corpses have been laid to rest, so to speak. This makes it difficult to identify the demon haunting you. Has he identified himself to you?"

"No."

Chapter 23

Kill the bastard. Kill the fraudster.
The voice again.
"Did you hear that?" she said.
Was she the only one who could hear the voice?
"Hear what?" said Brady.
Kill him. He's a sham. He doesn't know what he's talking about. He just wants your money.
"Oh, nothing," said Libby.
She felt the sudden urge to confess to Brady that she had killed Bill. It was madness. The guy would report her to the cops. But there was no corpus delicti. No evidence a crime had been committed. The DA could never get a conviction, or so she thought.

However, she still had Bill's personal belongings in her desk drawer. The DA might be able to get a conviction with circumstantial evidence. She needed to dispose of the belongings without delay.

Every time she thought of Bill she felt sick to her stomach. She kept seeing his bleeding body in front of her.

"Are you all right?" said Brady.

"Oh, something I ate for lunch didn't agree with me," said Libby, massaging her stomach.

Brady looked concerned. "Be careful what you eat. The demon might try to poison your food."

"You said before that it wouldn't poison me but my victims."

"I meant, poison with the intent to kill."

"It can't possess me if it kills me."

"It will poison you to make you ill and lower your defenses to make it easier for it to possess you. It won't poison you to kill you."

"That makes me feel a lot better," she said, continuing to feel sick.

"Demons are masters of deceit. You can't believe what they tell you. Almost everything they say is a lie. They use lies to manipulate you."

He's lying. He knows nothing. It's all an act. I'm your only friend. Listen to me. He's trying to scam you. Kill him.

The voice. Always nagging her.

"Can't you leave me alone?" she erupted, tired of listening to it.

"What?" said Brady, startled. "I thought you wanted my help."

"I'm sorry. I'm under a lot of stress. My boss was here earlier and gave me a hard time. I guess I just lost it. I *do* want your help."

Should she tell him what the voice was saying to her? For some reason she felt she shouldn't. Maybe it was the voice's sway over her. It had actually gotten her to kill someone. If it could do that, it could do anything—like getting her to kill again, which terrified her, but she didn't know how she could get the voice out of her head.

"Do you have any idea who might be haunting you?" said Brady.

"None."

"Do you keep a list of all the people you have cremated?"

"I keep a record of every corpse burned," said Libby. *Except Bill's.*

"Good. We need to study your records and find out which of the deceased would have an unsettled spirit that would seek to harm you."

"I've never cremated anyone I knew on a personal basis."

"Which makes it difficult to figure out who's haunting you."

"Is it *that* important?"

Brady nodded yes. "Unsettled spirits have a motive for trying to possess a person. If we can uncover the motive, we'll be better able to identify the entity and exorcise it."

The furnace clanked three times.

"What's that?" said Brady.

"The furnace has been acting up lately. I need a repairman to look at it."

"Does it make that noise only when you're here?"

Libby chewed it over. "I—I can't be sure. I don't know what goes on when I'm not here, and nobody else works here but me."

"Did the clanking start when you began feeling like you were possessed?"

"Why, yes, now that I think about it."

"The entity is causing that sound."

Bullshit. Get rid of the scammer. Cut his head off and smoke it in the retort.

Libby wished she could get rid of the voice. Nevertheless, she felt an overpowering urge to grab a knife from the kitchen and behead Brady.

"Are you OK?" said Brady.

"The noise gets on my nerves."

Brady inspected the furnace.

"Can you fix it?" said Libby, watching him.

"I don't know anything about machines."

"Can a machine be haunted?"

"I suppose. But I believe a demon is causing these inexplicable noises and fetid smells in this building. It's haunting the entire building, not just the machine, and it's targeting you. I can feel its presence in this building."

"I *have* been smelling really sickening odors lately."

"That's part of the process of possession."

"I wish that noise would stop," she said, wincing at the clanging.

Chapter 24

Libby wished Bill had fixed the retort before she had knifed—

"What do you know about the people you've cremated?" said Brady.

"Not much. I make it a point not to know too much about them. I don't want to feel like I know them. I try to keep my job on a business level without getting involved with my customers."

"I understand."

"I did get a serial killer yesterday. The transporters who dropped the body off made a point of telling me about it. He weighed over three hundred pounds and took up the whole furnace."

"Interesting. Did he die of natural causes?"

"As a matter of fact, no. Another inmate in the prison shanked him in the throat."

"That would give his spirit a motive for revenge. Which makes him a strong suspect." Brady paused a beat. "But why would he target *you*?"

"Beats me."

"Unless he wants to use you to get at his killer," said Brady, looking studious.

"Why does he want to involve me? I never go to the prison. There's no way I can get to his killer."

"I don't mean to be disrespectful, but is there any way you could have cremated somebody who was still alive?"

"Absolutely not. The deceased are declared dead before they get here. I have nothing to do with deciding who's dead. Each corpse is presented to me with an accompanying death certificate. I would never burn a living person."

The idea of cremating a living person horrified Libby. She had in fact had nightmares about doing just that. She would wake up screaming and covered with sweat whenever she experienced such a nightmare. It was her worst fear. She couldn't imagine being burned alive in a cremation chamber. It was too horrific to comprehend being trapped in an airtight coffin with flames surrounding you and eating you alive, vaporizing your flesh, your eyeballs bursting out of your head. She felt herself breaking into a sweat at the thought of it.

He dissed you. Called you unprofessional. With all due respect, get the carving knife and cut his head off. I'm your only friend. Listen to me. I'm trying to help you. Invite me in and I can help you.

"I didn't mean to upset you," said Brady. "We need to find the truth in order to battle the demon that is trying to possess you. We can use the truth to set you free. Maybe the entity mistakenly believes you harmed it in some way."

Libby felt fidgety. She glanced into the kitchenette at the knife block containing knives on the Formica countertop.

"Are you OK?" said Brady.

"Just don't accuse me of killing people."

"If someone had been burned alive in the crematorium chamber, it would've been an accident. Certainly not murder."

"The idea of it turns my stomach. I'm meticulous at my job."

"I'm sure you are. I was just wondering if it was possible for someone to be cremated by accident. Say, for instance, the so-called cadaver was in a catatonic trance."

"We have all sorts of checks and balances to prevent a living person from being cremated. And, like I said, I'm not the person who determines death. A coroner would do that."

"I'm thinking of premature burials. They've been known to happen—"

"That was in the past. They don't happen anymore. Science is much more advanced now. Can we change the subject?" she said, irked.

"Unfortunately, it does still happen, but it's rare. One cause is the Lazarus Syndrome."

"Never heard of it."

"In the Lazarus Syndrome a person is declared dead after CPR fails to resuscitate him. However, the supposedly dead person can come back to life an hour later."

Libby trembled. "You're bumming me out, making me think I burned someone alive."

"I don't think we can rule it out."

"Thanks for making me feel guilty."

You see. He hates you. Get the knife. Kill him.

"Leave me alone," said Libby, talking to the voice in her head.

"What?" said Brady. "We must find the truth before I can exorcise you."

"Just stop accusing me of burning someone alive."

"I'm not accusing you of it. I'm just saying it's possible. I'm trying to establish a motive for an unsettled spirit to want to possess you. We can put the spirit to rest if we know what's agitating it. Especially if it's mistaken in targeting you, thinking you're the one who did it harm. We can tell it the truth and it might leave you alone."

"'Might'?"

"It could have another motive beyond punishing you. It might want to possess you in order to use you to get revenge against someone else, someone who harmed it."

Libby heaved a sigh. "There's no way you can prove I burned someone alive."

Was Bill still alive when she burned him? No, he couldn't have been. She had felt no pulse in his wrist.

"True," said Brady. "We can't. But we can't prove you didn't either." He thought for a moment. "Do you know if a murder ever took place inside the crematorium?"

Nonplussed, she stared at him.

Brady scoped out the crematorium. "I'm sensing an evil entity's presence."

"If a murder *did* take place here, nobody ever told me about it."

Was there any way a psychic could read her mind and know she had killed Bill? She didn't believe psychics could read minds. They got in touch with the spirit world, but they couldn't read minds. He couldn't know she had killed Bill.

"Maybe a murder was committed in the crematorium before you started working here," suggested Brady. "The murder victim could be haunting you since you're the new manager."

"I guess it's possible."

"It would give an unsettled spirit a motive for possessing you. Vengeance is a powerful motive."

"My boss would know better than me if somebody got murdered here before I started the job."

"Maybe he'll fill you in if you ask him."

"We're not on good terms, especially after today."

Kill the scumbag and be done with him. I'm your only friend. Listen to me. Go to the knife block.

Screwing up her face Libby held her hands over her ears, trying to prevent the voice from harassing her.

"Are you ill?" said Brady.

"I—uh—it's been a trying day."

"Let's continue our discussion at another time," said Brady, fixing to leave.

Don't let him escape. He's going to the cops. Kill him. Slash his throat. Hurry.

Gnashing her teeth, her eyes bugging out of her head, Libby launched herself toward the kitchenette to retrieve the carving knife. Anything to make the voice stop echoing through her head, deafening her, turning her into a nervous wreck.

She froze in her tracks when she heard knocking on the front door.

Chapter 25

Saved by the bell. Libby sneaked a smoldering glance at Brady.

"Want me to get the door?" said Brady.

"I'll get it," said Libby, trying to collect herself and subdue the rage that was erupting inside her, bursting to vent itself in his murder.

"Who is it?"

"Another delivery probably. Plenty of people die every day. They keep the oven busy."

"Have you thought about closing down the business while you deal with the demon that's lurking here?"

"It's not my call. The owner makes those decisions. He's not gonna shut down the place if I tell him it's haunted. He'll laugh in my face."

"You're in grave danger."

"He doesn't care about me. He cares only about his precious business. If we close down, his profit margin will shrink. We never close. We're even open on Sundays. The truth is a lot of people like to have their dear departed relatives cremated on Sundays. It's the religious aspect of the thing."

The knocking resumed.

Libby flung open the door and gasped.

Two LAPD cops in dark blazers stood in front of her. The one on her left was a blonde in her forties with wide hips. She sported a sassy short haircut with fine hair that looked windswept over her forehead. Her lips had a downward curl on their edges. Her intense blue eyes targeted Libby's face.

The female's partner was a stocky thirtysomething guy with a large vein that pulsed across his forehead like an earthworm burrowing through his flesh. His cropped black hair glittered like gasoline-dipped lead filings under the bright sunlight. His black eyes regarded Libby with a flat gaze.

She could tell they were cops because they had badges clipped to their belts.

Libby's heartbeat was off the charts. She didn't want to talk to cops. What were cops doing here?

"Hello, ma'am," said the guy. "I'm Detective Rafa. And that's my fellow detective Anna."

"Hello," said Anna, offering a brief smile.

"We're from the LAPD. Who do we have the pleasure of speaking to?"

"I'm Libby Genet. Would you like to come in?"

"Thank you," said Rafa.

Rafa and Anna entered the premises.

Libby didn't see a hearse in the driveway. She saw a police cruiser. She doubted the cops were delivering a corpse. Then what did they want? She tried to slow down her heartbeat by force of will. Cops made her nervous. They had a way about them that made her feel guilty for no reason. But in her case there *was* a reason. She had murdered Bill.

"Are we interrupting something?" said Anna, noticing Brady.

"Not at all," said Brady.

"You're probably wondering why we're here," said Rafa. "We got a report from a cremation oven repair shop that a repairman they dispatched here has disappeared. They have been unable to contact him since he reported to his dispatcher that he had arrived here. His name's Bill."

"That's strange," said Libby, her anxiety stoked by the info.

There was no way they could know she had killed him, she told herself to calm her nerves. Her nerves refused to listen.

"The repair foreman says you recently filed a request to have your oven repaired. Is that correct, Ms. Genet?"

"It is."

"When did he show up here?" said Rafa, digging a pad out of his trouser pocket and withdrawing a pen from his brown blazer's black vinyl pocket protector.

"I did request a repair order." Libby paused a beat. "But the repairman never showed up."

She wasn't sure why she had lied about Bill not showing up. Maybe it was a case of nerves. She figured it would make her look more innocent if she said she had never met Bill.

"That's odd," said Rafa. "The last call the dispatcher got from Bill was from him saying he had arrived at your business."

Should she change her story? If she did, it would make her look like she was lying.

"He never showed up here," she said.

"Why would he say he was here if he wasn't?"

"You'd have to ask him."

"That's the problem. We can't ask him. We can't find him. The foreman believes Bill might have met with foul play. It's not like the man to go AWOL. It's not in Bill's character, says the foreman."

"I was getting ready to call the company and complain because their repairman never showed up."

"Hmm," said Rafa, absently pulling his earlobe.

The scumbag Brady what's his face sicced the cops on you. You see. You should've cut his throat when you had the chance. This is all on him. He knows you killed Bill.

Libby cleaned out her ear with her pinky, trying to blot out the voice. There was no way Brady could know she had killed Bill. The voice was full of lies.

Anna cast around the crematorium.

"Did you happen to see Bill's van today, Ms. Genet?" said Rafa.

"Nope."

"Why would he lie about reporting here? It makes no sense."

"Maybe he had something he'd rather do."

"Mind if we look around?"

"Uh, why?"

"Maybe he came here when you weren't here."

"You think he's hiding here?"

"You never know. You'd be surprised where we find missing persons."

"Uh, go ahead."

Kill the cops. They're not your friends. They'll find out you killed Bill. They'll throw you in the joint. I'm the only one who can help you. I'm the only one who cares about you.

How could they find out? Bill was gone. There was nothing left of him but ashes.

Rafa and Anna moseyed around the crematorium, trying to pick up on any evidence that might indicate Bill had been there.

Brady approached Rafa. "I don't understand what you're looking for. Do you think Libby's lying?"

Rafa gave him a no-nonsense stare. "Not at all, sir. What is your name again?"

"Brady."

"Do you work here?"

"I'm just visiting."

"Did you see a furnace repairman here while you've been visiting?"

"No. Do you really think he's hiding here?"

"We don't think anything. We have open minds. A missing person's report has been filed, and the filer believes there has been foul play. Bill was supposed to report here for a work assignment. We don't understand why he didn't. We're just doing our job, trying to find clues."

"Why did Bill say he was here if he was never here?" said Anna, approaching them.

"I can't help you," said Brady.

"You see our dilemma, don't you? Somebody's lying."

"You seem to think it's Libby."

"We don't think anything," said Rafa. "We're trying to find out what happened to Bill. Is that all right with you?" he said, his voice edged.

Shrugging, Brady retreated.

Libby saw Rafa amble toward her office.

"Is this your office?" asked Rafa.

"Yeah," answered Libby, remembering with apprehension that Bill's pocket litter was stuffed in a plastic bag in her office desk's bottom drawer.

Rafa nodded and peeked into the office, surveying it.

Her palms sweaty, Libby willed him not to enter her office and open the desk drawers.

Anna wandered toward Libby's bedroom. "Do you live here, Ms. Genet?"

"Saves on rent," said Libby.

Anna nodded and made for the kitchenette.

Rafa approached Libby. "Did you have any visitors here today?"

"I received the delivery of a cadaver," said Libby.

"Uh-huh. Anyone else?"

"Uh—my boss dropped in." The instant she said the words she regretted them.

Stringfellow had seen Bill's corpse in the crematorium. However, Libby had never told him the corpse's name. Maybe she was in the clear.

"Who is your boss?"

"Herbert Stringfellow."

Rafa scribbled the name on his pad. "I have terrible handwriting. I have trouble reading it myself. This is what I get for not listening to my penmanship teacher in grade school. Do you spell *fellow* like it sounds?"

"Right."

Libby hoped the cops never contacted Stringfellow. The guy might start talking about the bloody corpse she said the cops dropped off at the crematorium, which would pique the cops' interest. Not much she could do about it now. The damage was done.

"Thank you for your time, Ms. Genet," said Anna as she headed to the front door with Rafa.

"One more thing," said Rafa. "If Bill shows up here, could you give us a call?"

He handed his business card to Libby.

Chapter 26

Libby was relieved when the cops left.

"You live here?" said Brady.

"I live and work here," said Libby.

"Isn't it depressing living in a crematorium?"

"No."

"Don't you feel cut off from people?"

"I want to be cut off from people. They've treated me like dirt most of my life."

"Then you're taking refuge here."

"If you want to call it that."

"I don't mean to pry, but what exactly happened to you?"

Libby turned on him. "Why is that your business?"

"It might have something do with the demon that's trying to possess you."

Libby didn't like talking about it. She didn't like thinking about it. She wanted to forget it had ever happened, because there was nothing she could do about it. Recalling it was torturing herself pointlessly. You couldn't change the past. It was best to forget it and get on with your life.

"I don't like talking about it," she said.

"If we can find the demon's motive for haunting you, it will help us defeat the entity."

Libby hesitated. Every time she thought about it she felt angry. Then she felt frustrated, because there was nothing she could do about it to redress the wrong.

"Maybe the cops can help you," said Brady.

"Nobody can help me. That's why I don't like thinking about it. I feel so helpless."

"I'm not gonna tell anyone if that's what you're worried about. It's strictly confidential."

Feeling hungry, Libby made her way to the kitchenette. She withdrew a plastic bag of bread from the breadbox, removed a slice of white bread, and took a bite of it.

Brady followed her.

"Want a piece of bread?" she said.

"Thanks," he said, withdrawing a slice from the bag she held out to him.

He chewed the bread.

"A guy named Ed Grainger is the son of a rich hedge fund manager," Libby found herself saying despite her reservations about discussing the subject. "He shot my mother and sister dead."

He stopped chewing. "How awful. Why would he do such a thing?"

"He claimed he was out of his mind at the time because he was taking magic mushrooms prescribed by his shrink. When he was high on psylocibin, he saw my mom and sister in a restaurant and became convinced they were plotting to kill him. He took out a gun and shot them."

"Did he get convicted?"

"The DA's office dropped their case against him."

"What?" said Brady in astonishment. "How could he get away with murder?"

"He claimed the magic mushrooms made him insane. He had no idea what he was doing."

"They let him go?" said Brady, his voice ringing with disbelief.

"There was another reason they had to drop the case. The cops who recovered the murder weapon from his car did it illegally. 'Fruit from the poisonous tree' they call it in legal terms. The DA couldn't use the gun at a trial because of the technicality. Combine that with Grainger's claim that he was insane at the time, and the DA refused to prosecute. Plus . . ."

"Plus what?"

"Plus Grainger's father donated millions of dollars to the DA's political campaign. Another incentive for the DA to drop the case."

Brady shook his head. "So unfair. I can see why you're distrustful of people and take refuge here."

"I don't like talking about it. I get so angry and frustrated by it when I remember it that I get headaches and ulcers."

"Can't they retry him?"

"Why bother? They have no interest in pursuing the case. Don't forget Grainger is the son of rich Bel Air parents who can hire the best lawyers in the business. There's no way the DA could get a conviction. The DA doesn't want to take on the moneyed classes with such a weak case. He knows which side his bread is buttered on."

"At least if they put this Grainger on trial, it would embarrass him being accused of murder. It would hurt his reputation."

"The DA's office doesn't think like that. If they don't believe they can get a conviction, they don't prosecute. They say it's a waste of taxpayer's money to pursue an unwinnable case."

Brady swallowed the remainder of his slice of bread. "Bummer."

"It burns in my craw that he got away with it. That's why I can't think about it. I have to forget it happened. It's the only way I can continue to function. I can't accomplish anything if I'm constantly filled with outrage at the injustice of it."

"The legal system is a joke," said Brady, his face drawn. "Evil rules the world."

"There's another reason I live here. I came here to disappear from my enemies."

"Go on."

"Ed Grainger swore he'd get even with me for trying to put him in jail for murdering my mom and sister. If he can't find me, he can't harm me."

"It's sad we have to live like pariahs in hiding in this day and age because of the power of evil people."

"I'm worried he'll find me even if I keep my head down. He has a ton of money and endless resources to track anybody he wants."

"Is there some way I can help?"

He doesn't give a damn about you. He wants your money. Kill him.

Libby wished she could kill the voice.

Kill him or you'll regret it. I'm the only one telling you the truth. Listen to me. I care about you. Nobody else does. Trust me. Let me inside you and together we'll kill him.

Clenching her jaw Libby resisted the compulsion to run to the kitchen and retrieve the carving knife to cut Brady's throat.

"Is something the matter?" said Brady, noticing her discomfiture.

"I think you better go."

"You need to smudge the crematorium with sage ASAP. You can't delay. I feel the presence of the entity. It is becoming more powerful even as we speak."

"I don't have any sage."

"Buy it at Jean Baptiste's House of Voodoo in Hollywood."

Libby feared it was too late. The entity had already forced her to kill Bill. And now it wanted her to kill Brady. She felt her body go rigid as she fought off the demon. Her teeth began to chatter as she stood opposite Brady.

"Are you religious?" he said with concern.

"I'm not into superstition," she managed to say, trembling.

"You don't look well."

"I'm OK," she said, continuing to tremble.

"Can I drive you to the hospital?"

"You need to leave."

"You look like you're having a seizure," said Brady, widening his eyes as he watched her quiver.

"Leave me alone," she lashed out at him.

Grudgingly Brady walked backward to the front door, keeping his eyes on her, worried she was having a stroke.

"Is it the demon?" he said.

"Go away."

Was it her voice or the demon's that issued from her mouth? She couldn't tell.

"Fight it," said Brady at the front door. "You need to keep fighting it. Don't give up. After you smudge this building we'll have a séance to make sure the demon is gone."

Cut him. Cut him good. Give him a Colombian necktie. Cut his throat and yank his tongue through the slit.

Unable to restrain herself any longer, Libby bolted to the kitchen to retrieve the carving knife.

Hurry. You have no time to waste. Kill him before he leaves.

Brady opened the front door and departed.

Chapter 27

Brady climbed into his rental Jeep Gladiator and backed out of the crematorium driveway, convinced Libby was in the final stages of possession.

If he couldn't free her from the demon shortly, it would gain complete control of her, and there was no telling what she would do.

It was hard to help her though, because she kept fending him off. He figured it wasn't her fighting him but the demon as it continued to wage war to possess her.

He knew how difficult it was to fight a demon. He recalled Theresa's demon possessing him and forcing him to kill and wreak vengeance on her murderous mother.

Preoccupied, he almost rear-ended the SUV slowing in front of him. He slammed on the Gladiator's brakes in the nick of time. He had to concentrate on his driving.

He didn't know how he could help Libby if she refused to let him. He couldn't force her to smudge the crematorium. It was important she do it on her own initiative. She was the one who had to fight the demon. Brady couldn't fight the demon for her. He could help her only if she wanted his help.

For the time being it appeared she was resisting the demon. He could sense an internal conflict being waged inside her. Libby's nervousness and tenseness were outward manifestations of the conflict between her and the demon. She was still strong enough to resist the evil entity.

Brady didn't think she would be able to fight it off by herself. She needed his help. He wished he had more knowledge of exorcising demons. He had experience with possession, and he had learned from the occultist Dr. Armitage how to fight it. But a cult of satanists had slashed Armitage's throat and left him to die on Brady's front lawn. Brady was on his own with his exorcism of Libby. He had nobody to consult.

He had dealt with only one demon in his life, the one that had possessed him when he was ten years old. From that experience he had learned how demons controlled the wills of their victims and forced them to do things they would never do on their own, such as commit murder.

Brady wondered if Libby's demon was trying to get her to kill. He figured it was, for he had sensed the evil emanating from it and permeating the crematorium. He had to exorcise the demon before it succeeded at turning Libby into a murderer.

On her own she could stop the process of demonic possession for only so long. Eventually the demon would have its way with her—unless it was exorcised.

The smudging of Brady's house with sage hadn't accomplished exorcising the demon in his case, because the demon had been too strong, according to Armitage. Brady hoped the crematorium demon was weaker and would retreat when Libby smudged her home.

He turned his Gladiator into the Von's parking lot to buy a carton of orange juice.

Parking his rental he happened to notice a crematorium furnace repair van parked a dozen slots away. According to the cops who had paid Libby a visit, they were looking for the repairman who had never showed up to fix Libby's crematorium oven.

Brady wondered if this could be the repairman's vehicle. After all, how many crematorium furnace repair shops could there be in this section of LA? He strode over to the van and picked up on a parking ticket wedged under one of its windshield wipers.

The van must have been there a long time. It seemed like a good bet it might be Bill's. Making sure nobody was watching him Brady tried to open the driver's-side door. It was locked.

Libby had said Bill had never showed up at her business. Maybe something had happened to Bill while he was at the Von's. The problem was this Von's was only a couple of miles from the crematorium. In the cops' eyes, the van's presence in the lot might throw suspicion on Libby in the case of Bill's disappearance.

Brady didn't want to get Libby in trouble with the cops.

Then again, maybe the cops could find Bill in the vicinity of the Von's if they knew his van was parked here. Maybe something had happened to him while he was here.

Shielding his eyes from the sun's glare, Brady peered into the van at the steering wheel. He thought he saw dried blood on it. He couldn't be sure. He scoped out the van's front seats. He didn't see any more blood. Maybe it wasn't blood. Or maybe Bill had smashed a blood-gorged mosquito on his steering wheel, though Brady didn't spot anything resembling a dead mosquito near the blood. Granted, mosquitoes were small, and the mosquito corpse could have fallen into the footwell, he supposed, though he couldn't see it there.

Brady decided to call the cops and report the van. If the cops found Bill nearby, they would leave Libby alone.

Chapter 28

Now that there was nobody but her in the crematorium the voice stopped pestering her. She was grateful to be rid of its nagging. She couldn't keep fighting it. She felt herself becoming weaker the more it continued to assert itself in taking over her life. The voice was obsessive. The only thing it wanted her to do was kill.

Entering her office she thought about Bill's belongings in the desk drawer. She needed to get rid of them before the cops paid her a return visit. The cops would become suspicious of her involvement in Bill's disappearance if they found his personal effects in her office.

She inspected Bill's belongings in the plastic bag stored in her desk drawer. The only metal in the bag was Bill's keys. They weren't made of titanium, so the retort would burn them along with his other stuff. Titanium and a few other metals were the only things the retort couldn't incinerate because it didn't get hot enough.

She dumped his wallet, comb, keys, and other possessions into the retort and turned it on. Say good-bye to Bill.

She wouldn't have to worry about the cops returning and connecting her to Bill's murder. There was no evidence and no corpus delicti.

The knocking at the front door disturbed her train of thought.

Maybe it was a delivery, though they normally called her in advance to let her know they were on their way with a corpse.

She became nervous. What if it was the cops? Were they suspicious of her and returning to grill her about Bill? Why should she be nervous? She had just destroyed all the evidence. There was nothing left to incriminate her in Bill's murder.

Libby relaxed after a fashion and approached the door. Composing herself she answered it.

Dumbfounded, she saw a sixtysomething man in a wheelchair sitting at her doorstep. His ash grey hair tumbled rakishly over his ears. His hazel eyes had a cantankerous glint to them. Dry complected with a receding hairline, he thrust his narrow jaw at her.

"Finally," he said with chapped lips. "I thought you were never gonna answer the door."

"Dad—uh—how did you get here," she said, seeing no vehicle in the driveway.

"I hired an Uber. It was a bastard, getting in and out of it with this wheelchair, let me tell you. I didn't have enough money to pay him to wait around. I'll have to call another Uber when I'm done here. Are you gonna just stand there and make me sit out here all day?"

"Of course not," she said in astonishment at his presence. "Come in."

Dan Genet piloted his electric wheelchair into the crematorium.

"I can't believe you call this place home," he said, taking in the dreary surroundings, including the morbid brick oven. "Why would you want to live in a crematorium of all places?"

"How did you find me?" she said, bemused.

She had never told anyone where she lived, not even her father. The fewer who knew, the better.

"There are ways on the Internet to find anyone if you know what you're doing," he said.

If *he* could find her, it meant anyone could, including Ed Grainger, the man she was hiding from. Not good.

"What happened to you?" she said, remarking his wheelchair with commiseration.

"I was in a car accident. I would've told you sooner, but I had no idea where to find you. You never gave me a way to contact you. It was thoughtless of you if you ask me."

"I—uh—I don't want to be a bother to you."

"You're not a bother. You're the only one I have left in the world after they took your mother and sister from me," said Dan, his face dour.

"I'm sorry to hear you were in a car accident."

Kill him. He doesn't give a damn about you. He never did.

"Leave me alone," said Libby, raging in exasperation at the voice.

"What?" said Dan, flabbergasted. "I came all this way to see you, and this is the thanks I get?"

"I wasn't talking to you."

Puzzled, Dan looked around the room. "Who were you talking to?"

"I—I—thought I heard my cat yowling. He wants to eat every three minutes."

"I didn't hear anything."

"I can't believe it's you," she said, changing the subject.

"Yeah, well, it took forever for me to find you. If you want to throw your life away and bury yourself in a crematorium, that's your decision. But at least you could have told me where you live. I'm your father for the love of Mike."

Chapter 29

"I have no choice but to hide," said Libby.

"What do you mean? Are you in trouble, Libby?" said Dan, his eyes solicitous.

"It's Ed Grainger. I told the DA not to drop the case against him for killing Mom and Wendy. Grainger heard about it. He swore he'd get back at me."

"Don't get me started. They dropped the case against the asshole because of his fancy-dan, high-powered Beverly Hills shysters and a stupid legal technicality they dredged up. The law exists only to protect the rich. It's a freaking jungle out there if you're ordinary folks like us." Dan scratched his temple. "I have a friend who told me the wheels of justice grind slowly. I told him he's deluded. They don't grind at all. He said I needed patience. I told him I'd be dead before the wheels started to grind. Justice delayed is justice denied."

"Get this through your head. Grainger still wants revenge against me."

"You don't have to worry about me telling him where you're hiding if that's what's bugging you."

"Not at all. I figured if I told you where I lived, it would put your life at risk because Grainger would threaten you to find out where I lived."

"No spoiled rotten rich kid is gonna threaten me and get away with it. I'll shove the silver spoon in his mouth so far down his throat it'll come out his other end."

Libby paused. "How do you know he wasn't the one who arranged your car accident?"

Dan did a double take. "I never even considered it."

Libby had a faraway look in her eye. "What if there are no such things as accidents? What if all accidents are manifestations of evil? Evil is everywhere."

"What's gotten into you, Libby? Accidents *do* happen, you know. You're starting to sound paranoid."

"Do you deny evil exists?"

"Not at all."

"It's always out there ready to strike."

"That doesn't mean you have to think about it all the time."

"Grainger killed Mom and Wendy. That's not paranoia. It's real."

"Life is brutal and cruel, and suffering is everywhere. Babies cry when they're born. They don't cheer. Suffering is our lot. I'm not denying that. But not everyone is your enemy. There are some OK people out there."

"That's what I thought till I met Ed Grainger. I never met an eviler man."

"He thinks he can do whatever he wants because he's a trust-fund baby." Dan paused. "Actually, he's right. We have to be careful out there. I'm not saying otherwise. But not everyone is as rotten as Grainger."

"I don't share your faith in people. I'm a victim of my experience with others."

Dan shrugged imperceptibly. "In the end I don't trust anyone but myself. But I cut slack for most people. They're not all a bunch of Ed Graingers. The world would collapse into anarchy if they were."

"If you're trying to get me to change my mind and move where I can be found, you're not succeeding. I'm staying incommunicado."

"I'm not trying to get you to do anything. I came here because I haven't seen you in a dog's age. You're my daughter and I care about you."

Kill him. He's lying. He led your enemies here. Believe me. You can trust me. I'm you're only friend.

Pulling a face Libby covered her ears. "No."

"No what?" said Dan, confused. "Are you denying you're my daughter?"

"I—I—was—I was thinking of something else," said Libby, her voice tense.

"You sound confused. Maybe it's because you don't socialize anymore. You can't shut yourself away in a crematorium and never come out. It's not good for you. You burn dead bodies here. It's no place for a young woman. You need to experience the world and grow like a flower in the sun," he said, making an expansive motion with his arms. "Ye gods, this vault of death is stunting your growth. Cooped up here, you're turning in on yourself. It's not healthy. You're imagining evil is everywhere. It isn't."

"I feel safer here."

"Think of your emotional well-being."

"Don't you understand? He'll kill me if he finds out where I am. My emotional well-being doesn't matter if I'm killed."

"Why don't you move in with me? I have a nice house. This corpse joint is a bummer. Surrounded by burning bodies, you must be chronically depressed. How can that be good for your mental health? Don't you have nightmares, sleeping under this tomb's roof? This is like something out of Poe. You shouldn't be obsessed with death."

"I'm not obsessed with death. I'm trying to stay alive. I feel safe from the mass murderer Grainger here."

"I can protect you in my house. You won't need to live in constant fear for your life."

"Then I'd have to live in constant fear for your life too."

Dan shook his head. "Don't worry about me. I'm not scared of that bastard."

"He's vindictive. He hates me and wants revenge. He will never forget I told the DA not to drop the case against him. He'll come after me till he finds me and he'll take his revenge."

Dan sat back in his wheelchair and gazed up at Libby. "Why bother? He got off scot-free. He got away with murder. Why should he care what you told the DA?"

Libby didn't know how she could make him understand.

"You don't understand evil people like him," she said. "They're consumed with hate. They're vindictive. They don't let their enemies go on living. He won't be satisfied until I'm dead."

"I can't protect you here," said Dan in frustration. "I *can* protect you at my house."

He wants you to take care of him and push his wheelchair around. You'll be his slave. Don't you see? Kill him before he takes control over you.

The never-ending voice. Her constant companion from the dark side. How could she get rid of it? Maybe smudging the crematorium like Brady had said would help.

"I can take care of myself," she said.

"Do you ever look at yourself in the mirror?" said Dan. "You're a bucket of nerves. You're shaking all over and you look pale. You look worse than Shelley Duvall when she was shaking with fear in *The Shining*. You're letting yourself go to pot. This place is a dungeon." He sniffed the air. "It smells in here too. What's that stink?"

He rolled his wheelchair around the room, searching for the source of the stink. He came to a halt.

"And it's colder than hell here," he said.

She realized he had parked his wheelchair in the middle of the crematorium cold spot.

Watching his breath turn to vapor, he rubbed his arms, trying to keep warm.

He's the one making you nervous. Kill him. He won't let you live your life like you want.

"I like my job, and I don't want to lose it," she said.

"Who said anything about losing it? You can continue to work here if you move in with me. What's the problem? You got a car. You can commute."

He could be overbearing at times. She felt like he was smothering her when she was with him.

"I would put your life in danger if I moved in with you," she said. "Don't you understand? Grainger's gonna come after me when he finds out where I live. He'll kill both of us."

"I'm not gonna tell him."

"I can't live out in the open like other people. He'll find me."

"I'll protect you. He has to come through me to get to you."

"How can *you* protect me? You can't even walk."

Dan flinched at the withering insult.

"I didn't mean it to sound like that," said Libby, regretting her phrasing.

"Yeah, you did. You make me sound like a helpless invalid," said Dan, wheeling himself away from her, his pride hurt.

"*I care about you.* That's why I don't want to endanger your life by moving in with you."

He's manipulating you. Cut his face off. Cut his tongue out and nail it to the door.

"Stop it," said Libby, at the end of her rope.

Dan turned his wheelchair around to face her. "Stop what?"

"Not you," she muttered.

"We're the only two in this room. Now you're talking to yourself. I'm telling you this death chamber is driving you nuts. You can't lock yourself up here. It's not good for you."

"Do you believe in possession?"

"You mean, like in that movie *The Exorcist*?"

"Yeah."

"Of course not. You see, that's what I mean. You got all these morbid thoughts in your head because you live in a crypt. You gotta move outa here."

"It's not safe for me to move."

"I got a gun back home. And I know how to use it. Just because I'm in a wheelchair doesn't mean I can't fire a gun."

"I don't want you to have to fire a gun."

Kill him. He wants you to be his sock puppet. Get the carving knife. Kill him. They're gonna use him to get to you. Cut his eyes out and eat them like lollipops.

Libby's right hand started shaking. She couldn't control it. She grabbed it with her left hand to steady it. The hand kept shaking. She needed to go to the kitchenette and get the carving knife. She couldn't resist the urge any longer.

"What's wrong?" said Dan. "I'm telling you, you're heading for a nervous breakdown if you keep living under these dreadful conditions."

I'm heading for the kitchen to get a knife to cut off your head.

She couldn't keep the thought out of her mind. Her right hand was dragging her toward the kitchenette no matter how hard she tried to resist it.

He wants you to be his slave. Cut his head off.

The voice kept tormenting her.

She staggered to the kitchenette behind her right hand which led the way.

"What's gotten into you?" said Dan, watching her with consternation. "Do you want me to call a paramedic? Do you have Parkinson's? You need to calm down. You're a nervous Nellie. What's wrong with your hand?"

Shaking uncontrollably, Libby returned from the kitchenette, carving knife in hand, her teeth bared as she glowered at Dan.

"I'm calling 911," said Dan, alarmed at her sinister aspect. "You need an ambulance. You're having a heart attack."

She lurched toward him, gnashing her teeth, holding the knife in front of her below her waist, pointing the blade in her quivering hand at Dan.

"Hello," said Dan into his cell phone, his widening eyes trained on Libby in apprehension. "This is an emergency."

Kill him. Kill him.

Libby thrust the knife into Dan's throat and severed his carotid artery, unleashing a fountain of blood from his ragged throat.

Dan gasped into his cell phone.

"What is your address, sir?" said the dispatcher on the other end of the line.

Dan dropped his blood-soaked cell phone to the floor, where it clattered at his feet and slid in his blood.

"Sir? You need to speak up, sir." The dispatcher waited for an answer. "Keep the line open, and we'll trace you. Do you understand, sir?"

Libby stamped on the cell phone with her heel, shattering the glass face. She stamped on the phone two more times. She picked it up, took it to the kitchenette, filled the sink with water, and tossed the phone in the sink.

Nobody could trace the cell phone now. She gloated in triumph.

Bloody knife in hand, she returned to Dan's lifeless body slumped in the wheelchair, his blood-smeared mouth with its withered lips hanging agape.

"Dad. Oh, Dad," she said, breaking into tears. "What have I done?"

Weeping, her head bowed, she fell to her knees, letting go of the knife.

"I'm turning into a monster," she moaned in despair.

Chapter 30

Ed Grainger knew a thing or two about the black arts. He had been dabbling in them for years. Magic mushrooms had paved the way for his initiation into black magic, introducing him to the gateway to hell, where demons lurked, demons who could be summoned by anyone knowledgeable in the black arts.

It gave him a heady sense of power to be able to summon and control an evil demon that wreaked havoc on the world. Few had the power to do it. He was one of those select few.

He didn't need to hire hit men when he could use a demon to do his evil bidding. He didn't like wasting money on hired guns. A demon would do the job for free. And nobody could trace the crime to Grainger.

He never let anyone get away with dissing him. His father had taught him long ago to never suffer disrespect at the hands of others without retaliating, to always get even if anyone dared to disrespect him. Ed Grainger had learned his lesson well.

He had gone his father one better. Ed had communicated with demons via magic mushrooms, something his father had never dared to do. His father didn't even drink booze, let alone use psychedelic drugs. His mind closed to the doors of perception, his father used battalions of lawyers to do his dirty work instead of summoning demons.

Which made his father weaker than him, decided Ed, sitting in the driver's seat of his late model Grigio Ingrid Ferrari Spider parked in the driveway of his Bel Air Dutch Colonial mansion. It amused him to know that the color "Grigio Ingrid," a warm grey, was created by the multimillionaire film director Roberto Rossellini to match the color of his movie-star wife Ingrid Bergman's eyes.

Rossellini was a mental pigmy compared to him. Rossellini had no idea how to summon demons from the bowels of hell.

Ed could safely say to his father that nobody had ever gotten away with dissing him. They had all suffered payback, meaning they had led brief lives. The best thing about Ed's kind of payback was that it could never be traced back to him. Demons didn't leave a trail of clues for the cops to follow.

At the steering wheel of the convertible Ferrari, eying the picture-postcard blue California sky overhead, Ed yawned. He never had to fear getting caught by cops. In some ways it was too easy to get away with murder like he did. However, it wasn't easy summoning a demon. Which was the hard part of exacting retribution against his enemies.

He had to drop psilocybin to enter the doors of hell. Ingesting the drug was the only way he knew of to contact the world of demons.

The one thing he had to fear on his journeys into Hades was losing his sanity. Experiencing the drug was tantamount to experiencing madness. There was always the chance he might never return from his treks to hell and the outer limits of sanity. His mind could end up in hell for the rest of his life and he could die screaming in a madhouse. It was a risk he was willing to take to wreak vengeance on his enemies. Not a single one of his enemies must be allowed to go on living.

You had to dance with the devil if you wanted to be a billionaire, which took balls. Most idiots were cowards and weren't willing to take the risks necessary to become rich.

Ed considered himself fearless. To venture into the bowels of hell after dropping magic mushrooms you had to be bold enough to dance on a tightrope strung over the Grand Canyon. There was always the chance you could fall into the abyss of madness.

The sky was a blinding blue today. His pale blue eyes glittered in the sunlight. Sometimes, when he had ingested enough psilocybin, he had the crazy thought that he could look directly at the sun and not go blind. But he didn't stare at the sun, because he knew his enemies would love for him to go blind. Then they would walk all over him.

They had no idea how terrifying it was to journey into hell to summon a demon to deal with his latest enemy. They were too scared to even consider it. Which was why he would always defeat them.

In the case of Libby, he didn't think summoning a demon would be enough. He wanted to use his own spirit to enslave her and make her pay for her attempts to get him imprisoned. With his own spirit possessing her, he could watch her suffer at his every whim. He would be able to see what she saw as she committed the heinous crimes he commanded her to enact.

He was going to make her pay for the war she had waged against him after he had killed her mother and sister.

Chapter 31

Libby cleaned up the evidence of Dad's murder in the crematorium. She had to steel herself to the brutal fact that she had murdered her own father for no reason she could think of. It was the demon that was taking over her very being who had forced her to kill Dad.

Crippled with guilt for committing patricide, she could barely mop his blood off the floor. Each stroke of the mop was a dagger thrust of guilt into her, plaguing her conscience. She kept looking at his lifeless body sitting in the blood-streaked wheelchair as if he was watching her with his glassy dead eyes fixed in an accusing stare.

She never wanted to kill him. Why did he have to come here in the first place? How did he find her? She had thought she had covered her tracks well and that nobody would ever find her in this godforsaken house of death. She had thought wrong.

What about Grainger? Could he find her? Maybe not. Her father had known her better than anyone else had, which had given him an edge in locating her. Grainger had no edge that she could think of, other than money, which, truth to tell, was advantageous to the nth degree in accomplishing any project, including tracking her.

She continued mopping the blood off the floor. Her second murder victim today. How many more would die at her hands? It might have been her hand that had wielded the knife, but it wasn't her. It was the demon that was becoming increasingly dominant inside her.

Libby's back was beginning to ache from all her mopping. Exhausted, she squeezed more blood from the mop into the galvanized steel pail, listening to the blood tinkle as it impinged on the several inches of blood already inside.

Libby Genet, murderer. How could she live with herself, knowing she was a murderer? But she wasn't. It was the demon that had committed murder, using her hand to stab his victims.

She finished mopping up the blood on the floor and looked at her father, who was continuing to stare at her with unblinking eyes.

She would incinerate him in the cremation chamber and be rid of the corpus delicti.

She couldn't bear to look at his eyes that condemned her for murdering him.

Overcome with grief, she clutched her brow, bowed her head, and covered her eyes. She wanted to scream. But she didn't want anyone to hear her. It was isolated here, but you never knew who could be approaching the front door. Another cadaver could be waiting for her in a hearse parked in the driveway with the deliveryman walking toward her door even now.

She had to dispose of the body.

Quashing her reluctance, she grabbed the handles on the wheelchair and rolled her father toward the oven.

She struggled to load the corpse onto the conveyor belt. She gripped his lame legs and strained to load the rest of the body onto the belt. The wheelchair kept sliding backward and away from the oven.

She released Dan's legs, pushed the wheelchair back toward the oven, and, leaning over, locked the wheels. She resumed lifting his legs and dragging the rest of him onto the conveyor belt that fed the oven.

At last, breaking into a sweat, she managed with a grunt to horse the entire body onto the belt.

Breathing hard she backed away from the oven and stretched her sore back.

She stepped toward the computer, pushed the button that opened the oven door, and pushed another button that operated the conveyor belt, sending the cadaver into the core of the oven. Convinced he was staring at her from inside the oven, she closed the door quickly to get him out of her sight. She couldn't bear looking at him any longer. Especially his eyes—those eyes that kept staring at her, condemning her. She wanted to cut them out of his head to get them to stop staring at her. Didn't he understand it wasn't her fault she had killed him? The demon had forced her to do it. *Those horrible, dreadful eyes.*

Using the computer she initiated the cremation.

The wheelchair. How was she going to dispose of it?

If parts of it were made of titanium, the cremation chamber wouldn't destroy them because it didn't get hot enough to burn

113

titanium. But she had to do something with the chair. It had bloodstains on the leather which might not come out. If she cleaned them before they dried, she could remove them with cold water alone.

She retrieved a paper towel in the kitchenette, soaked it in cold water, and returned to the wheelchair to scrub the blood off it with the damp towel. She needed to repeat the process with paper towels several times before the wheelchair was clean.

How was she going to explain a wheelchair in the crematorium?

She noticed it was collapsible. Wearing nitrile gloves she would fold it, load it into her car, and abandon it in a parking lot. Nobody would know where it had come from. It sounded like a good plan.

She set to work scrubbing off the bloodstains on the wheelchair.

Some of the blood wouldn't come off.

She obtained hydrogen peroxide from the bathroom, poured a little on the remaining bloodstain, and rubbed the stain with another damp paper towel, scrubbing the wheelchair clean.

She couldn't believe how tired she was.

She collapsed in a chair to rest her legs.

Chapter 32

The crematorium was dark and still. In the corner she could barely make out what looked like a large spiderweb with a dark object lurking behind it. Drenched in shadows, the object skulked out from behind the web and, hunched over, slunk toward her.

She couldn't make out its features from this distance in the poor lighting. She thought she could see fangs in its mouth which were dripping with saliva. The creature sent a shiver of fear down her spine as it slouched toward her.

"I am you," it hissed. "Do you welcome me?"

It was covered with black fur like an animal, yet it walked on two legs like a human.

"No," she managed to say, sitting on her chair, petrified and filled with loathing of the creature.

"I am here for you."

"Go away."

It made a sound like a dreadful laugh.

"I am you," it said. "If I go away, you cease to exist."

Convinced it was the demon, Libby wished she had some sage to banish the revolting creature. She couldn't stand the idea of the monstrosity taking over her body. This was the creature that was turning her into a murderer. It had to be.

It wanted to displace her and take over her body.

She had to fight it.

Its bloodred rat eyes transfixed her. Indeed its entire face had the aspect of a rat's. It was something so hideous it couldn't exist in daylight. It could only exist in the darkest corners of a pitch-black nether world.

The creature kept slinking toward her.

"I am you," it said in an unnatural, slimy voice that displaced its hiss. "You can't exist without me."

She recognized its voice. It was the voice she kept hearing in her head, telling her to kill.

She wanted to run for her life. But she couldn't move.

The idea of that grotesque monstrosity taking over her body repelled her and filled her with abhorrence. It was the demon.

She must not let it inside her. She must fight it. But how?

"Say that you want me," it said. "Say that you need me."

"No."

"Say that you want me inside you."

"Never."

"You need me as much as I need you," said the demon, approaching her with its fetid breath.

Libby gagged on the stench. "No."

"Together we are better than alone. Ask me to enter you."

"Go away," said Libby, frozen in her seat with fear.

"Ask me to enter you. It will be the best choice you ever made."

Reeking of death and rot, it sounded like it was purring as it neared her.

Libby shuddered. How could she get it to leave?

"I'll protect you from your enemies," said the demon. "I'll kill them. But you have to let me in first. Invite me in," it cooed in a salacious voice.

Libby shook her head no.

"Nobody can stop us when I am you and you are me," it said. "Let me in and see what I say is true. We are stronger together."

"Liar. You want me gone."

"Nobody can stop us when I am you and you are me," said the demon, sidling up to her, hissing, its bloodred eyes glowing like embers in its rat face.

"Who sent you here?"

"You did. I am you and you are me."

"No, I didn't."

"Ask me to enter you," it said, inflating itself to twice its size and hovering over her with its back arched, raising its hackles, intimidating her. "I will show you a world where you are all-powerful, a world that will be putty in your hands. A world where you can rule like a god."

Libby woke from her nightmare with a start, gasping for breath, her face bathed in sweat. She thought she was going to have a heart attack. Her tongue felt sore. She must have bitten it in her sleep when she was dreaming.

She looked around her bedroom, wide-eyed, fearing the demon would dart out of the shadows and attack.

The bedroom was empty save for her.
A wave of relief swept over her.

Chapter 33

Brady opened his laptop on his desk in his West LA apartment and googled serial killers who had died recently. It didn't take long to find one who had died last week in Terminal Island Penitentiary in Los Angeles.

The killer's name was forty-two-year-old Wayne Bobinsky. He was a 320-pound welder who would get drunk and kill prostitutes. He had strangled seven prostitutes, cut them up with a chain saw, and buried their pieces in his backyard garden, not before he had eaten their calves.

Bobinsky had to be the killer Libby had cremated yesterday.

Brady couldn't find any other serial killers who had died recently in LA. Could it be Bobinsky's tormented spirit that was trying to possess Libby? It seemed possible. The problem was Libby said she had cremated many prisoners who had died in the nearby prison, which must have been the Federal Correctional Institute, Terminal Island. Any one of those prisoners could have died with tormented spirits that could be haunting her.

Brady googled Terminal Island. It incarcerated many Mafia mobsters. Even Charles Manson had done time at Terminal Island.

If Bobinsky was the demon trying to possess Libby, her life was in danger, since he preyed on women.

He read more about Bobinsky on the Internet.

The serial killer used to hold black masses for the murdered hookers, complete with black candles and an altar, before he cut the women to pieces, wrapped their body parts in butcher paper, and buried the parts in his garden, save for their calves, which he dined on after microwaving them.

His wife had never suspected a thing. She filed for divorce after he went to prison.

If Bobinsky was indeed the spirit trying to possess Libby, she would become a murderer if he succeeded. His murderous spirit had to keep on killing. It was the reason he couldn't rest in peace.

In the end, Libby would be convicted and put in prison or killed by one of her intended victims if she became possessed and turned into a serial killer. Brady had to find a way to exorcise her before it was too late.

Brady couldn't be certain Bobinsky was the demon trying to possess Libby, but Bobinsky seemed like a good suspect. Of course, it could always be another spirit from one of the many corpses Libby had cremated that was haunting her.

If it was Bobinsky's spirit, it would never be satisfied if it possessed her. His spirit existed only to commit murder. It would go on killing for the rest of Libby's life, which would be short because she would inevitably be caught.

Brady had to prevent the completion of the possession. The fact that Libby was seeking help from him meant she could still be saved.

He would buy sage from Jean Baptiste's House of Voodoo in Hollywood, charge it to Libby's account, and take the sage with him to smudge the crematorium.

Chapter 34

Libby didn't think she could live with herself after murdering her father.

And yet she was convinced she wasn't the one who had done it. It was the demon in the act of possessing her that had committed the horrific murder. The entity hadn't taken control of her entirely, though she could feel it becoming stronger and harder to fight off. She couldn't fight it off by herself. Its supernatural force was too strong. She needed help from the medium Brady.

She listened to the crematorium furnace burning her father's body. *She had killed her own father*. How was she supposed to come to grips with the abominable act?

She hated herself for murdering him. Why couldn't she fight off the demon? She needed to resist the evil creature. But the demon's power was growing. Each murder it forced her to commit strengthened the entity.

Why was evil focusing on her? First Ed Grainger had murdered her mother and sister, and now evil had revisited her in the guise of the demon that was turning her into a mass murderer. Why her of all people?

Maybe there was no reason. Maybe shit just happened. And it could happen to anyone at any time in a world of chaos. Nobody was safe.

A knock on the door roused her from self-pity.

A customer. She needed to concentrate on her work to fight off her depression at her helplessness at resisting the demon.

She opened the door.

It wasn't a customer.

It was the cops. The two detectives Rafa and Anna were back.

Libby's nerves were already stretched to their limit. Why had the cops returned? They couldn't possibly know she had killed her father.

Her rapid heartbeat was echoing in her ears like the surf crashing on the beach during a storm.

"Hello, Ms. Genet, we have a couple more questions to ask you," said Rafa. "Could we come in?"

She could barely hear him through the roar of the thunderous surf.

"Oh, sure," said Libby, motioning for them to enter, dissembling her fear with a courteous smile.

"We thought you'd be interested to know that we found Bill's repair van abandoned in the Von's parking lot near here."

"Did you find him?"

"No. Just his vehicle. It proves he was in this area, however, since the supermarket is only a couple of miles from here."

"Do you use a wheelchair?" said Anna, picking up on the wheelchair standing near the furnace.

"Uh—oh—no. A bereaved customer was here earlier, planning to cremate a deceased relative. It's hers."

"That's odd. Why did she leave her wheelchair here?"

"She was in a hurry."

"But how could she leave without it if she was an invalid?"

Libby had to think fast. She was becoming entangled in the web of lies she was spinning.

"She's not confined to a wheelchair," she said. "She is able to walk. She finds it convenient to use to get around."

"Why would she forget it? Those things aren't cheap."

"She was grief-stricken and preoccupied with her mother's recent death."

Anna nodded.

Libby was getting tired of lying all the time. Every time she turned around she found herself telling another lie. But she didn't want to go to jail.

"We also talked to your boss Herbert Stringfellow," said Rafa.

As if entranced by it Libby stared at the vein palpitating on Rafa's forehead. It was one of the largest veins she had ever seen. It seemed to be expanding. She felt short of breath.

"Oh," she muttered.

"We seem to have a problem."

"A problem?"

"He says he was here at the crematorium and when he came here he saw the repair van parked in the driveway."

"I see," uttered Libby, starting to lose her voice.

"Do you see our problem?"

"No. The repairman must not have gotten out of his van, because I never saw him."

"Why would he sit in his van and not come out after driving all the way here?"

"Maybe he had an emergency and had to leave."

Rafa and Anna exchanged looks.

"I guess that's possible," said Anna.

"You're welcome to inspect the building again if you want," said Libby. "He's not here."

Rafa scratched his head in bafflement. "It seems strange that Bill wouldn't tell you he was here before he left for his emergency or whatever."

"You'd have to ask him," said Libby, shrugging.

"That's the thing. We still haven't found him. His wife is very upset and is convinced something happened to him." Rafa paused. "Why would he abandon his van in a supermarket parking lot?"

"I'm not very good at solving mysteries. I can never figure out who the killer is on those TV cops shows."

Rafa pricked up his ears. "Do you think Bill met with foul play?"

"I dunno."

"You said 'killer.'"

Libby felt her heart pumping faster if that was possible. If she could get through this cop grilling without passing out, she should get by without incriminating herself. After all, there was no corpse. What did she have to fear? As long as the cops didn't trip her up she would be OK.

"I meant, I'm not very good at solving mysteries," she said. "That's all."

"Of course," said Anna, nodding, playing the good cop.

"Didn't you see the van in your driveway, Ms. Genet?" said Rafa in an accusatory tone.

"Nope. As you can see, there are no windows in this building," said Libby, gesturing with her arm.

"Don't you get claustrophobic in here?" said Anna.

"A little."

"I don't know how you do it. I'd be claustrophobic all the time. This is Southern California. I need to be out in the sunshine."

"I don't understand why Bill would park his van in your driveway and not come in and see you," said Rafa, "especially since you were the one who called him to fix your furnace. It wouldn't've taken longer than a minute or two to tell you he was here."

"I can't read minds," said Libby. "I wish he had fixed my furnace. It still makes weird noises."

"Are you sticking to your story that you didn't see him in your driveway?"

"Why do you call it a 'story'?"

"He doesn't mean anything by it," said Anna. "That's just the way we talk. Cop talk."

Libby didn't think they believed her. But she didn't see how they could charge her with anything, since there was no proof a murder had been committed. All the cops knew for sure was that the repairman Bill was missing.

Yet the cops continued to press her with the third degree.

Chapter 35

"Maybe Bill fled the country," said Libby, trying to get the heat off her. "He could be in Timbuktu by now."

"Why would he do that?" said Anna.

"Who knows? People do strange things."

"There's one other thing that flies in the face of that possibility," said Rafa, staring at her, searching her face. "We found Bill's blood on his van's steering wheel."

Libby felt her heart sink. She must have gotten Bill's blood on her gloves and it had gotten on the steering wheel when she had driven the van to the Von's parking lot. Too late to do anything about it now.

"Maybe he cut himself," she said, amazed at her ability to lie on a dime and lie convincingly, it seemed to her.

The vein on Rafa's forehead looked like it was swelling and throbbing faster, like it would burst any second. What did it mean? Did it mean he suspected she had something to do with Bill's disappearance? Did the vein swell and pulse faster when he was about to make a bust?

She felt an overpowering urge to confess to Bill's murder even though she wasn't the murderer. The demon was. It had forced her to kill Bill. Still she felt guilty. She was the one who had plunged the knife into Bill's throat and torn his carotid in half. Part of her was screaming inside her head to confess.

Rafa was gazing at her as if he expected her to come clean.

Libby managed to keep her mouth shut. What was the point of her doing time in the joint? It would accomplish nothing. The demon wouldn't go to jail with her. The demon would remain free and able to murder at will. It would possess someone else and carry on its mission of wielding death. Libby's imprisonment would not prevent the demon from continuing its rampage of murders.

"Do you have anything to say to us?" said Rafa, no doubt expecting a confession.

She returned his gaze. His expectations were about to be dashed.

"About what?" she said.

"Bill's disappearance."

"I can't help you."

"We don't mean to pry," said Anna. "We're just doing our job. We have a lot of questions about this case."

"People don't up and vanish into thin air," said Rafa.

Libby kept her mouth shut. She figured they were trying to trap her into incriminating herself. The less she said, the less chance they had of trapping her with her own words. And yet she still felt the urge to confess to Bill's murder.

Kill them. They know too much. Kill them.

She flinched. The damn voice. Why wouldn't it leave her alone? Would it hound her for the rest of her life?

"Are you OK, Miss Genet?" said Rafa.

"I'm fine."

Kill them.

How was she supposed to kill cops, anyway? They both had guns. They'd end up killing her if she attacked them.

"Are you finished?" she said. "I need to get back to work."

Rafa gazed at the furnace. "You're cremating someone, aren't you? I can hear the furnace working."

"Uh—why yes."

There was no reason for her to deny it. The machine was obviously in operation, since it was rumbling at a steady pace.

Rafa strutted toward the cremation chamber. "Do you mind if we take a look?"

"It would interrupt the cremation in progress," said Libby, worry fraying her nerves.

"I'm afraid I must insist."

"Why don't we wait till the job is done? Then I can open the furnace."

Rafa snorted. "I don't want to have to get a warrant."

The cremation would be completed by the time he got a warrant, Libby knew. Could he even get a warrant? Was there a reasonable cause to obtain a warrant from a judge? She wasn't a lawyer. She didn't know. All she knew was it would make her look like she had something to hide if she refused the cop's request to open the oven. She had no idea what shape her father's corpse was in. Would he be identifiable if she paused the oven and opened it?

"I'm not trying to be difficult," said Libby, sweating. "Cremation is a time-consuming process. Stopping and starting the oven before it's done isn't good for the machine."

"I understand, but this is an active police investigation of a possible murder," said Rafa, inflating his chest, thinking it made him look authoritative.

Kill him and be done with it. Then kill his partner.

Libby wanted them to leave. She couldn't stand dealing with them any longer. Maybe if she paused the oven they would leave. She wasn't going to kill them no matter what the godforsaken voice said. They were two armed cops trained to kill for Chrissake.

"You're not off the hook," said Rafa. "We have too many questions that remain unanswered. Let us see the corpse you're cremating."

Chapter 36

Libby gathered herself. The cops wouldn't see Bill if she opened the oven. They would see her dad. Even if he was recognizable, her dad's face would mean nothing to them. It was just another corpse being cremated for all they knew. How would that incriminate her?

She had nothing to fear, she told herself, but herself wasn't listening. She felt fear. But she saw no way out. She would have to open the retort.

"If you insist," she said, trying her best to sound calm.

She angled across the floor to the computer and turned off the retort, which wheezed to a halt.

"Thank you," said Rafa.

"Don't stand too close to it. It's gonna be hot."

When she opened the door, a blast of heat hit them.

"Whew," said Rafa, brushing the sweat off his forehead with his hand.

Libby feared she would see her dad's eyes staring accusingly at her. She narrowed her eyes in apprehension.

Everybody in the room trained their eyes on the charred corpse.

The stench of burning flesh that emanated from the oven was overpowering. Grimacing, Rafa backed away.

In its present charred shape the cadaver was unidentifiable. Libby couldn't see her dad's eyes. Maybe they were shut.

"Satisfied?" she said.

"No," said Rafa. "I want a piece of the cadaver for a DNA test."

Fuck, thought Libby. That was when she saw her dad's eyes snap open and glower at her.

"What?" said Anna, staring at Libby in puzzlement.

"Nothing," said Libby, cringing. "I didn't say anything."

"You looked terrified when you eyed the corpse."

"No, no. I—uh—was surprised to see—uh—it was all in one piece still."

"You looked scared to me," said Anna, glancing at the corpse.

"Why would I be?" said Libby, trying to regain her composure. "When you've seen one corpse, you've seen them all. If anyone should know the truth of those words, I should, since I work at a crematorium."

Libby snuck a peak at the sooty cadaver, fearing she might see her dad's eyes open again.

They were either closed or covered with soot. She must have imagined they were open before.

"You're gonna burn your hands if you touch the corpse now," she told Rafa.

"We need a pair of tweezers," Rafa told Anna.

Anna made her way to the bathroom and returned with tweezers, which she handed to Rafa.

"Do you have an evidence bag?" he said.

Anna removed a polyethylene baggie from her trouser pocket and handed it to him.

Wincing, holding his breath, Rafa approached the sooty corpse and picked pieces of tissue off the burnt kidney with the tweezers, doing the job hastily so he wouldn't burn his hand. He deposited the tissue inside the baggie and handed the baggie to Anna.

Gasping for air he backed away from the oven. "Close it. I can't stand that stink."

Libby shut the oven.

However, the stench of burnt flesh permeated the building.

"I'm gonna be sick," said Anna, her face ashen.

"Let's go," said Rafa.

They bustled out the door without saying a word.

Libby turned the retort back on. It hummed to life.

And then the clanking resumed.

Taken aback, she wondered if it was the malfunctioning machine or it was her father trying to get out. Was he pounding on the oven wall? How could he? He was dead.

Nevertheless, she halted the retort and opened its door to inspect the interior, not knowing what to expect, her pulse racing headlong. Were his eyes going to be glaring in accusation at her again?

She peered into the open oven.

Everything looked OK. Dad's arms hadn't moved. They must not have been pounding on the retort wall. It was the faulty machine that was kicking up again with its nerve-racking clanking.

But his eyes were glaring at her again.

Libby gasped.

They couldn't be staring at her. They were dead eyes. Dead eyes couldn't see.

Sweating, Libby closed the oven door and restarted the machine. There would be nothing left of those eyes after the retort was through with them. They would turn into ash like every other body part on her dad's corpse. All she had to do was let the machine do its thing, and no evidence would be left to incriminate her in the murder.

No more damn eyes to haunt her.

She needed some air.

She crossed the room to the front door, opened the door, and left it open to air out the room after the cops had left. She turned on the fan in the building to help remove the stench of death. Even so, she went outside to clear her lungs. Nobody ever got used to the mephitic odor of death.

The cops had his DNA.

But it wasn't Bill's DNA. It was her father's. It would do them no good in their investigation of Bill's disappearance if they could even get DNA from a charred kidney. Libby didn't know the science.

She was safe from the cops for the time being. Nevertheless, she got the feeling they'd be back to harass her. If Stringfellow hadn't told them about Bill's van parked in the driveway, she would have been in the clear. Leave it to the boss to mess up her life.

Who was she trying to kid? Her life was a train wreck. She was in the middle of being possessed by a murderous demon. She had the blood of two murders on her hands. And her hands would become bloodier unless Brady could exorcise the evil entity that was turning her into its killing machine.

At least the sun was out. She took in the monolithic azure sky as a slight breeze rippled her hair and wafted the sweet scent of jasmine flowers in her direction.

A carmine Jeep Gladiator pickup pulled into her driveway and came to an abrupt halt.

Chapter 37

Libby watched Brady clamber out of the Gladiator with something in his hand.

"I bought sage from Jean Baptiste," he said, approaching her. "I did research on the Internet. You cremated several brutal killers here. Your life is in extreme danger."

"Can you help me?"

"That's what this sage is for. I charged it to your account."

"What do you do with it?"

"I'm gonna smudge your crematorium with it."

"I'm airing it out right now."

"What happened?"

"The cops wanted to inspect the furnace so I had to open it before it completed its job."

"Cops?" said Brady, suspicious.

"They're looking for a repairman who went missing. They've been harassing me about it."

"I researched that serial killer you cremated here. His name's Wayne Bobinsky. He killed a bunch of hookers and worshiped Satan. He could be the demon trying to possess you."

"How can we know for sure?"

"That's the problem. We can't. You've cremated a lot of people from prison here. Any one of them could be haunting you. But Bobinsky was the most recent."

"What does the creep want with me?"

"He wants to kill and keep killing."

"Wonderful. What if it isn't him? What if it's some other demon after me?"

"Same difference. We still need to smudge your crematorium. Let's do it."

Gripping the bundle of sage, Brady made a beeline for the crematorium.

"It smells like death in there," said Libby in tow. "I turned the fan on full blast."

"We'll need to turn it down. Otherwise, it will blow out all the sage smoke. We need only a little ventilation during the smudging."

Brady lit the bundle of sage and entered the crematorium, shielding the sage with his hand to prevent the gusts of air from the fan from blowing out the flame. The wind generated by the massive fan became more intense and extinguished the burning sage.

"We need to turn down the fan," said Brady, the wind from the fan blowing his hair every which way.

Libby made for the fan, fighting the juggernaut of wind generated by it. She had no idea the fan could produce gale-force wind. She battled her way through the powerful gusts and tried to turn down the fan. The wind was preventing her from reaching the fan dial.

Leave it alone. Kill him. He's one of them.

The voice was in her head again, plaguing her. One of who?

They hate you. They want to rob and kill you. Don't trust him.

Libby couldn't concentrate with the voice harassing her. How could she get it out of her head?

"I can't light the sage with the fan on so high," said Brady.

"I can't reach the dial," said Libby.

"Be gone, demon," said Brady, waving the bundle of extinguished sage in front of him. "Do you hear me, Bobinsky? Be gone. Leave this building and never come back."

The fan increased its speed.

"The fan's fighting me," said Libby. "I didn't know it had such a high speed."

"Can you pull the plug?"

"I can't move an inch. The wind has me pinned here," said Libby, struggling to keep from being blown backward.

"Be gone, demon," said Brady.

"Is it gone?"

Kill the scammer. Kill him now.

It wasn't gone. It was still screaming in her head.

"Wayne Bobinsky, be gone," said Brady, screwing up his face in the fan-generated hurricane winds. "Leave this building, Bobinsky. You are dead meat. Return to your grave. I have sage in my hand."

Kill the scammer before the cops get back.

"He's still here," said Libby.

"How do you know?" said Brady.

"I can feel his presence."

"Return to the grave, Bobinsky."

The fan made a loud buzzing sound as its steel blade whirled faster. The blade reached a fever pitch before the fan exploded, hurling its metal screen and gyrating blade across the room in Brady's direction.

"Watch out," cried Libby, ducking out of the way.

Brady dove to the floor just as the swiveling blade screamed over his head like a five-foot-wide Frisbee, missing his scalp by less than an inch. The blade buried itself six inches into the wall beside the doorjamb.

The air in the crematorium became calmer, disturbed only by the breeze that blew in through the open front door.

Stunned by the near miss, Brady rose to his feet and ran his hand through his wind-tousled hair.

"Close shave," he muttered, turning around and eying the steel fan blade embedded in the wall.

"Are you all right?" said Libby, striding toward him.

"Yeah."

"That thing could've cut off your head."

He should be dead. Why did you warn him to get out of the way?

"Bastard," said Libby.

"What?" said Brady.

"Nothing. I didn't mean you."

"The demon? Do you hear his voice in your head?" said Brady, hanging on her every word.

"I . . . ," she trailed off.

"Is it Bobinsky?"

"I—I'm confused. My mind is a jumble."

She didn't know if she should tell him the truth. For some reason she thought she shouldn't. Or was that the voice restraining her from revealing its presence to Brady?

Let me inside you so we can kill him. You and me are one. We are one together. Stop fighting me. When we are one, we are perfect. You must let me in.

"I feel the entity's presence," said Libby.

"So do I," said Brady.

"Can you tell if it's Bobinsky?"

"No."

Chapter 38

Brady relit the sage with his lighter and fell to smudging the building. Holding the smoking sage bundle in front of him, he walked around the room perimeter, guiding the smoke into every nook and cranny. He walked in and out of Libby's kitchenette, office, bathroom, and bedroom, making sure every room was smudged.

"Is the cremation furnace empty?" he said.

"It's in operation," said Libby, racked by the memory of murdering her father. "A cadaver needed to be cremated."

"Are you all right?"

"Uh—yeah. I can still see that fan blade flying over your head," she said, her face wan.

Brady blew out his cheeks at the memory. "I'd like to smudge inside the furnace too, just so we get every space inside the building."

"You'll have to wait till it's finished."

Brady waved the smoking sage bundle around. "Be gone, Bobinksy. You are dead."

"How does smudging get rid of the demon?" said Libby, her face regaining some of its color.

"It works in various ways. It purifies the air. Some believe it kills bacteria. It also calms the nerves and boosts your mood. It relieves stress and clears the negative energy in the room."

"I never heard of it."

"Release the negative energy of this space," intoned Brady, addressing the room, wheeling slowly around, waving the burning sage.

"Can you get rid of obnoxious guests with that?"

Not that Libby did any entertaining. She was just curious.

"It's better to knife them," said Brady.

The blood drained from Libby's face.

Did he know she had killed Bill and her father?

"It was a joke," said Brady, shifting uncomfortably on his feet as he picked up on her discomfiture.

Libby shook her head. "I'm stressed out. This demon stuff is messing up my head really bad."

"You've got to keep fighting it. You can never give up. When you give up, it will win, and you'll never be able to get rid of it."

The woodsy aroma of the sage suffused the air. Libby hoped it was working to repel the demon from the crematorium. She had already killed two people at the demon's behest. She couldn't let the murder spree continue. Crippled with guilt, she couldn't stand any additional guilt heaped on her. How was she supposed to atone for the two murders she had committed? She had killed her own father. What the hell was she doing?

It wasn't her that had committed the murders. The truth was it was the demon that had taken over her body and soul.

"Be gone, Bobinsky, and never return here," said Brady, brandishing the sage bundle.

"Don't we need a priest to make sure the exorcism works?"

"I'm not a priest. I can't help you there. I'm not religious."

"Then why are you an exorcist?" she asked, puzzled.

"Because I believe in evil," he answered. "I was a victim of a demon when I was younger, so I should know."

Libby nodded in understanding. "Then you know the hell I'm going through."

"I know how helpless you feel. It was the most terrifying thing for me. I felt so powerless when the demon possessed me and commanded me to do its bidding. I had no power to stop it."

"It's like it *becomes* me. There is no *me* left to fight it."

"We've got to get it away from you before it completes its possession of you."

"Is there anything else I can do to fight it?"

"Don't take any sedatives. They weaken your resistance and make it easier for the demon to possess you. Also, don't sleep too much."

"Why shouldn't I sleep?"

"Sleeping lowers your resistance like sedatives. The demon can sneak into your dreams and take over."

"I had a nightmare about the demon. It seemed so real it scared me to death."

"Demons flourish in the dream state."

Libby mulled it over. "Should I take speed to keep me awake?"

"Any kind of mood-altering drug could make you susceptible to being possessed, because it lowers your resistance. Satanists have been known to drop magic mushrooms to enable them to summon demons, who take advantage of any opening that presents itself in order for them to enter the world of the living."

"You're giving me the willies."

"A demon forced me to . . ."

"To what?" said Libby, agog.

Thinking better of answering too specifically, Brady cleared his throat. "It forced me to do something evil."

She wished she could tell him the demon had forced her to kill someone, but she couldn't take the chance lest he report her to the cops. But if he believed she was possessed when she had committed murder, why would he tell the cops? He was a medium. He knew about demonic possession and how helpless the victim was in thrall to a demon. He would understand she wasn't in control when the demon forced her to kill.

"That's why we need to exorcise you," said Brady. "Otherwise, the demon will force you to commit a series of despicable acts until it has achieved its goal."

"What *is* its goal?"

"It depends on the identity of the demon. The demon I encountered when I was younger wanted revenge for being murdered."

"What does my demon want?"

"If it really is Bobinsky, he must want you to go on a murder spree that never ends."

"Jesus. You mean, he's gonna turn me into a serial killer like him?"

"It might not be him. Has he identified himself to you in some manner?"

"No."

"He wants to keep his identity hidden. Demons are notorious for practicing deception. They're consummate liars. They rarely tell the truth. They use lies to gain power over their victims. Do you still feel his presence?"

Libby didn't hear the voice in her head for the moment. "I don't think so."

"Good. I don't feel his presence either. The smudging must have worked." Brady paused a beat. "Or . . ."

"Or what?"

"Or he's in hiding until the smudging dissipates."

"Crap," said Libby, downcast. "How do we get rid of the demon forever?"

"A séance."

"What good will that do?"

"We might be able to determine the entity's true identity and its motive for haunting you. We can use that information against it."

"Let's do it."

Chapter 39

Brady had never conducted a séance, though he had participated in one when he was ten years old. He didn't know for sure if he could get in touch with a spirit, but he figured he might be able to because the demon Theresa had possessed him.

He knew how to conduct a séance because Dr. Armitage had shown him before his untimely death.

"Are you the only one who lives here?" asked Brady.

"Me, myself, and I," answered Libby.

"Then we can have the séance with the two of us."

He wondered if he should tell Libby that the demon Theresa had possessed him and made him kill his mother. He figured knowing he was a murderer might upset Libby. Which was why he hadn't told her earlier. He continued to be reluctant about telling her. She could fire him if she found out he had committed matricide.

He didn't want to instill in her the fear that she too might become a murderer like him if he told her the truth about his committing murder. Also, she wouldn't want to associate with a murderer and like as not would fire him, rendering her defenseless against the demon haunting her.

He wanted to help her, so he kept his mouth shut about his shooting his mother.

"How do we do a séance?" said Libby.

"We sit at a table and hold hands. Then I summon the unsettled spirit and communicate with it and try to find out what it wants from you."

"What do I do?"

"You ask it questions after it manifests itself using me as its medium."

"Is it dangerous?"

"The séance shouldn't be. We're just trying to communicate with the entity. As long as we don't break the circle we should be safe."

"What circle?"

"Holding hands. We need to keep holding hands through the séance to protect ourselves from the demon. He can't enter the circle."

"When should we do it?"

"If the smudging worked, the demon is gone and shouldn't bother you anymore. If that's the case, it won't appear when we have a séance. Which is a good thing."

"OK. So when do we do it?"

"Let's air out the crematorium," said Brady, heading for the front door to open it wider. "Too bad you don't have any windows in here."

"I thought you wanted the sage aroma to remain in the building to keep the demon out."

"If the demon's gone, it won't come back, because the building has been cleansed. The entity can't exist in a building cleansed of negative energy. If the demon left, it should be in its grave by now."

Libby glanced at the broken fan. "We can't use the fan. That's for sure."

"Let's keep the door open a little while longer to clear the air. Then we can hold the séance."

"If the entity is gone, the séance won't bring it back, will it?" said Libby, gnawing her lower lip.

"No," said Brady quickly, though he wasn't sure.

He didn't have enough experience with séances to know what to tell her.

"Why's it so cold in here?" she said, shivering.

"Do you have the A/C on?"

"No A/C."

Libby stepped outside. "It's warmer out here than it is in there."

She reentered the crematorium and watched her breath turn into mist in front of her face.

"I'm getting my jacket," she said.

She retrieved a lilac puffer jacket from her closet and put it on.

"Is it normally this cold in here?" said Brady.

She shook her head no. "The oven is usually working, and it keeps the building warm. It's working now. I have no idea why it's so cold in here."

Brady shivered, watching his breath vaporize. It was a bad sign. Haunted houses frequently had inexplicable cold or hot spots in them. The demon could be present. It must have hid somehow from the smudging smoke. Perhaps it had hidden in the retort or the cremulator.

He closed the front door.

"Let's go ahead with the séance," he said.

"The heater must be broken. It would've gone on by now with the temperature this low." Libby fetched a sigh. "Something else I have to get fixed. Did you ever notice how everything breaks down at once?"

She zipped her puffer all the way up to the collar.

"We'll sit at the table in the kitchen," said Brady. "Can you kill all the lights in the building?"

Libby went around the crematorium, turning off all the lights.

The only one that remained on was the one in the kitchenette ceiling.

"It gets nice and dark in here without widows," said Brady. "We normally do séances at night, but this should work fine."

Exhaling puffs of vapor Libby sat at the small kitchenette table for two.

Brady killed the overhead fluorescent light with the light switch on the wall and found his way to the table in the dark. Groping, he found his chair and sat down.

"Let's hold hands on the tabletop," he said.

The lime digital light on the stove was providing enough light for him to see her in the dark.

Libby extended her hands on the tabletop. Brady did likewise and clasped hers.

Brady wished he had brought a jacket. The cold was getting to him. Shivering, he felt his fingers becoming numb. The only thing that kept them warm was Libby's hands.

Chapter 40

Brady took three deep breaths and relaxed, trying to open himself up for the demon to enter him and use him as its medium.

"Wayne Bobinsky," Brady intoned, tilting his head upward at the ceiling. "Are you here?"

No response.

"Wayne Bobinsky, give us a sign that you are present," said Brady.

"Is he here?" said Libby, her breath vaporizing as she spoke. "I'm gonna get frostbite."

"Shh," said Brady. "We need absolute quiet."

No response.

"Give us a sign, demon."

Brady heard the cremation chamber clanking in the other room.

"In this room, demon," he said. "Are you in *this* room?"

The table started jumping up and down three inches off the linoleum floor.

Libby gasped in astonishment and tried to pull her hands free of Brady's.

"Don't break the ring," warned Brady, tightening his grasp on her hands.

Libby stopped trying to pull away.

The table continued to buck up and down.

"Fuck me," said Libby with a husky voice.

Brady gazed at her.

She tore her hands away from his.

She unzipped her puffer and ripped open her button-down blouse to expose her breasts, her nipples erect.

"I'm a whore," she said. "Fuck me on the table. You know you want to. Fuck me in the ass. What's your problem?"

Brady stared at her with wide eyes.

"You broke the circle," he muttered.

"Fuck the circle. Fuck me. I'm a whore. Can't you get it up?"

Her face took on a ratlike aspect with saliva-dripping fangs and bloodred eyes.

Brady figured it was ectoplasm, but it should have been exuding from him, the medium, not from Libby. The medium was the conduit for the demon. Then why was the demon manifesting itself through Libby? He could think of only one explanation. The demon wasn't responding to him.

Libby bolted to her feet, tore off her puffer and blouse. Bare-chested, she threw off her jeans and underwear, leapt onto the tabletop, and sat in front of him with her legs spread.

"Then lick me, since you can't get it up," she husked, her drooling rodent face knotted with lust, her bloodred eyes leering at him.

Appalled, Brady stared at her.

"That's good pussy," said Libby. "Don't you like girls? Are you a goddamn priest?"

She snagged his hand and thrust it into her, sawing it back and forth inside her. She moaned with pleasure.

Brady yanked his hand away from her.

"Be gone, demon," he managed to say, pulling himself together.

"Fuck me. I'm for dinner tonight. Get it up and dig in."

"Be gone, Bobinsky," said Brady, forcing himself to concentrate on the exorcism. "You are *dead*. Your life is over. Return to your grave."

Libby laughed at him with her lust-twisted rat face.

"Be gone, Bobinsky," said Brady. "Leave her alone."

"You said you wanted me to show myself. Here I am. Now you want me to leave. Make up your fucking mind. Fuck me. What's holding you back? Homo," spat Libby, cupping her bare breasts and pushing them toward Brady. Twitching her whiskers she puckered her rat lips. "Suck me."

"Leave this house, demon. You're not welcome here."

Libby crabbed around on the table so she was on her knees and facing away from Brady. She spread her legs.

"Fuck me in the ass," she said, looking back at him with lecherous rat eyes. "You like ass meat, don't you, homo? Come on. I'm your whore. Don't you have a dick? Stick it in me."

"Leave her alone. Go back to your grave, demon."

"What's wrong with you? I'm a cougar. I want your hard dick inside me, boy," Libby growled.

"Be gone, Bobinsky," yelled Brady.

Sweating with apprehension, Brady didn't know what else to say to the demon to exorcise it from Libby. If he was religious, he would make the sign of the cross. But he didn't believe in a God that was always silent and gave no evidence of existing. Brady knew his exorcism wasn't working, but he didn't know what he was doing wrong.

Libby whipped around and faced Brady.

"Stick your dick in my mouth," she said, hanging her fanged mouth open inches away from him and slavering.

"Be gone, demon. *You are dead.*"

"I want to suck your dick, stupid. Stick it in my mouth. I give good head. Don't you like blowjobs?"

"Return to your grave, demon."

"Say the Lord's Prayer and I'll leave," said Libby, cackling with laughter. "After I suck your hard dick. I can see it bulging in your pants."

"You are not welcome here," said Brady, his throat tight. "You are cast out."

"Say it or I'll unzip your pants and suck your dick," said Libby, reaching for his trouser zipper. "Let me see it," she said, ogling his crotch.

"Be gone, demon."

"Let it out of your pants. My mouth is watering," she hissed through her obscene, gaping rat mouth.

"I said be gone, demon," Brady said louder.

"Say the Lord's Prayer and I'll leave," laughed Libby. "You don't even know it, do you, you stupid fag?"

Brady struggled to remember it. How did it go? Would it do any good? He had nothing to lose by trying it.

"Our father who art in heaven," he said.

"Bye-bye, putz," said Libby, waving at him. "I'll be back."

She collapsed on the tabletop, her body limp, her face morphing back to normal.

Brady resented the demon toying with him. It infuriated him. He wanted to lash out at it. But where was it? Was it here? He didn't believe it had left.

"Bobinsky," he said in white heat. "Are you here? Show yourself."

Libby stirred on the tabletop, groaning.

"Jesus," she said, embarrassed, realizing she was naked and covering herself with her hands as she sat up. "What did you do to me?" she said, staring at Brady, aghast.

"Nothing. The demon possessed you."

"I blacked out," she said, scrabbling off the table and retrieving her clothes that were scattered on the floor.

"Is it gone? Do you feel it inside you?"

"No. Did you give me a drug?" she said suspiciously, donning her clothes as rapidly as she could.

"I didn't give you anything."

"Did you give me roofies?"

"Don't you remember? We had a séance. The demon possessed you," said Brady, hitting the switch on the wall and flicking on the overhead light.

Squinting thanks to the sudden light, Libby shook her head, trying to clear the cobwebs out of it.

"I can't remember," she said in frustration. "Why was I naked?"

"The demon did it."

"I thought you said there was no danger."

"You broke the circle. There wasn't any danger if we had kept the circle intact."

"Are you sure you didn't give me some drug?" she said, not convinced he was leveling with her.

"I'm sure. The problem is the demon is still here. The smudging didn't work. The entity must have hidden in the cremulator while I was smudging the building."

"Now what do we do?" she said, remaining suspicious of him. She winced. "Why am I sore down there if you didn't rape me?"

"The demon was making you do things," said Brady, nervously remembering her lewd acts on the tabletop. "It had complete control of you."

"This is hard to believe," she said, zipping her puffer up tight.

"It's getting warmer," he said, noticing his breath wasn't vaporizing.

Libby held her arms around her. "I don't know what's going on. What the hell happened? I totally blacked out."

"You're lucky it left you. I don't know how I'm gonna exorcise it. I don't know why it left. It told me to recite the Lord's Prayer then left. It got tired of playing with me, I guess."

"The Lord's Prayer? Are you telling me I need a priest to exorcise it?"

"I don't know what else I can do," said Brady, befuddled. "Unless . . ."

"Unless what?"

"Unless the demon isn't the serial killer Wayne Bobinsky. I was addressing it as Bobinsky. If it wasn't Bobinsky, nothing I said to it would affect it."

"Then why did it leave?"

"It must have felt like it. It said it would be back. It wants to let me know it's in charge and I can't control it."

"I don't understand how it took my clothes off."

"It made you take them off."

"Me? I would never . . . in front of a complete stranger," she said, incredulous. "You have the wrong idea of me. I don't do that type of thing."

"I had nothing to do with it. It was the demon controlling you."

"This is hard to believe," said Libby, trying to get her head around it.

"We shouldn't've broken the circle. The demon can get inside us when the circle breaks. It got inside you."

"Why didn't it go inside you?"

"Maybe you're more receptive," said Brady, unsure. "In any case, you're the one it wants to possess, not me. I'm merely acting as a medium trying to get it to show itself and leave you. If it isn't Bobinsky, it wouldn't pay attention to anything I told it. The way it acted I don't think it was Bobinsky."

"You helped it get inside me?" said Libby, disconcerted.

"That wasn't my intention. I was trying to get it to leave you alone. It was toying with me, goading me by making you take off your clothes to seduce me."

Libby clutched her head. "This is hard to believe. Why can't I remember any of it?"

"It doesn't want you to remember. It's gaining more and more control over you. Pretty soon, unless we stop it, it will possess you entirely, and no force on earth will be able to save you."

Frowning, Libby shut her eyes and rubbed her brow. "I can't remember any of this."

"The demon is clever. It doesn't want you to remember. It wants you to think I took advantage of you."

"Why?"

"Because it wants you to fire me. It knows I'm dangerous to its existence."

"I wish I could remember what happened during the séance," said Libby in frustration. "Why do I hurt down there? Are you sure you didn't rape me?"

Brady gulped. He didn't want to go into the details of what had happened, but he thought he should explain.

"You took my hand and put it inside—"

Brady heard knocking on the front door.

"Tell me later," said Libby, flushing. "I can't believe . . ."

Chapter 41

Brady accompanied Libby to the door.

Libby was trying to look composed after her trying experience during the séance.

She opened the door to reveal the two cops Anna and Rafa.

"We don't want to disturb you, but we wanted to let you know what we discovered," said Rafa. He remarked Brady. "You look familiar. Do I know you?"

"No," said Brady, feeling his palms sweat.

He thought the cop might recognize him as the kid who had killed his mother and did time in an asylum for the criminally insane. But Brady had been a ten-year-old boy at the time. He was sure he looked different now. After all, he had become an adult.

"What's your name?" said Rafa.

"Brady."

"Oh, that's right. You were here the last time we were here."

"Yeah."

"Are we interrupting something?" Rafa asked Libby, who looked ruffled from her torment during the séance, her face pink.

He cut his eyes back and forth between Brady and Libby.

Edgy, Brady hoped Libby wasn't going to tell the cops about the séance and her suspicions about his raping her.

"Not at all," said Libby. "Why are you back?"

Brady breathed easier. He got the impression Libby didn't want to talk to the cops.

"We wanted to tell you what we found," said Rafa. "The DNA we found in your cremation oven wasn't Bill's."

"I know," said Libby. "I told you his corpse wasn't being cremated."

"Is it still being cremated?" asked Rafa, peering over her shoulder at the cremation furnace.

"As a matter of fact, yeah. It takes several hours."

Rafa kept glancing suspiciously at Brady, unnerving him.

Had the cop recognized him as the killer ten-year-old?

"Have you heard anything from Bill, Ms. Genet?" said Rafa.

"Not a peep," said Libby. "If he's not coming, I hope the repair company sends someone else to take his place. The oven keeps making noises. It's driving me crazy."

"You'd have to ask them. We're involved in a missing person investigation which is looking more and more like a homicide."

"I wish I could be more helpful."

"How do you two know each other if you don't mind my asking?" said Rafa, eying Libby and Brady.

"I'm an occultist," said Brady. "This place has bad mojo."

"I'm trying to get rid of the negative energy here," said Libby.

"You believe in that stuff?" said Rafa, his visage skeptical. "I thought everybody believed in feng shui."

"I don't even know what it is. Is it like kung fu?"

"Good vibes, basically."

"Cops don't deal with good vibes. Just the opposite. We deal with the garbage that nobody wants to think about."

"I deal with a lot of dead people," said Libby. "It can get depressing."

"Bad mojo," chimed in Brady.

"Has your memory gotten any better?" Rafa asked Libby.

"What?" said Libby, confused.

"You said Bill's van was never in your driveway, but your boss said he saw it there."

"I never saw it in the driveway."

Anna sniffed the air. "It smells like some kind of smoke. Were you burning something?"

"I smudged the building, cleansing it of evil spirits," said Brady.

"What makes you think there are evil spirits here?" said Rafa.

Maybe he had said too much. Why was the cop acting so suspicious of him? Brady doubted the guy could have recognized him as the matricidal boy in the Hollywood Hills murder rampage many years ago. Brady didn't look like an innocent little kid anymore.

"I'm superstitious," said Libby. "I hired him."

"Same question. Why do you think you have evil spirits?"

Libby's eyelid twitched. "I—I don't want to take any chances with evil spirits, since I spend most of my time around dead bodies. I have nightmares about ghosts."

"I wouldn't want to do this for a living," said Anna. "I don't know how you do it."

"That'll be all," said Rafa.

Brady felt relieved. He didn't want Rafa to recognize him. It would open a can of worms.

Rafa and Anna turned to leave.

"Oh, one more thing," said Rafa, slewing around to face Libby. "Can you remember what you and Bill talked about? Did he say something that annoyed you?"

"We—"

Libby caught herself before finishing her sentence.

"Yes?" said Rafa, eager to hear her out.

"We never met. I told you he didn't keep his appointment with me."

"You see, that's what's so strange. His boss said Bill called him and told him when he arrived here. Why would Bill lie?"

"I can't read minds."

"You don't think it's strange for Bill to lie?"

"I don't know anything about Bill. How can I know what's strange and not strange about him?"

"Your boss told us he saw Bill's van in your driveway. Which proves he was here."

"I'm not denying he was here. I'm denying I met him."

"What about you, Mr. Brady? What did you say to Bill?"

"Bill who?" said Brady.

"The cremation oven repairman."

"I never met him."

"He didn't interrupt you two in one of your sessions?" said Rafa, leering.

"What are you trying to say, Detective?" said Libby, teed off.

"You looked a little flushed when we knocked on your door. Like maybe you two are in a relationship—"

"I don't have to answer any more of your questions."

"Of course not. You aren't under any obligation to answer our questions."

"Exactly."

"But it makes you look suspicious if you don't."

"Suspicious of what? What are you trying to say?"

"We're just asking questions. That's what cops do. We're trying to find the truth."

"Are you insinuating I'm lying?"

"Certain things about Bill's disappearance don't add up."

"I have to get back to work," said Libby with a resolute expression.

"After all, why would you lie?"

Brady saw that Libby was on the verge of responding to his question when she changed her mind.

"I'm not answering any more of your questions," she said.

"There you go," said Rafa.

He and Anna turned to leave again.

"We'll let you know if we have any more questions," he said, waving good-bye over his shoulder at her.

"Prick," muttered Libby.

Chapter 42

Brady watched Libby close the door.

"Cops," she said.

"Why are they bugging you?" said Brady.

"The oven repairman's missing. They think I had something to do with it."

"Maybe you should get a lawyer."

"They *are* getting to be a pain."

"The less I deal with cops, the better," said Brady, remembering being busted for his mother's murder. "They don't understand the supernatural."

"Does anyone?"

"What I mean is they don't believe in ghosts and demons."

Libby stared at him. "Did you exorcise that demon that's trying to possess me?"

"Not yet. We need to know its true identity before I can exorcise it. I'm beginning to think it's not the serial killer Wayne Bobinsky. If it was him, he should be back in his grave by now and you would be exorcised. But he isn't, and you're still in danger."

"It's not Bobinsky?"

"I was working under the assumption it was, but I couldn't be sure. Now I'm sure it's not him. It couldn't be him, or you would be free of him. We need to know who it really is. Do you keep a record of all the corpses you've cremated here?"

"Yeah."

"Could I take a look at it?"

Libby led him to her office and withdrew a notebook from the top drawer of her desk. She handed the notebook to him.

"You said you cremate a lot of convicts," said Brady, flipping through the pages.

"Some. Not a lot. They come from Terminal Island."

"Did you know any of them personally?"

"I don't know any convicts," she said in a huff.

She froze.

"You *do* know a convict?" said Brady, picking up on her reaction.

"Not a convict. I know someone who's the vilest person I ever met. He murdered my mother and sister."

"That guy you told me about? What's his name?"

"Ed Grainger."

"Is he dead?"

"Not that I've heard. Evil people tend to live a long time, is my experience."

Brady furrowed his brow. "If he's not dead, I don't see how he could be trying to possess you."

"Then it must be some other demon."

"I can research the names in this book. It might bear fruit. Could I borrow this for a while?" said Brady, holding up the notebook.

"Sure. I can use a temporary notebook for the new corpses I get."

"Good."

"Is it possible I'm going insane?" said Libby, distraught. "Maybe I should go back to my psychiatrist."

"I believe you're sane. A demon is in the act of possessing you. A psychiatrist can't help you fight a demon."

She grimaced. "I feel like I'm at war with myself."

"You're not fighting yourself. You're fighting the demon. You must not let it win. It wants you to commit evil acts. I will help you fight it."

"I think it's already won," she said, resigned to defeat.

"Don't think like that. It hasn't won yet. If it had won, you'd be acting out of character *all* the time, not just occasionally. But you're not. You wouldn't think you were going nuts if the demon had completed its possession of you." Brady paused. "In fact, you as a person wouldn't exist. The demon would be in complete control of your mind and body."

Horror warped Libby's face.

Chapter 43

Libby dared not tell Brady she had murdered two people already, including her own father. She didn't like talking about the voice in her head either. If she kept talking about it, Brady might think she was going insane. He claimed hearing voices was part of becoming possessed, but maybe he was saying that to humor her. Maybe he thought she was nuts and therefore he could scam her.

The demon was taking her apart piece by piece from the inside, dismantling her wall of resistance so it could take permanent residence inside her.

"Do you think I'm a sex maniac?" she said.

"No," said Brady quickly.

"I had this nightmare that I was doing horrible things, ripping off my clothes and acting like a hooker."

"It's part of the demon's efforts to possess you."

It wasn't a nightmare. He raped you. Kill him.

Not the voice again. Libby felt terrified.

Don't let him get away with it. He violated you. Be strong. Kill the rapist.

"I think you better go," she said, grinding her teeth, clenching her fists at her sides, trying to resist the voice.

"The demon forced you to do those things. It wasn't you."

"Why didn't you stop it?"

"I wasn't in contact with it. It was in contact with you. I tried to get it to leave you, but it didn't respond to me."

I didn't force him to rape you. He did it on his own. You turn him on. Make him pay. Kill him.

"I don't know who to believe," said Libby, exasperated.

"I feel the presence of the demon," said Brady. "Is he trying to contact you?"

"This has got to stop," said Libby, clutching her forehead.

"I'm telling you the truth. The demon forced you to commit obscene acts. What else has it forced you to do?"

"Why should I believe you? I can't remember what happened. All I know is I was naked when I came to after the séance."

"A demon is a master of deception. It manipulates people with a tissue of lies. Don't believe anything it's telling you."

He's a liar and a rapist. Kill him. He raped you when you blacked out. Kill him.

Libby couldn't get the voice out of her head. She didn't know who to believe. She doubted she could believe the demon. It had forced her to kill. How could she believe anything it told her? And yet she continued to do as it commanded. Even now she felt a powerful urge to kill Brady the same way she had killed Bill and her father by cutting their throats.

Her face broke into a sweat.

"Is he here?" said Brady, his eyes riveted on her. "Resist him. Resist his lies."

He's a lying scammer. He's trying to manipulate you. Kill him now. He's a scammer and a rapist. Kill him.

Where was the carving knife? She wanted to cut the voice out of her head. It was like a cancer growing inside her, becoming bigger and stronger.

Kill him or he'll rape you again.

Her body writhed as she stood. She needed to retrieve the carving knife from the kitchenette. She couldn't let Brady rape her again.

"Go," she managed to tell Brady.

"Fight the demon."

"You have no idea. Go."

Snarling at him she began frothing at the mouth, losing control of herself.

"All right," he said, reluctant to leave her alone. He held up her notebook. "I'll research the names of these corpses you cremated and see if I can find the demon that's attacking you."

Her face flushing, Libby shook uncontrollably, foaming at the mouth like a racehorse chewing a bit.

"Is there some way I can help you?" he said, concerned for her safety.

She continued trembling in the grip of her paroxysm, her face twitching.

Getting no response from her, Brady retreated to the front door.

Unable to restrain herself any longer, Libby bolted to the kitchenette to retrieve the carving knife.

Kill him. Cut the rapist's dick off. It was inside you. Don't let him get away with raping you. Kill him.

Libby whipped the carving knife out of the knife block on the Formica countertop. Brandishing the knife in front of her, growling, she burst out of the kitchenette, searching for Brady, her eyes wild and flashing. She didn't see him in the crematorium.

She stormed to the front door and flung it open.

She saw Brady's Jeep Gladiator reversing out of the driveway.

Whipped into an insatiable fury by the goading demon, knife in hand, Libby pelted down the driveway after the retreating Gladiator.

When Brady reached the road, he burned rubber and sped away, with Libby chasing after him like a hissing maenad, waving her knife at him in orgiastic rage, her body and soul intoxicated with burning revenge.

The Gladiator raced into the distance.

At last Libby stopped running after it and breathed maniacally in the middle of the road, her mouth gaping, her throat burning, her body shaking with exhaustion.

A yellow Honda sped by and honked at her to get out of the road.

She gave the finger to the trampy young brunette driver and trudged out of the road, shoulders slumped, holding the knife at her side.

What was she doing out here? Her mind muzzy, she couldn't remember why she had left the crematorium.

When she eyed the knife gripped in her hand, her face registered horror. Had she knifed someone else? She looked in the road and in the grass verge for a dead body. She breathed easier when she didn't see one. No blood on the knife blade either. A good sign.

Another blackout. She must be cracking up. Why would she be walking outside with a carving knife in her hand? She must have tried to kill again. Whoever the intended victim was had gotten away.

Squinting, she tried to remember how she had got outside in the road. Brain fog. She couldn't remember. Maybe she should

156

have herself committed. At least, being locked in an insane asylum she wouldn't be able to pursue her murder spree.

How else could she prevent herself from killing again? And how could she stop blacking out and forgetting things?

Woozy from her forgotten escapade, she entered the crematorium. The stench of a foul odor emanating from the bowels of the crematorium wafted into her face. It smelled like death and sulfur.

This place never used to smell so bad. She never should have paused the cremation chamber for the cops while it was in operation. The pause and her opening the retort door must have caused the dreadful stench. However, she didn't want to get on the wrong side of the cops. She needed to allay their suspicions by going out of her way to be cooperative.

Did you kill him?

Just what she needed. The voice to cheer her up. Kill who?

Did you kill the rapist?

What rapist?

Can't you remember? Are you losing your mind?

It looked that way.

I'm the only friend you got. You killed all the rest of them, because they were false friends. I know what you're thinking. What friends?

She told herself not to listen to the voice.

Don't worry. I'm on your side. The rapist did this to you. He violated you. You need to kill him.

She *did* feel sore down there. Could the voice be speaking the truth? Had she been raped while she was passed out? Was that why she had lost her memory? Because Brady had raped her and traumatized her? She wanted to scream to vent her frustration at not being able to remember things.

Memory blackouts. The path to madness? Or to possession? She knew the demon was out there and wanted to get inside her. Maybe the demon had raped her. But a demon was incorporeal. It couldn't rape a living human.

She heard the cremation chamber wheeze to a halt. Now the corpse's leftover bone fragments needed to be placed inside the cremulator and turned into ash. What corpse? She didn't recall a client leaving a corpse for her to cremate.

Her father was the corpse, she remembered. She had slit her own father's throat. Overcome by the heinousness of her crime, she collapsed against the nearby wall, which prevented her from falling to the floor. She couldn't escape some of her memories despite her amnesia attacks. The memory of her murdered father would forever haunt her.

I'm the only one that cares about you. When are you going to understand that?

When you shut up. But the voice would never shut up. It was her curse. It had come to turn her life into a nightmare. Or was her life already a nightmare, and she didn't know it? At least, she wasn't a murderer before the demon had commenced to possess her.

Chapter 44

Brady worried Libby was too far gone. The demon seemed to have a near total grip on her.

He drove back to his apartment, laid Libby's receipt notebook on his desk, and sat in front of his laptop. He booted up his laptop, accessed the Internet, and researched the names in the notebook.

He wasn't sure what he was looking for. Anybody with a criminal past was a good bet. Such a person might have an unsettled spirit. The question was, why would the spirit choose to possess Libby, especially if it didn't know her? She had told him that she didn't know any of the people she had cremated at her business. Then why would the demon target her? Maybe because she was the only one in the crematorium when the corpse burned and gave up the ghost, which, if true, would mean she had burned someone alive despite her denials.

Brady didn't know. He wasn't an expert on possession. Nor was he an expert on psychosis. He had read hundreds of books about possession when he was locked in the insane asylum. He also had firsthand experience when Theresa had possessed him. But he would be the first to admit that there was a lot about the supernatural that he didn't comprehend.

He discovered that one of the corpses Libby had incinerated named Victor "The Stick" Dimagio, aka Vic the Stick, had been a Mafia enforcer for the Genovese Family in New York. He got his nickname from being a semiprofessional pool player. He had whacked out over forty people for the mob before the cops caught up with him.

A guy with a hot sheet like Dimagio's would be a prime candidate for the embodiment of an evil demon. Had the demon escaped from Dimagio's corpse as he burned in the cremation furnace and transferred itself to Libby? But, as Brady understood it, demons needed a motive to possess someone. Possession wasn't just a random occurrence. Dimagio didn't know Libby. On the other hand, if Libby had burned him alive, it would give him a motive to possess her.

Libby had cremated Dimagio over a year ago, according to her bookkeeping records. Why did the demon wait a year before it attempted to possess her? Where had it gone in the meantime?

The serial killer Wayne Bobinsky seemed like the best candidate as the demon because Libby had cremated him recently. But why didn't Bobinsky respond to Brady's attempt to contact him at the séance? The demon had never acknowledged that it was Bobinsky during the séance and it hadn't returned to the grave despite Brady's entreaties for it to do so.

If Brady was trying to exorcise Bobinsky and the demon wasn't Bobinsky, the exorcism was doomed to fail. Somehow Brady had to determine the identity of the evil entity.

Chapter 45

Rafa and Anna shared a cheese margarita pizza with a bacon topping at an Eight Hundred Degrees restaurant. Rafa retrieved a Coke and a Diet Coke from the soda fountain. He returned to their table and handed Anna the Diet Coke.

"What do you think about Libby Genet?" said Rafa, sitting down opposite her.

"She acts like she's got problems," said Anna.

"Like maybe she's lying to us about Bill the repairman."

"She looked nervous when we spoke to her."

"I noticed," said Rafa, and took a bite of his pizza.

"Why should she be nervous if she has nothing to hide?"

"She could be involved somehow with Bill's disappearance. How could she not know that his repair van was parked in the crematorium driveway like her boss told us?"

"I don't understand why she would lie about it."

"I'm pretty sure Bill met with foul play."

Anna sipped her Diet Coke. "Looks that way."

"I'm not seeing a motive, though. Why would anyone harm a crematorium oven repairman?"

"We must be missing something."

"What about that guy Brady who was with her? Didn't you recognize him?"

"No."

Rafa wiped cheese from his mouth. "I swear I've seen him before. He looks different, but I bet it's the same guy I saw somewhere before."

"Where could you have seen him?"

"I dunno."

"Do you go to psychics?"

"No," said Rafa, pulling a face. "I don't believe in that nonsense."

"Why's Genet seeing a medium? That's what I want to know. That whole medium/psychic stuff is suspicious to me."

Rafa chuckled. "You mean, you don't believe in ghosts?"

"Supernatural stuff makes me suspicious. There's a lot of scamming in that line of work. Fortune tellers, psychics, mediums, mind readers, palm readers, the lot. Ya know?"

"Another thing. He looks kind of young to be a psychic. He's not even twenty. Those guys tend to be older."

"It's weird how he turns up at Genet's when Bill disappears."

"You think there's a connection?"

Anna finished chewing her bite of pizza. "I think we need evidence. And a motive. I don't see any reason for Genet to harm Bill."

"And yet she's lying about his being at the crematorium," said Rafa, scratching his chin.

"Well, we know one thing. Bill's corpse wasn't the body Genet was cremating while we were there."

"This is true. You can't argue with the science of DNA." Rafa paused. "That guy Brady. What did he say his first name was?"

"He didn't say."

"It might help jog my memory if I knew his first name."

"This Libby Genet is up to something."

"She ain't off the hook as far as I'm concerned."

"We don't have any hard evidence that any harm came to Bill. Maybe he just wanted to start a new life and took off for parts unknown."

"Then why did Genet lie, saying Bill's van wasn't in her driveway? It keeps bugging me. She's involved up to her neck in his disappearance."

"Didn't you ever feel like you just wanted to chuck everything and start a new life somewhere else?"

Rafa did a double take. "Don't tell me you don't want to be a cop anymore."

"I got two kids to feed. No way am I quitting. I meant, sometimes I feel like moving and starting out fresh. It's just a *feeling*."

"I *feel* a lot of stuff, but I don't do them. And I *feel* Libby Genet is up to no good."

"I don't know how she can stand being locked up in that crematorium all day. And did you notice she sleeps there too?"

Rafa nodded yes. "I saw her bedroom and kitchen."

"The nightmares she must have. Phew."

"Are you afraid of the dark?" said Rafa, grinning.

"A dark crematorium, yeah. The place even smells like death. I don't know how she does her job without it warping her mind. I mean, she's there 24/7. Alone with the stiffs."

"You make it sound like a horror movie."

"The horror here is this pizza," said Anna, grimacing and throwing down her unfinished wedge on her tray.

Rafa laughed. "I think it's pretty good—for a margarita."

"You got no taste."

"Taste is for the Hollywood rich kids who tool around in Lamborghinis with their designer French bulldogs. Guys like us are better off without it."

"I should've been born rich, I guess."

"And miss out on all the fun of busting scumbags? That's not you. You'd be bored to tears being rich."

Anna sniggered. "You read me like a book."

"Ain't it the truth."

Chapter 46

Libby found herself on the stage that night, dancing under the spotlight as Megadeth's "Countdown to Extinction" blasted through the Stacked Deck Strip Club, numbing her ears. Nursing drinks, patrons sat at tables scattered in front of the stage as sinuous clouds of tobacco smoke drifted above them.

Some of the patrons waved dollar bills at her, leering.

Gyrating to the music, she tossed off her blouse. She stepped out of her green plaid miniskirt and danced in white vinyl go-go boots as the besotted, boisterous crowd consisting mostly of men roared its approval.

She was wearing only a lavender bra and a gold lamé G-string, continuing her uninhibited dance and flirting with the crowd, who catcalled and cheered.

She made a show of removing her bra slowly during her dance routine, relishing the hundreds of eyes trained on her in the smoke-hazed joint. She danced closer to the crowd that ringed the stage. Writhing sensuously, she knelt down and allowed patrons to stuff dollar bills into her G-String while she stared at a bald, beefy fortysomething guy with three days' growth and tattoo sleeves. He ogled her and unleashed a toothy grin.

She retreated to the center of the stage, finished her dance, gathered her discarded clothes from the stage, and scampered behind the curtain, brushing past a muscular Asian stripper getting ready to start her routine.

Libby dashed into the dressing room and threw on her clothes.

Other strippers were sitting in front of their vanities working on their makeup and fixing their hair.

Libby didn't say anything to them. She didn't even favor them with a look. The light bulbs on the vanities blinded her. She kept her face averted from them. She had never been here before.

She left the dressing room and mingled with the crowd. She headed for the bald guy with the tat sleeves. He wasn't her type. She didn't know why she was fixated on him. He saw her at once. He got up and approached her. He must have been over six feet tall.

They went to the bar and ordered beers. She found out his name was Chuck. She told him her name was Vanessa.

She didn't want to chitchat. He got the idea.

They left the strip joint and made for his blue and white striped Dodge pickup that had dented fenders. The pickup had not been washed in weeks, a veneer of grime coating it.

He climbed into the driver's seat.

Clutching her purse she claimed the shotgun seat, her miniskirt hitching up her thighs as she sat.

His eyes widened with lust at the sight of her white thighs.

This guy wasn't her type at all. What was she doing with him? And she had never done a strip routine in her life. None of this was making sense to her.

"Want a cigarette?" he said, lighting up.

"Sure."

She plucked a cigarette from the package of Marlboros that he offered her. She inserted the cigarette into her mouth. He lit her up with a Bic lighter.

She almost gagged on the smoke as she inhaled it. She recovered her poise rapidly, not wanting to look like she had never smoked. The fact was she wasn't a smoker. Then why was she smoking?

"Are you OK?" he said.

"I hiccupped when I inhaled, is all."

Chuck laughed. "I do that sometimes too."

"You got a nice truck," she said, noticing a pair of oversized foam dice hanging from the rearview mirror. "You like to gamble?"

"Yeah. I go to Vegas every chance I get. I got this there."

He fished out his house keys from his trouser pocket and showed them to her eagerly. The key ring had his keys and a miniature plastic flesh-colored phallus with balls hanging from it.

"I hope yours is bigger than that," she said.

He guffawed. "It is."

She picked up on the white silhouette of a provocatively sitting naked woman stenciled on his windshield's right lower corner.

"I couldn't believe it when I first laid eyes on you," he said, putting his keys back in his pocket.

"Me either," she said.

"You saw it too? It was like a lightning bolt hit me when I saw you."

"Yeah," she said, wishing she could get rid of her cigarette that was stinking up the pickup.

He reached for her head. "How about a blowjob to start things off?"

Grabbing her head he intended to guide her mouth toward his crotch.

She flicked her cigarette out the window.

"I'll get a rubber," she said, resisting the pressure of his hand on her head. "I believe in safe sex."

"I don't like those things," he said, but released her head.

He unzipped his jeans.

She reached into her purse, withdrew her carving knife, and plunged it into his throat, slashing his carotid artery.

His eyes popped out of his head as much in astonishment as in pain. He grabbed his throat, trying to stanch the fountain of blood that was jetting out of the gaping, tattered wound torn in it.

His last words were, "Why?"

She didn't know why. She didn't even know what she was doing here.

She replaced the bloody knife in her purse, snapped the purse shut, and climbed out of the pickup as Chuck slumped in his seat with glazed eyes, his throat awash in blood.

She didn't see anyone watching her in the parking lot. She beat a hasty retreat down a dark side street to her Fiat, which she had parked near the curb at a parking meter.

What the hell was she doing at a strip joint of all places? She barreled into her car and fired the ignition.

She must be going insane. This wasn't her at all. She was acting like another person.

I'm with you. We'll be one soon.

The damn voice. Did she have a split personality? Or was it a demon like Brady had told her that was possessing her? Whatever it was was taking over her personality, and it scared the hell out of her.

She couldn't go on like this. She was becoming two different people who were polar opposites. Dr. Jekyll and Ms. Hyde at your service.

Distracted, she pulled away from the curb and cut off a black Camaro, whose driver leaned on his horn and shook his fist at her.

Chapter 47

Libby woke up the next day with a throbbing headache to the sound of Tandy meowing in the kitchenette, demanding to be fed.

Libby crawled out of bed and sat on the edge of the mattress, nursing her headache. Why did her head ache? Had she gotten drunk? She barely touched booze. Opening her mouth she held her cupped hand in front of it, exhaled, and smelled her breath. She winced. It smelled like a distillery.

That cinched it. She must have gone out drinking last night. But she couldn't recall last night. It was a blur in her memory bank. She figured excessive drinking could diminish her memory.

Out of character. She wasn't a heavy drinker. What had prompted her to go out and tie one on? It must have been the demon.

Tandy yowled louder.

Libby got out of bed and shambled to the kitchenette.

"Good morning to you too," she said to Tandy, who was standing near the table.

Then a strange thing happened.

He took one look at her, arched his back, and hissed at her.

"What's with you?" she said.

Hissing, he swiped his claws at her.

"Calm down," she said.

Tandy yowled and pelted out of the kitchenette.

"I thought you wanted to eat," said Libby, watching him with bafflement. "Do I look that bad?" she said, picking at her hair.

She must look like shit. Oh, well. What could you expect from a hangover? Who ever looked good waking with a hangover?

Still, she felt like running after Tandy and strangling him or cutting off his head for disrespecting her.

She retreated to her bedroom and changed out of her pajamas into her clothes.

Hearing the phone ring she entered her office and picked up the handset.

A cadaver was going to be delivered to her later this morning. She agreed to accept the corpse for cremation. At least she would get paid for this cremation. She hadn't gotten paid for Bill's or Dad's cremations.

She hung her head in despair, thinking about her father's murder at her hands. She clutched her head. She needed to stop the killing. He was her father for Chrissake.

She couldn't go on like this. She had to exorcise the demon. She phoned Brady.

"Am I possessed?" she asked, her face haggard.

"I believe so," he answered.

"Can you exorcise the demon inside me?"

"If it's not too late."

"Does that mean yes or no?"

He didn't answer for a while.

"I don't believe it has complete control of you," he said at length. "There's still time to save you, but we have to act fast."

"What am I supposed to do?" she said at her wits' end.

"Have you ever heard of the Mafia hit man Victor 'The Stick' Dimagio, aka Vic the Stick?"

"No. Should I know him?"

"He's a killer from Terminal Island and you cremated him about a year ago."

"I'm not following."

"He could be the entity trying to possess you."

"Why would he take a year to start doing it?"

"That's the part I can't get my head around. It makes more sense that it's the serial killer Wayne Bobinsky possessing you because you just cremated him. But he didn't respond to me when I summoned him at our séance yesterday. I doubt Bobinsky is the demon who's after you."

"Then who is?"

"That's why I mentioned this Vic Dimagio guy, but you said you never heard of him. That leaves us back at square one. Unless you burned him alive."

"I don't burn people alive," snapped Libby. "Are you calling me unprofessional?"

"You don't have to bite my head off. I meant no disrespect. I'm trying to establish a motive for Dimagio to possess you."

"You've got to exorcise me before I go nuts," said Libby, distraught. "I can't take this any longer. I'm doing things I don't ordinarily do. I can't control myself. You gotta help me. Even my own cat hates me. He hisses at me and runs away from me every time he sees me even when he's dying of hunger."

"I'm doing the best I can." Brady paused. "Do you know anybody who practices black magic?"

"You mean, a satanist? I don't hang around with satanists."

"A practitioner of the dark arts might have the power to summon a demon to possess you."

Libby mulled it over. "The evilest person I ever met was Ed Grainger, the guy who murdered Mom and Wendy. I have no idea if he's a satanist. I believe he takes hallucinogens if that helps."

"Not all people who take hallucinogens are satanists."

"He hates my guts. He swore he'd get back at me for trying to put him in jail. That's why I took refuge at the crematorium. Nobody would look for me here."

"Could he have found out where you live?"

"I don't see how—"

She caught herself, remembering that her father had been able to track her to the crematorium. If he could do it, why not Grainger? A frisson of fear ran down her spine.

"What?" said Brady.

"Nothing. I thought I saw Tandy coming toward me. Nope. False alarm."

"What about Grainger?"

"If he found out where I live, he would send a hit man to kill me. He has all the money in the world. Why would he bother sending a demon to me?"

"Maybe he doesn't want you to know that he knows where you live. If you knew, you'd take a powder."

Libby shrugged. "Anything's possible."

But Libby didn't believe it. Why wouldn't the billionaire hire a hit man? One could be headed her way even now for all she knew.

"Maybe you should consider moving out of the crematorium," said Brady.

"Grainger will find me if I move. This is the last place he would look for me."

"The demon will complete its possession of you unless we can find a way to stop it if you continue to live there."

There was truth in what he said. But moving was such a hassle. And she was convinced she would fall into Grainger's net if she moved. She was sure he had spies everywhere. When you had as much money as he had you could buy anything you wanted, including spies on the lookout for her.

"I'm not moving," she said. "It must be this Vic Dimagio enforcer you're talking about. He must be the demon."

"We could try another séance to find out. If it's not him, he's gonna possess you again. There are only so many times you can fight off the demon before you become too weak to resist it."

"Then what happens?" she said with dread.

"Then it becomes you. There will be no more you."

"You're scaring me," said Libby, gripping her phone tighter.

"You *are* in grave danger. We have to exorcise the entity before it's too late."

She was in more danger than he knew. She had murdered three people. She couldn't tell him about it, though. He might turn her into the cops even though he knew she wasn't the one doing the killing but the demon that possessed her. He was the only one who might believe it was the demon committing the murders and not her. Still she didn't trust him. Hell, she didn't trust herself. After all, it was *her* hand that had plunged the knife into her victims.

Sometimes she wished she could go mad and escape her debacle of a life. Insanity might be the only solution.

She started when she heard somebody knocking on the front door.

"I have to go," she said, and hung up.

Chapter 48

Libby opened the door and saw a middle-aged man clad in a navy blue uniform standing at her door. Past his shoulder she could see a black hearse parked in the driveway.

"We have a new job for you," said the florid-faced, stocky delivery man, sounding vaguely Russian, grimacing at the noxious odor emanating from the crematorium. "I'm Yuri. We have a delivery from the Sweet Farms Nursery Home." He made a face. "You need to have your furnace repaired. It smells like it's leaking."

"The repairman went missing."

"I'd try a different company if I was you."

His younger, rangy partner with an equine face and shoulder-length black hair opened the hearse's tailgate, revealing a black-painted wooden coffin.

"You didn't need to paint the coffin," said Libby. "It's gonna burn in the oven with the corpse."

"The customer wanted a nice-looking coffin. We aim to please our customers."

"I'll open the side door for you."

"We got a gurney for the coffin. We'll roll it to the loading entrance. I'll get the papers for you to sign."

He strutted back to the hearse on his bandy legs.

Libby retrieved the loading cart and rolled it to the side door, which she opened. She waited for the deliverers.

I'm the only one who cares about you. We are one. Accept me and we will be stronger together. You need me. You are better with me. Resisting me is futile.

The voice. Always the voice.

Open your heart to me and we will be one.

She wished there was a way to block the voice. She didn't want it inside her. It was pure evil. It killed and killed.

Yuri and his partner rolled the gurney bearing the coffin to the loading door. Yuri removed a clipboard bearing forms on it and handed it to Libby for her signature.

"Please sign these while we load the coffin on your cart," said Yuri, grimacing as he breathed the noisome odor that wafted out of the crematorium.

Libby accepted the clipboard and commenced signing the forms with the ballpoint that hung from the clipboard on a brass chain.

"You should keep your doors open," said Yuri. "That awful odor is gonna make you sick. This place reeks of death. Can't you smell it?"

"You get used to it," said Libby, signing a form.

"I dunno," he said, searching her face. "You look kinda pale. Are you sure you're OK?"

"Yeah. The place is haunted," she said dryly, wanting them to leave.

"Haunted?" said Yuri, wide-eyed. "You mean, like Amityville?"

"I was joking. I don't believe in that stuff. Do you?"

"The air in this place is toxic, I'm telling you. Do you have any Vicks VapoRub?"

"No. I don't have a cold."

"It's also good for blocking stenches. You smear it under your nostrils. You can't smell anything else when you stuff it under your nose. All you smell is menthol."

"I don't like menthol."

"On the count of three," Yuri told his partner. "Hold your breath and lift." He counted.

Holding their breaths Yuri and his partner hefted the coffin off the gurney and onto Libby's cart that was parked inside the crematorium. They hustled out of the crematorium and resumed breathing.

She finished signing the forms and returned the clipboard to him.

Hawking and spitting, Yuri hustled away with his partner to their hearse.

See how they run? Nobody likes you, but I do. You should open up to me and welcome me.

"They don't like the smell of death," she muttered.

They insulted you. They said you looked sick.

"Leave me alone," said Libby, wheeling the cart carrying the coffin to the retort door.

You're nothing by yourself. I'm here to help you. I'll look after you. I'll take care of you. Open up to me and we'll be one.

"You're here to help yourself."

"Hello," said Jackie de Matteo, sticking her head through the open delivery door. "Libby?"

"Hi, Jackie," said Libby, lining the coffin cart up with the conveyor belt, surprised to see Jackie.

Chapter 49

"Did you hear the news?" said Jackie, approaching Libby and turning up her nose at the stench. "Wow. What's that smell?"

"The furnace is on the fritz. And the cops made me stop it in the middle of a job and open it. The smell of burning flesh escaped into the room."

"Why did the cops make you open the furnace?"

"They wanted to get DNA from the corpse."

"What for?"

"The cremation oven repairman is missing. They're trying to find him."

Jackie chuckled. "Did they think he fell into the oven while he was repairing it? I'm sorry. I shouldn't laugh. 'Crematorium Repairman Cooks Self in Oven.' You know me. I'm always thinking of titles of articles for the newspaper I work at."

"I suppose."

"Well?"

"Well what?"

"I'm dying to know. Was it the repair guy in the oven?"

"No."

Jackie coughed. "Don't you have a fan to get rid of the stink in here?"

"The fan broke."

"*Fawlty Towers*, huh? Everything's falling apart."

"What can you do?" Libby paused. "What brings you here?"

"Did you hear the news?"

"What news?"

"A guy was stabbed to death in the parking lot of the Stacked Deck Strip Joint."

"I didn't know," said Libby, sliding the coffin onto the conveyor belt.

"Aren't you worried? There's a psycho killer on the loose."

"I don't go to strip joints."

"Me either. But he could be anywhere. I'd keep my doors locked if I was you. I know I'm locking my doors *and* windows." Jackie coughed. "How can you breathe this toxic air?"

"You get used to it."

Jackie shook her head no. "Not me. It's making me nauseous. I hear my stomach rumbling."

"Who do they think did it?"

"The killer?"

"Yeah."

"They don't have any suspects. Drifters go in and out of strip joints. It could be anyone."

"Why do you think it's a psycho killer?"

"The guy didn't steal the victim's wallet. What was his motive? If there's no motive, he's nuts."

"Do they have any clues?"

"If they do, they haven't told anybody about them. I've been thinking. Maybe the psycho killer took out your missing furnace repairman."

"Maybe you should tell the cops."

"The cops aren't gonna listen to me."

"Why not?"

"I have no evidence. I'm just speculating." Jackie eyed Libby's face with concern. "You look anemic. Are you getting over something? You don't have Covid, do you?"

"I feel fine."

"I bet it's this rancid air you're breathing that's making you lose your color. You can't be too careful about your health. We only live once. Enjoy it while you can. That's my motto."

"I keep busy. That's the best thing for your health."

"Not if you're breathing toxic pollution from a cremation oven at your job. How can that be good for you?"

"The smell will go away eventually."

"Are we still on for *The Wicker Man* at the Nuart this Friday? If you're still alive?" said Jackie, cracking a smile.

Libby shot her a paranoid look.

"I was kidding," said Jackie.

"We are," said Libby, relaxing. "I want to see that movie."

"An oldie but goodie. What would we do without the Nuart Theatre?"

"There's always the Aero on Montana. They show old movies. And so does Tarantino's New Beverly."

"I must admit I've never been to either of them." Jackie eyed the coffin. "That's a nice coffin."

"I don't know why they bothered. It's just gonna burn along with the body."

"It's the thought that counts."

"But the corpse doesn't care one way or the other."

"Oh, I almost forgot. The cops said a witness at the Stacked Deck told them she saw a blonde running away from the parking lot about the time of the murder."

Libby's pulse ratcheted upward. "Did she get a good look at her?"

"Uh-uh. Just saw the back of her head."

Good, decided Libby. She was glad she had worn a wig to the Stacked Deck. Now the cops would be searching for a blonde, not a brunette.

"Maybe she was running away from the psycho killer," she said.

"She's a person of interest, according to the cops."

It was dumb luck nobody saw her kill him. Why did she kill him anyway? Because she thought he was going to break her neck when he grabbed her head. Why did she even get into his pickup? What the hell was she doing stripping at the Stacked Deck in the first place? She had never been there before, and she had certainly never stripped before a live audience. Becoming a stripper wasn't her burning ambition in life.

She was heading for a nervous breakdown if she kept up this sort of thing. Her alter ego was a homicidal maniac. A straitjacket and a padded cell with her name on it were waiting for her at the local loony bin.

Her hands were steeped in blood. Didn't the witness see her bloody hands? So what? As long as the witness didn't see her face, Libby was safe from the cops. Unless someone else had seen her too? *Look, it's the stripper running away with blood on her hands.* After all, everybody had seen her up close and personal as she had danced onstage. How could they *not* recognize her if they had seen her in the Stacked Deck parking lot?

She felt her palms sweating.

"Are you all right?" said Jackie, eyeballing Libby.

"Why did you really come here?"

"I told you. I wanted to tell you about the murder."

Did Jackie suspect she was the killer? How could she? Jackie couldn't know. Unless the cops had told her a witness had ID'd Libby. No, no, she was getting paranoid.

She knows you killed him. You'll have to kill her.

Not the fucking voice again. Libby wanted to tear her hair out. Why did Jackie really come here?

She came here because you're a suspect in the strip joint killing.

As though she could believe anything the voice of doom told her.

She wanted to see how you would react when she told you a witness saw the murder. She wanted to see how nervous you got.

"Shut up," said Libby.

"What?" said Jackie, startled. "I didn't say anything."

Libby rubbed her forehead in anguish. "I'm having a bad day."

"I hear ya. My boss says he's gonna can me for being too slow at my job."

"I can't take much more of this."

· "You need to go outside and breathe fresh air. The toxic stench in here is messing you up. You can't keep breathing poison day and night. I mean, you work *and* live here."

"Maybe I'll lie down for a while."

Get the carving knife. She knows you killed Tattoo Sleeves. She'll tell the cops. Kill her.

"Why don't you lie down outside in the sun?" said Jackie. "The air is cleaner."

It's a trap. The cops are waiting for you outside. Get the carving knife.

Libby gripped her right hand, which was leading her toward the kitchenette to retrieve the carving knife, and yanked it back toward her. The hand kept fighting her.

"What's wrong with your hand?" said Jackie.

"Spasms," said Libby, gritting her teeth.

Jackie glanced at her wristwatch. "Uh-oh. I lost track of the time. I gotta get back to the office."

She bustled out of the crematorium.

The demon was trampling through Libby's defenses and crushing her will. Soon Libby wouldn't have enough energy left to fight back.

Get Jackie and cut her throat before she gets away.

Libby's right hand lunged toward the kitchenette. Libby had no choice but to follow it. Its strength overpowered her resistance.

She seized the carving knife from the knife block on the counter and pelted to the front door. Her heart beating furiously, her eyes wild, she flung open the door, baring her teeth, aching to slash Jackie's throat.

Jackie's gold VW Bug was gone.

A black-and-white pulled into the driveway.

Now you're fucked. She ratted you out to the cops.

Chapter 50

Libby raced back into the crematorium and returned the carving knife to the knife block. She doubted the cops had seen the knife, because she was holding it behind the doorjamb when they had arrived.

She had recognized the two cops sitting behind the windshield. They had questioned her about Bill before.

Despite her anxiety, she fixed her hair and tried to look calm, waiting for them to knock. She had no idea what they wanted, but it couldn't be good.

They rapped on the front door.

Even though she was anticipating the knock, she jumped at the sound because of her wired nerves.

She strode to the door and answered it.

"Hello," said Rafa, flashing a smile. "Mind if we have a word with you?"

"Phew, what's that odor?" said Anna, grimacing.

"I'm busy loading a corpse into the oven," said Libby.

"This won't take long," said Rafa.

To avoid looking guilty Libby decided she better let them in.

"Come in," she said. "I need to get back to work ASAP or the boss will chew me out."

Rafa and Anna entered the crematorium. They glanced at the black coffin resting in front of the cremation furnace.

How could they possibly suspect her of killing Chuck at the strip joint? Libby felt her armpits sweating.

"We just got a report that your father is missing," said Anna. "His neighbor filed the report. He's worried something happened to him."

"My father?" said Libby, her heart missing a beat.

Why did they come here to tell her?

"Isn't Dan Genet your father?" said Anna.

"Uh—why yes."

"He left his home yesterday and never returned. His neighbor said your father never stays overnight anywhere. He's confined to

180

a wheelchair and can't get around very well. But of course you know that."

"I haven't seen my father in years. I had no idea he was in a wheelchair."

She felt relieved she had hid the wheelchair in the backyard. If the cops saw it here, they would never stop grilling her.

"He was in a car accident, apparently," said Anna.

"How awful."

"I remember seeing a wheelchair here last time."

Shit. She would have to remember that. Libby fidgeted.

"I told you it belonged to a customer who forgot it in her haste," she said, trying to maintain her composure.

"Where is it now?" said Anna, looking around the room.

"The customer returned and picked it up."

"Then it wasn't your father's wheelchair?"

"Of course not."

"His neighbor said Mr. Genet was planning to see you when he left his house yesterday," said Rafa.

Libby shook her head. "Like I said, I haven't seen him in years."

If her nerves were stretched any tighter, she thought she would explode.

"He didn't come here yesterday?" said Rafa, bemused.

"No," said Libby. "How could he? I never told him where I lived."

Rafa cocked an eyebrow. "You never told your own father where you live? Isn't that strange?"

"Uh—well—you know, we haven't been on the best of terms."

"Still, he *is* your father."

"Yeah, he is."

"Aren't you concerned about him?" said Anna.

"I am, of course. Is there any way I can help?"

"We thought maybe he had come here, since this was his destination and we saw a wheelchair here last time."

"Maybe something happened to him before he made it here. God forbid," said Libby, biting her lower lip.

"Do you see our problem?" said Rafa, searching her face.

"Um—no. We're not close. I don't see how I can help."

"Our problem is this is the second person who was supposed to come here and never made it, according to you. Bill the repairman and now your father. Don't you find that bizarre? What are the chances? The odds must be astronomical against it happening twice."

They suspected her, decided Libby, her heartbeat hammering in her ears.

"A coincidence," she said.

"I don't believe in coincidences."

"What other explanation is there?"

Rafa harrumphed. "Who's in the coffin?"

"A customer's relative. She bought the deceased a pretty coffin even though it's gonna burn with the body."

"It's a nice gesture," said Anna, eying the coffin.

"Mind if we open it?" said Rafa.

"Why would you want to do that?" said Libby.

"Curiosity."

"I doubt the grieving relatives would appreciate it."

"I'm not gonna tell them. Are you?"

"No."

"Do you have a crowbar?"

"You don't think . . . ?"

"I just want to satisfy my curiosity."

Libby repaired to her office, withdrew a crowbar from the closet, returned to the cops, and handed Rafa the crowbar.

He approached the coffin and, using the crowbar, pried open the nailed-shut lid, which squeaked as it rose. He lifted the lid high enough to see a white-haired woman in her eighties lying dead in the coffin. He closed the lid.

"Do you have a hammer?" he said.

"I'll take care of it."

"Why doesn't the stiff smell?"

"This one was embalmed before it got here. The embalming prevents bacteria from growing and causing a stink."

"Why do they embalm the body if it's gonna be cremated?"

"This body was on display at a wake before it arrived. You didn't really think my father was in the coffin, did you?"

"I never think anything. I'm naturally suspicious. It's part of my job." Rafa stared hard at her. "Why would you think I suspected your father was in the coffin?"

"Why else would you want me to open the coffin, since my dad was reported missing?"

Rafa grunted but said nothing.

"Why does it stink in here if the corpse doesn't smell?" said Anna.

Because you stopped the oven in the middle of a cremation, Libby wanted to say but didn't. She resisted the temptation because she didn't want to antagonize the cops.

"We're having a ventilation problem in the crematorium," she said. "The fan broke."

"I see."

"You seem very composed for a person whose father has been reported missing," Rafa told Libby.

She didn't feel composed. She had murdered her father, Bill, and Chuck. She must be putting on a good act.

"He can take care of himself," said Libby. "He may be getting on in years, but he's very independent. I bet he'll show up any time now."

"His neighbor isn't so optimistic. He's worried sick about your dad," said Anna, her face grim.

Rafa cast around the crematorium.

"Looking for something, Detective?" said Libby, watching him.

"Why? Does that bother you?"

"Not at all," said Libby, amazed at her coolness under pressure.

But then again why shouldn't she be cool? She had cremated her father's corpse. There was nothing left of him except ashes. The same held true for Bill the repairman. The only corpse that remained of her murder spree was that of tattoo-sleeved Chuck. And it wasn't in the crematorium. Why should she worry?

"If your dad shows up, could you give us a call?" said Anna. "His neighbor would appreciate it."

"Sure," said Libby.

They suspect you. They'll be back. Kill them.

What would she do without the voice nagging her?

Get the carving knife. Saw their necks off.

Libby clenched her jaw. She struggled to control herself. Don't listen to it, she told herself.

"Are you all right?" said Rafa, fixing his gaze on her.

She wanted to gouge the throbbing vein out of his forehead and stamp it on the floor as it wriggled like an earthworm. Maybe then he would stop coming here and pestering her.

"I'm fine," she managed to say through her teeth.

Rafa shook his head and angled across the floor to the front door, Anna at his side. They exited the crematorium.

Go outside and cut their throats.

"They're cops," said Libby, sick of the voice. "They got guns."

They'll be back.

She refused to listen to the voice.

You'll be sorry. Never put off to tomorrow what you can do today.

"Shut up," said Libby.

You're gonna have to kill them sooner or later.

Chapter 51

"She's hiding something," said Rafa, sitting in the driver's seat of their parked black-and-white.

"You picked up on that too?" said Anna, riding shotgun.

"She doesn't look well. Something's preying on her mind."

"Yeah, but what?"

"A couple of murders maybe?"

"We have no evidence she had anything to do with the two disappearances."

"But both of the missing persons came here to visit her before they vanished off the face of the earth."

"We don't know if either Bill or Genet's father is dead."

"True. But something hinky is going down. I can feel it."

"Did you notice her reactions?" said Anna, looking pensive.

"What do you mean?" said Rafa, facing her.

"When we left, she didn't even ask us to let her know if we find her father. Wouldn't you care if your father was reported missing? Wouldn't you want to know as soon as someone saw him?"

"Yep."

"Although she *did* say she and her father weren't on good terms."

"Which could mean they hate each other's guts."

"Enough for her to kill him?" said Anna.

"Great minds think alike." Rafa paused. "She's as suspicious as hell. She always looks antsy. Why would she be nervous if she has nothing to hide?"

"It could be her personality. Maybe she's neurotic. We can't bust somebody for their personality. I'd probably be neurotic too if I worked at that creepy place."

"I half thought the stiff in the coffin was her father."

"I could see your face droop when you found out the truth."

"I know she's up to something. But I can't figure out what."

"Why would she harm the crematorium repairman?" said Anna, furrowing her brow. "I don't see a motive."

"I know. And yet Genet looks nervous every time we show up at her digs. Why if she has nothing to hide?"

Anna drummed her fingers on the dashboard, thinking.

Rafa fired the ignition and reversed the squad car out of the driveway.

"Why does she live in a crematorium?" said Anna. "That's what I can't figure out. Why not live in an apartment?"

"Maybe she's in hiding."

"From what?"

Rafa jacked up his eyebrows. "Dunno. She could just be a recluse who wants to be left alone."

"Which makes me want to know more about her."

"Me too."

"Or maybe she's on the lam from the law and figures a crematorium is a good place to hole up."

"She might have a rap sheet. Let's see what we can dig up on her. Too many people are heading to her place and ending up missing."

Anna looked at him. "Two is too many?"

"One is too many in my book."

"There could be innocent explanations for their disappearances."

"Nobody's innocent. Everybody's got something to hide. Some people are more guilty than others—and they're the ones we gotta bust. That's why I became a cop. What about you?"

"I joined because I wanted to kick ass."

Rafa laughed. "A nice girl like you? Ex-cheerleader and all. I don't believe it."

"You're too suspicious of people. You think everybody's lying."

"Most of the time they are," said Rafa, his eyes hooded.

"That reminds me. Do you remember where you saw that Brady guy who was visiting Libby?"

"Not yet. He looks a little different. But I've seen him somewhere. I need to find out his first name. If he hangs around with Libby, I'm suspicious of him. Too many people are disappearing around here."

"They ought to rename it the Bermuda Triangle."

Rafa chuckled. "Good one."

186

Chapter 52

Brady sat at his laptop in his apartment.

He needed help with the exorcism. After all, he was new to this game. Most of his knowledge of exorcisms was anecdotal, besides his learning from books that he had checked out at the insane asylum's library when he was incarcerated. He had also learned from the occultist Dr. Armitage by watching him, but he hadn't learned enough, it seemed.

Brady didn't understand why he couldn't contact the demon haunting Libby. He figured it must be because he hadn't identified the demon, but he could be wrong. He needed another opinion.

Brady couldn't consult Armitage, because a satanic cult had murdered him at Brady's former residence.

Brady searched the Internet and found an occultist who went by the name of Quentin, who claimed to know more about the occult than anyone on earth. Brady called Quentin and made an appointment with him.

Brady drove his rental Gladiator to Quentin's office in West Hollywood and was lucky to find a vacant parking space at a meter on the curb three blocks from Quentin's office.

Brady knocked on Quentin's door, strode into the occultist's office, and was surprised to see black-painted walls with stars painted on them. In the dim lighting he spotted a sixtysomething man with a full head of white shoulder-length hair, wearing rose-tinted, wire-rimmed spectacles. He sported a moth-eaten short white beard.

"Have a seat," said Quentin in a voice booming from deep within his chest.

He gestured to a worn leather chair that stood in front of the desk where he sat.

"I spoke to you on the phone," said Brady, sitting down.

"Before we begin, my fees are five hundred dollars an hour."

"Do you take credit?" said Brady, running low on funds.

"Of course. Now what seems to be your problem?"

"I'm an occultist like you. It's not my problem that's baffling me. It's my client's."

"Go on."

Brady smelled sage in the office. Quentin must purify his own office to keep evil entities at bay.

"My client is being haunted by a demon who is trying to possess her," said Brady. "I held a séance, but the demon didn't respond to me. Instead it possessed my client, forcing her to commit obscene acts on the table in front of me. She is so far gone she doesn't even remember committing the acts."

Quentin stroked his ragged beard. "How did you address the demon?"

"By his name. At least, I thought it was his name. Now I'm not sure."

"If you're addressing the demon by the wrong name, it will not respond to you. What did you tell it?"

"I told it to leave my client alone, that it was dead and should return to the grave where it came."

"You seem awfully young to be an occultist. Where did you study?"

"I have personal experience with possession. A demon possessed me when I was a boy. I've also read many books on the subject. What about you?"

"I have a PhD in parapsychology from the University of Edinburgh," boasted Quentin. "Their Koestler Parapsychology Unit is world renowned."

"Impressive," said Brady, eager to learn from Quentin.

"With my doctorate I set up shop here in Hollywood. As a result I have a very low opinion of human nature. You wouldn't believe how many of my clients want me to put curses on other people."

"I had no idea."

"Nobody ever went broke pandering to the depravity of the human race," said Quentin, grinning.

"I guess not."

"You have to have a sense of humor in this line of work."

"I need—"

"For the record, I don't put curses on other people. Enough of me. Let's get back to your problem," said Quentin, becoming serious.

"I need help. My client needs help. I believe her life is in imminent danger."

"Did you smudge your client's house?" said Quentin, all business.

"I did."

"And then you held a séance? Correct?"

Brady nodded yes.

"How did you find out the identity of the demon?" asked Quentin.

"My client works in a crematorium. She recently cremated a serial killer who died in a nearby prison. A fellow inmate murdered him, actually. Soon afterwards, she experienced acts of possession—"

"Such as . . . ?"

"Such as changes in her personality. She began acting out of character and smelling repulsive odors in her building. She heard weird sounds. She located a cold spot in the crematorium. She started hearing voices."

"Go on."

"She suspected she was going insane. I figured the unsettled spirit tormenting her was the serial killer."

"It could be. But it could be someone else. Why would a serial killer choose your client to possess?"

"Because my client was in the crematorium where the killer's body was incinerated."

"Your client works in a crematorium, you say?"

"She also lives there."

"I see."

"I came up with another motive. I thought it was possible my client might have accidentally burned the serial killer alive and he is seeking revenge."

"Does your client think that's what happened?"

"She denies it. She said she's never cremated a living person."

"Not even a cataleptic?"

"She says no."

Quentin nodded. "Burying people or cremating them alive is pretty rare nowadays because of modern science. She's probably right."

"Then what's going on? Who is trying to possess her?"

Quentin chewed it over. "It could be any number of spirits haunting her, since she's in the business of cremating many corpses."

"That's what makes exorcising her so difficult. I have to figure out which spirit is tormenting her out of all of the corpses she has cremated."

"There is another possibility."

"I'm listening."

Chapter 53

Quentin took a deep breath as he prepared to disabuse Brady. "The evil entity could be that of a living person."

"What?" said Brady in surprise. "Is that possible?"

He had never heard of anyone being possessed by the spirit of a living person, though he had heard of satanists conjuring demons when they put curses on people.

"It is indeed," said Quentin. "A practitioner of the black arts could be sending his spirit to haunt your client."

"I had no idea."

"The ways of evil are many. You're too young to have encountered all of them. They are also in great demand by people."

"This is a question that continues to puzzle me. Maybe you can answer it. Why does evil exist?"

"Ah, I wish I knew the answer to that," said Quentin, leaning back in his chair and looking up at the black-painted ceiling constellated with silver stars. "If we knew the answer, maybe we could get rid of it."

"Maybe there is no answer."

"I don't want to wax philosophical on your dime," said Quentin, leveling his gaze at Brady. "Do you know of a living person who might want to inflict harm on your client by means of possession?"

"I didn't think it was possible. I thought unsettled spirits acted on their own, possessing their chosen victim."

"The spirit of a living person trying to possess your client might explain why you can't exorcise the demon. You must identify it correctly before an exorcism can be successful. Demons are masters of deception and will say anything to dissemble their true identities."

"If a living person is siccing his spirit on my client, can I still exorcise it? I mean, I can't tell it to go back to its grave because it's dead. It won't obey, since it's not dead."

"True. It will not heed you if you tell it to return to its grave, for it has no grave. It will continue to possess your client until it has claimed her completely and can never be exorcised."

"Are you saying it's hopeless?" said Brady, perplexed.

"It's not hopeless. You must act swiftly, though. Listen to me." His visage intense, Quentin leaned forward over his desktop toward Brady. "You must tell the spirit to return to its living master, and you need to tell it the name of the master. You must identify the name of the master correctly or your séance won't work. It's the only way you can exorcise the evil entity. Telling it to return to the grave will do no good."

"This practitioner of the black arts must be a monster."

"There are many monsters in the world in the guise of humans," said Quentin with a trace of fatalism. "We can only do our best to fight them." He paused. "Your problem will not be solved after you tell the demon to return to its living master."

"What do you mean?" said Brady, confused.

Quentin didn't answer right away.

Brady didn't understand what Quentin was getting at.

"You will have to kill the master," said Quentin at length.

Brady started. "Why?"

"The master will send his demon to possess your client again if you let him live," said Quentin solemnly. "In the end the demon will possess your client. You don't want that, do you?"

"No," said Brady, rubbing the back of his neck in anguish. "This is worse than I thought."

"You have no choice but to kill the master in order to free your client permanently from being possessed. But first you must exorcise the demon from your client. If you kill the master without exorcising the demon, it will take up permanent residence inside your client."

"This is *much* worse than I thought," said Brady, overwhelmed, not sure he could bring himself to kill someone.

"It's difficult for humans to comprehend the vastness of evil."

Brady had no desire to murder again. He had already murdered his mother while a demon possessed him. He would never live down the guilt for committing the execrable act. Now Quentin was telling him he would have to commit another murder.

"You're telling me to commit an evil to get rid of another evil," said Brady.

Quentin heaved a sigh. "It can't be helped. Evil has tremendous power in this world. The evil person you're dealing with can continue to send out his spirit to possess people until the evil person is dead."

"Isn't there some other way to get rid of the demon?" said Brady.

"The necromancer you're dealing with is diabolical. He must be destroyed to free your client."

"I'm not sure I can do it."

"As I said, getting rid of the demon in this case isn't enough. You must get rid of the demon's master as well or he will send out his demon again to persecute your client."

"Then I'll send the demon away again."

"The necromancer can send the demon as long as he lives. You'll have to spend your entire life exorcising the demon from your client."

"I can't do that."

"Of course not. Nobody could."

"I don't know if I can bring myself to kill—"

"I'm not telling you this lightly." Quentin fiddled with a brass astrolabe on his desktop as he contemplated the rest of his answer. "I know full well the gravity of the act of committing murder. But it's the only way to free your client from being possessed. Banishing the demon won't be enough. The demon master must be destroyed afterwards. He hates your client and won't be satisfied until she's possessed."

Agitated, Brady stood up.

Maybe Quentin was wrong. Why should he believe this guy, anyway? Just because he claimed he was the most knowledgeable occultist in the world with a PhD from the University of Edinburgh and had a website on the Internet? Anybody could make the same claim and set up a website. He could be a fraud. On the other hand, what he said made sense if anything made sense when it came to the subject of demons.

"I want to make sure I understand you," said Brady. "Are you telling me to commit murder?"

"Let me be clear. I'm not telling you to do anything. I'm telling you what *needs* to be done to free your client from being possessed for the rest of her life."

Distraught, Brady furrowed his brow as he pondered committing another murder.

Quentin picked up on Brady's discomfiture.

"The world is full of evil, my son," said Quentin, his eyes morose. "If you can't do the deed, maybe you could hire someone to do it for you."

"Same difference. I'd be just as guilty of murder either way."

"Sometimes the only way to deal with evil is with evil."

"Then what's the difference between us and them?"

"I'm not a philosopher. I'm an occultist. I have told you what needs to be done to exorcise the demon tormenting your client. You must act quickly. It sounds like the act of possession is in its final stages. In her present stage your client is capable of violence, I believe."

"You think she's that far gone?"

Quentin nodded. "Her acting out of character means the demon is taking over. When people become possessed, they frequently commit acts of violence."

"They'll put me in jail if I do what you say."

"Demons don't obey the law. To fight them and win you can't obey the law either. You have to do what's right."

"How can murder be right?"

"It's the only way to get rid of the demon permanently. A demon sent by a living person is the worst kind. The most difficult to destroy because it's still alive."

Perturbed, Brady blew out his cheeks and massaged his brow.

"How do I proceed?" he said under his breath, not sure he wanted to hear the answer.

"Listen carefully. First, you must hold a séance and order the demon to return to its master to make sure your client is free of possession. Then you must kill the master to prevent him from resending the demon to possess your client."

"OK," said Brady tentatively.

"Your task is difficult. You must understand the gravity of what I'm telling you to do. The problem is it's the only answer. There's no other way. Demons don't obey the law. To destroy them you sometimes must go beyond the law, or in other words, take the law into your own hands."

Brady searched Quentin's aged, somber face and knew Quentin was leveling with him.

Chapter 54

Libby watched the retort cremating the most recent corpse. The machine made a pleasing hum when it was running smoothly, not that clanking, grating sound which the repairman was supposed to fix. She would have to file another service request. Fortunately, the retort wasn't clanking at this time.

She heard knocking at the front door. She hoped it was another customer. But she didn't trust her luck today.

Apprehensive it might be the cops returning to give her the third degree, she answered the door with caution.

Clad in a shocking pink minidress, a petite twentysomething peroxide blonde wearing false eyelashes and gobs of turquoise mascara greeted her.

"Hi, honey," she said, smiling with her puffy face.

"Do I know you?" said Libby, not recognizing her.

"I saw you last night in the dressing room. I'm Carly."

Libby still didn't recognize her.

"At the Stacked Deck," said Carly. "You look different." Staring at Libby, she made a face. "Oh, I know what it is. You were wearing a wig last night. You were blonde."

Libby felt her pulse accelerate. She didn't recall seeing Carly.

"I was in the dressing room when you came through," said Carly. "It's OK. I'm not gonna tell anyone you strip in your spare time. I do too. I'm going to college at UCLA to get my BA in Business. I gotta pay tuition, so I work."

"I don't think I know you," said Libby, wishing the woman would book. "How did you find me?"

Carly withdrew a plastic card from her scarlet vinyl clutch.

"You dropped your AAA card in the dressing room," she said, showing the card to Libby.

"Oh," said Libby, embarrassed. "But my address isn't on it. How did you find me?"

"I called them up and told them I found your card and I wanted to return it to you. So they gave me your address. And here I am. Aren't you glad?"

Libby reached for the card. "Thank you."

"Not so fast," said Carly, pulling the card away from Libby. "I'm having trouble paying my college tuition."

"You want a reward?" said Libby in surprise.

"Aren't you gonna invite me in?"

"Why?"

"I brought you your lost AAA card."

"Well, thanks," said Libby, reaching for the card again.

Carly wouldn't let her have it.

"I'm not in the mood to play games," said Libby, nettled.

"This isn't a game. I have valuable information for you."

Libby didn't know what Carly was talking about, but she knew she didn't like the shrewish glint in Carly's green eyes.

"I don't see how that's possible," said Libby, preparing to close the door in Carly's face. "I don't recall ever seeing you."

"I wouldn't do that if I was you. Or do you want me to go to the cops?"

Libby opened the door, her nerves tightening. "Why would you do that?"

"Do you really want me to tell you out here? I'd think you'd want some privacy."

Libby decided she better find out what Carly wanted. Why would the woman mention the cops?

"Come in," said Libby.

"That's better."

Chapter 55

Libby watched Carly enter the crematorium and screw up her face in disgust.

"What's that stink?" said Carly. "How can you stand it in here? What is this place anyway?"

"It's a crematorium," said Libby.

"What's that?"

"We cremate corpses here."

"Ugh. How can you stand the stink?"

"The cremation chamber is on the fritz. It's got a glitch."

"It does smell like dead things in here," said Carly, her face turning pallid. "And sulfur. I would never work at a crappy job like this. I work only at jobs I like."

"Like stripping."

"That's right. I think stripping's fun. I'm gonna run my own cosmetics company when I graduate from college."

"Could I have my card back?" said Libby, reaching out her hand.

"Not so fast."

"What?"

"I saw you leave the strip joint with that guy that got killed in his pickup in the parking lot last night."

Libby's heart stopped. She felt the blood rush from her face.

How could Carly recognize her? The blonde wig Libby had worn at the Stacked Deck must not have fooled Carly.

"The bastard was giving you a hard time and you had to defend yourself," said Carly. "Am I right or what?"

"I don't know what you're talking about."

"I saw you in his pickup. Am I getting through to you?"

"It wasn't me. What kind of a scam is this?"

"Oh, come off it. What did he want? A knob job?"

She saw you kill him. Kill her. Kill the ho.

Her friend the voice. What would she do without it to make her day?

"So it's OK if I tell the cops I saw you in the dickhead's pickup last night and I give them your AAA card?" said Carly, fixing to leave.

"Wait," said Libby, flustered. "Don't go."

"That's better. Maybe you should be a little nicer to me."

"I've had a rough day."

"I guess I could stay a little longer," said Carly, drawing up at the front door.

"Thank you. Maybe I was at the strip joint last night. But I didn't kill anyone. You saw somebody else in Tattoo Sleeve's pickup."

"Is that right? How did you know he had tat sleeves if you weren't in his pickup?"

Libby gulped. The more she talked, the more she incriminated herself.

"I'm telling you I didn't kill him," she said.

"Do you want me to tell the cops or not?"

"Not."

"That's what I thought," said Carly, looking smug. "Well?"

"Well what?"

"What's it worth to you to keep my mouth shut?" said Carly, prancing around.

"Uh—twenty dollars."

Carly burst out laughing. "You gotta be kidding."

She'll rat you out to the cops. Don't let this skank push you around. Kill her. Kill the tramp.

"How much do you want?" said Libby, testy.

"A hundred grand would do nice."

"Where am I gonna get a hundred thousand bucks?" blurted Libby. "Do you see where I work? Do you think I make that kind of money? I have to strip at night to pay my bills."

"Join the club. Maybe the cops'll go easy on you if you strip in the joint for them," said Carly with a puckish expression, retreating toward the door.

"Wait," cried Libby, holding up her hand.

Carly slewed around to face her. "You got a better offer?"

"I can't pay you a hundred thousand bucks. No way."

"OK. Fifty thousand today and the other fifty next week. How's that? Look, I'm trying to help you stay out of jail. That guy you killed was a dickhead. He gave all the girls a bad time. I'm glad you wasted the douchebag."

"Impossible. I don't have that kind of money."

"Then you better get it. Find a sugar daddy or something."

You won't last five minutes in jail. Kill the blackmailing bitch.

Why did the slut have to see her in Chuck's pickup? Libby clenched and unclenched her right hand.

"What's wrong with your hand?" said Carly.

"A cramp."

Crossing her arms over her chest, Carly tapped her foot. "I don't have all day. I'm a working girl."

"I can give you a hundred bucks as a down payment."

Carly snickered. "Not even close. Stop jerking my chain and pay up."

"Do I look rich?"

"This is serious. Five-O are gonna throw your sorry ass into the joint if I snitch to them I saw you with Chucky last night." Carly coughed. "This place stinks. How can you stand it? Open the windows." She cast around the room. "Where are the windows? Don't you have any windows? This place is a crypt."

Carly darted to the front door, flung it open, and breathed fresh air from outside.

"Don't leave," implored Libby.

Chapter 56

"I got your attention, huh?" said Carly, gloating.

"Let's work this out," said Libby, all but begging.

She hated debasing herself by begging, especially begging a tramp like Carly to go easy on her with her demands for money.

"I'm not leaving till you pay me," said Carly. "Don't you have a fan to air out this dungeon? I come from a good family and I'm very sensitive to smells. Do you want me to pass out?" said Carly, holding her stomach, looking ill.

"The fan broke," said Libby.

"You think I'm gonna leave because it stinks in here? Is that your plan? Forget it. I'm not leaving till you pony up," said Carly, rubbing her forefinger against her thumb.

"I can't . . ."

"You don't look well. Are you eating enough? You need to get out more often. This tomb is killing you."

"I have to work."

"Join the club, honey."

"Look, I'll give you a hundred dollars for the card. That's more than it's worth. The annual fee costs half that."

"I don't care about annual fees. Do I look like trailer trash who stands at bus stops selling blowjobs?"

"Of course not."

"You're the one with a job for poor white trash."

"Now hold on a minute—"

"This kind of job would make anyone sick, skulking around corpses 24/7. I'm gonna throw up if I have to stay here any longer. Want me to barf on your floor? Hurry up and grab the money and fork it over before I puke my guts out. What's wrong with your hand?"

Libby's right hand was leading her to the kitchenette.

"I'll get the money," she said, her face contorted with the anger welling inside her.

The two-bit sleazeball is acting like the Queen of Sheba. Cut off her head and hold it up by the hair.

The voice echoed through her head haranguing her. Unable to escape its demands, Libby retreated toward the kitchenette.

Cut the blackmailing white-trash bitch to pieces.

"Why are you going to the kitchen?" said Carly. "Don't you keep the money under your mattress like everybody else?"

Libby disappeared into the kitchen, gliding like a ghost. Her right hand behind her back, she returned in Carly's direction and stopped.

"Come here," said Libby, her face a conflict of expressions, one agonized, the other lusting for blood.

"What's wrong with you?"

"Nothing."

"You forgot the money."

"No, I didn't."

"Show me it," said Carly, approaching her warily. "You look messed up. If you don't move out of here, you're gonna end up burned up in your own oven. Burn, baby, burn." Carly studied Libby's face. "You look gravely ill, girl." Carly laughed. "I made a joke. Get it? *Grave*ly ill. This place is like a factory fueled by graveyard stiffs."

Gnashing her teeth, growling, Libby hurled herself at Carly and slashed her throat with the carving knife that she clutched in her right hand.

Carly screamed in horror. Backing up she groped in astonishment at the blood gushing from her severed carotid artery.

"You're insane," she gasped, crumpling on the floor, her eyes starting out of their sockets.

Make sure the slut's dead.

Libby pounced on Carly's writhing body like a tiger savaging its prey and plunged the knife into the dying woman's heart, listening with satisfaction to the bubbly death throttle escape Carly's shredded throat.

Libby threw the knife down, reeling backward, aghast at what she had done.

Clean up the mess and burn the body. You see, I'm the only one who cares about you. Everyone else is your enemy. You and me together are better than apart. All you need to do is let me in. Invite me in.

"No," screamed Libby, barely able to fight off the demon as she felt it attempt to gain complete domination over her.

I care about you. Let me in. You can't fight the world alone. You need me.

Libby couldn't stand the snake whispering in her ear. She told herself not to listen to the lying demon.

Your mother and sister are dead. You killed your own father. You are alone. I'm the only one who cares about you. Let me in.

"Get out of my head," cried Libby, clutching her ears.

She leered at the blood-soaked body of Carly sprawled at her feet. She knew she had to dispose of the corpse and clean the floor. Another customer could knock on the door any second. She dashed to the front door and shut it.

Energized by the adrenaline coursing through her body, she hauled the limp corpse onto the cart and lined the cart up with the conveyor belt that led to the oven.

There was one problem.

The cremation chamber was already occupied, and it wouldn't be finished for another hour.

Libby couldn't dispose of the corpse yet.

She retrieved the mop from the kitchen closet and set to mopping Carly's blood off the floor.

She wondered if anybody else had seen her with Chuck in his pickup. She didn't think so. But she hadn't thought Carly had seen her either.

There was nothing Libby could do about it now.

The demon was fast turning her into a mass murderer. She had to get the thing exorcised from her. There was no way she could go on like this. Where was Brady? He was the only one who could help her if it wasn't too late for her to be helped.

Mopping the blood off the floor, she wondered frantically what she was going to do with the body. Maybe she could hide it in the empty cremulator while the retort was occupied. A temporary measure before she could incinerate it.

She realized with a start that her dad's wheelchair was standing beside the retort.

How could the wheelchair be there? She had put it in the backyard. At least she thought she had. Was her memory playing tricks on her?

She would have to push the wheelchair out to the backyard again. She couldn't have the cops see the wheelchair if they returned, and she knew they would return.

Confused by its presence, she grabbed the handles on the wheelchair and rolled it rapidly into the backyard.

Chapter 57

Rafa and Anna were riding in the black-and-white, Rafa at the wheel, trailing a driver who was jacking his chrome-decked flashy orange Dodge lowrider up and down, as they crawled along in slow traffic just this side of gridlock.

"Do you think he's trying to mess with us?" said Anna, riding shotgun, watching the lowrider.

"It's not like we're in a hurry. Anyway, everybody else is stuck in traffic with us."

"Do you have one of those cars?" said Anna, nodding at the lowrider.

"I just thought of something. That guy Brady, the friend of Genet's. His last name isn't Brady. It's his first name. His full name is Brady Carney," said Rafa, turning away from the windshield to look at her.

"Who's Brady Carney?"

"Don't you remember? He's the kid who killed his mother when he was ten years old."

"Didn't he do time? I can't remember what happened with that trial."

"You must have been out of town. It was in all the media. 'Mother Killer Walks,' blared the news."

"Clue me in."

"He got off by reason of insanity. He claimed he was possessed by a demon when he shot his mother."

"The jury believed him?" said Anna, incredulous.

"The stupidity of jurors never ceases to amaze me."

"Not all jurors are idiots," retorted Anna. "Some of them have PhDs."

"They're the ones who are the stupidest, if you ask me," said Rafa, indignant. "They hide in their ivory towers and have no concept of the jungle of the real world surrounding them."

"Are you saying the court let him go?"

"They locked him in an insane asylum. I guess they must've released him. I knew I saw him somewhere. He's older now, but I still recognized his face. He has those weird eyes."

"The shrinks at the loony bin must think he's cured."

"The question is, why's Genet hanging around with a homicidal maniac? I'm getting more suspicious of her."

"Maybe she doesn't know he's a murderer. I didn't recognize him. He was just a kid during that trial. He's an adult now. It would be easy not to recognize him."

"Maybe she doesn't watch the news. She seems out of touch with the real world in that crematorium she lives in. Maybe she doesn't have a TV."

"'Out of touch.' That's a good way to describe her. She might have a disease too."

"A disease?"

"Like anemia. She's pale as a ghost."

"Log onto the laptop and google Brady Carney," said Rafa, glancing at the police laptop mounted in the squad car.

Anna awoke the laptop from Sleep mode.

"I'm not finding a Brady Carmy. There's a Brady Carmody."

"Not Carmy. Carney. C-a-r-n-e-y."

"Oh."

"What's he up to these days?" said Rafa.

"I can't find anything recent about him except that he was released from the Rosehill Asylum for the Criminally Insane."

"I figured out that much already."

"Nothing else."

"Are you sure?"

"You know, that picture of Brady Carmody looks a lot like Brady Carney."

Anna googled Brady Carmody.

"He could be using an aka," said Rafa. "What's it say about him?"

"He's got a website that says he's an occultist."

"An oculist?"

"No. An occultist. An oculist is an eye doctor."

"Then what's an occultist?"

"This Brady Carmody character claims he's an expert on the supernatural."

"A fancy way of saying he's a psychic. Everyone knows they're frauds."

"I'm not so sure. I have an actor friend who seeks the advice of her psychic all the time. She believes in astrology and all that."

"Maybe this guy isn't Brady Carney."

"It sure looks like him," said Anna, zooming in on his photo. "There's a photo of him on his website."

"Why would anyone patronize an occultist who killed his own mother? How can he stay in business?"

"Let me read further."

Rafa shook his head. "Does he really think everybody believes that cock and bull story he gave on the stand that he was possessed by a demon when he killed his mother?"

"You said the jury believed it when they found him innocent."

"Not everybody agrees with juries. Like the one in the OJ trial."

"All I can say is he's using his experience with demons to promote himself on his website."

"Does his website say he killed his mother because a demon possessed him? I can't believe he'd advertise that he's a murderer."

Anna continued reading the website on the laptop screen. "It just says he has experience with being possessed. It doesn't say that he killed anyone."

Rafa mulled it over. "He must realize nobody would hire him if he advertised himself as a murderer."

"So why is Genet consulting with a self-declared expert on the occult?"

Tired of driving behind the lowrider driver who kept jacking his Dodge up and down with customized hydraulics, Rafa switched lanes. He caught the mustachioed driver ginning at him.

"It's not illegal to consort with psychics, but it makes me suspicious," said Rafa.

"Do you think Genet believes in all that supernatural mumbo jumbo?"

"Ask your friend the astrologer."

"She's not an astrologer. She's an actor who believes in astrology. A lot of people do."

Rafa slapped the steering wheel in a pet. "Well, I don't. I say this Brady guy is a professional scammer. He scammed the court, and now he's scamming the public to make a fast buck."

"Do you think Genet hired him?"

"Hired him to do what? That's the question."

"Yeah. Maybe this guy's got a sideline as a professional murderer. He's killed before. Why not again?"

"First we need to find out what happened to Genet's father and Bill the repairman. I'm convinced they met with foul play. They both went to the crematorium or were on their way there and disappeared. Something's hinky."

Anna scratched her hair. "I don't understand the motive, particularly the repairman. Why kill the repairman who comes to service your machine?" She glanced at the driver passing her on the right whose eyes were staring at her and popping with anxiety. "Why does everybody look at a black-and-white like they're guilty?"

"Because they are."

Chapter 58

Ed Grainger laughed.

He was having the time of his life, tripping on his psylocibin in his bedroom in his Dutch Colonial mansion. It stood out in his neighborhood in Bel Air thanks to its gambrel roof and curved eaves. Everybody else in Bel Air owned a Spanish-styled mansion, a Tudor one, or an Italian palazzo. Everyone but Grainger. He wanted to be different, to be special, to be superior. Hence his Dutch Colonial home.

Lying on his back in bed in Tom Ford turquoise shorts and a Gucci white T, his eyes closed, he was enjoying watching his demon harass Libby and force her to commit another murder. In his hallucinogenic dream state he could see everything going on in the Elysian Fields Forever Crematorium.

He was going to own Libby Genet body and soul before his revenge was complete. The bitch had been arrogant enough to think she could get away with having him thrown in prison for the murder of her mother and sister. He was in the process of proving her wrong, of showing her why everybody shivered in fear at the mere idea of antagonizing the son of a hedge fund billionaire. He was teaching her a lesson.

Not only was he a billionaire feared by all thanks to his money, he could drop magic mushrooms and send out his spirit to destroy his enemies.

Libby Genet had demonstrated herself to be his enemy. Therefore, he would make her life a living hell.

He had shot her mother and sister because they were plotting to kill him. It was a clear case of self-defense. Kill or be killed. This was America for Chrissake. Everybody owned a gun and everybody knew how to use it. If he hadn't shot them, they would have shot him.

In any case, the trial was thrown out on a legal technicality uncovered by his filthy rich pad-their-paychecks, bill-by-the-hour team of lawyers who took six months to do the same thing an honest lawyer (if there was such a thing) could do in one day.

Libby would have to learn the facts of life the hard way, that nobody took on Ed Grainger without suffering his wrath. The best thing about tormenting his enemies with his demon was it put him above the law. Nobody could convict a demon of anything. Likewise, nobody could convict the conjuror of the demon. He was an Ubermensch.

Using the demon, Grainger wanted to possess Libby body and soul and turn her into his bloodthirsty slave, a homicidal maniac at his beck and call.

Grainger guffawed. It was hysterical.

He felt like a necromancer version of the Wall Street homicidal maniac Patrick Bateman, but instead of killing anybody himself like the inferior Bateman, other than Genet's mother and sister, Grainger used his spirit to possess Libby and force her to become a serial killer for him.

He was turning her into a raving lunatic, and nobody could figure out he was the one that was driving her nuts, since he had no contact with her. His only contact with her was through the demon he unleashed upon her. Nobody would ever suspect him, because nobody believed in demons, let alone demons conjured by necromancers like himself.

Not only could he control the real world with his billions of dollars, he could control the supernatural with his ability to conjure demons by ingesting magic mushrooms he bought along with bricks of blow from the invincible Mexican cartels that enslaved America the Beautiful.

With his eyes shut he could see even now Libby running around her crematorium like a madwoman hysterical with the fear of being arrested for the murder of the guttersnipe stripper Carly. Via his demon he could see trailer-trash Carly's blood-drenched body sprawled on the conveyor belt that led to the cremation chamber.

He thought about calling the cops and ratting out Libby for Carly's murder. But then the cops would throw Libby in the joint, and his cat-and-mouse fun with her would come to an end. In any case, he didn't possess her completely. His goal was to possess her root and branch. Once he completed his goal, there would be no need to have her thrown in the slam, because she would become his slave and would be unable to resist his commands.

A perfect master like himself needed a perfect slave. He had chosen Libby to play that role.

Chapter 59

Libby was standing staring at Carly's body wondering what to do with it when she started at the sound of knocking on the front door.

The person standing outside set Libby's nerves on edge.

She couldn't let them leave before answering the door, or they might report her to Herbert Stringfellow for being closed. Libby was already in Dutch with the boss. He wouldn't stand for her closing the crematorium, especially after he had chewed her out for doing the same thing earlier. She had to open the door and see who was outside.

With misgivings she angled to the front door, which vibrated whenever the visitor outside knocked on it.

Her palms sweaty, she latched onto the doorknob and cracked the door, hoping it wasn't the cops standing outside.

"Phew," said Jackie, standing in front of Libby. "Why does it stink so bad in there? It smells like you got a hundred decomposing cadavers lying inside. Are you running a charnel house?"

"Hi, Jackie," said Libby, sticking her head through the crack between the door and the jamb.

"Aren't you gonna invite me in? I came all this way to see you."

"I've never been busier than today. Can't this wait?"

"I heard on the radio that your father has been reported missing. I thought you should know."

"I already heard."

Since Jackie was a head taller than Libby, she was able to see over Libby's head and make out Carly's corpse sprawled on the conveyor belt behind Libby.

"Jesus, what happened?" said Jackie, putting her hand to her gaping mouth.

"What do you mean?" said Libby, sweating in apprehension, fearing lest Jackie had seen Carly.

"That woman on the conveyor belt behind you. She's covered with blood."

On pins and needles, Libby had to think of a plausible explanation. Shutting the door in Jackie's face wouldn't solve anything. Jackie had already seen the corpse.

"She's—uh—my next job," said Libby.

"Why's she covered with blood?"

Her heartbeat jackhammering out of control, Libby racked her brains, trying to think of an answer.

"Uh—well—uh—she committed suicide," Libby managed to say.

"Suicide? Here?"

"No, no. Uh—her parents brought her body here after she did it."

"Why didn't the mortician clean her body?" said Jackie, aghast.

"Well—uh—the mortician didn't see the body. The parents don't want anybody to know their daughter committed suicide. It's against their religion. They're terribly embarrassed."

"How horrible." Jackie paused. "Is it legal to drop off a body before getting a death certificate?"

"I—I don't know. What's the law say?"

"I'm not a lawyer. It just doesn't seem right to drop a bloody body here before cleaning it off."

"She'll burn just as well whether she's bathed in blood or spick and span."

"Gee, listen to us. What a morbid conversation we're having."

"You can't avoid death."

"I guess. Maybe this fresh corpse is what's making it smell so bad here," said Jackie, contorting her face with disgust.

"Maybe."

"Aren't you gonna invite me in?"

"Uh—you said it smelled. Why do you want to come in?"

"It doesn't feel right, standing out here while you're inside with the door between us. It's like you're trying to hide from me."

Libby heaved a sigh. "OK. Come in."

Chapter 60

There didn't seem any point to keep Jackie out of the crematorium now that she had already seen Carly's corpse. Libby opened the door and backed away from the entrance.

"Thanks," said Jackie, entering.

"You shouldn't get too close to the body."

"Don't worry." Jackie examined Libby's face. "You don't look well. I've never seen you this pale. Are you eating OK?"

"Sure."

"Do you eat enough spinach?"

"I do."

"I don't see how you can have an appetite being cooped up in this smelly tomb. How do you keep your food down?"

"You get used to it. You can get used to anything."

"Maybe. But it shouldn't smell this bad. It never used to stink like this."

"The cremation oven is on the fritz. Plus I had to interrupt a job and open the oven for the cops. The stench backed up into the room."

"Oh yeah. You told me about the cops looking for the repairman."

Libby nodded.

Jackie eyed Carly's corpse with distaste. "Are you gonna report the parents for dropping off their daughter here?"

"I don't want to get them in trouble."

"You're the one who could get in trouble for cremating the body without first getting a death certificate. You gottta look after yourself in this world, Libby. If you don't, nobody else will."

"The world's such a godawful mess. I'm trying to cope."

Libby had never told Jackie about the murder of her mother and sister and her subsequent retreat from the vicious world by taking refuge in the crematorium. She wasn't going to start now. She didn't want Jackie's pity. She didn't want anybody's pity, for that matter. She would just as soon keep the matter to herself. After all, it was personal.

There were some things you couldn't tell your BFF.

"The cops could put you in jail for not following the law," said Jackie.

"Not if they don't find out about it. I'm not gonna tell them. Are you?"

Yeah, she will. You can't trust her. Get the carving knife. Take her out.

The frigging voice. What would she do without it?

"I'm not gonna tell anyone," said Jackie. "We're friends. I got your six."

"Thanks."

Jackie stared at something on the floor. "What's that? It looks like a puddle of blood."

She knelt down and studied it.

"It must be from the body," said Libby, wishing Jackie would leave.

"How did it get over here?"

"Uh—I rolled the cart with the body from the side door to the oven."

"The body was still bleeding when the parents dropped it off?" said Jackie, bemused.

"Yeah."

"What if . . . ?" Jackie trailed off.

"What?"

"I devour mystery novels in my spare time. What if the parents killed their daughter and lied to you about it being a suicide so you wouldn't report the corpse to the cops?" Jackie furrowed her brow in thought. "It would be the perfect way to dispose of the corpus delicti and avoid the suspicion of the cops."

"You read too many mysteries," said Libby, eager to drop the subject.

"Think about it. Why would the parents want the body disposed of without anyone knowing about it?"

"Because it was a suicide like they told me. They don't want anyone to know their daughter died by her own hand. Suicide is a sin in the Catholic religion and is strictly prohibited."

"It sounds hinky to me," said Jackie, pacing around in a circle. "You don't want to be an accessory to a crime, do you? You could go to jail for that."

She knows you killed Carly. She's gonna tell the cops. Kill her.

"No," cried Libby.

"What?" said Jackie, startled.

"I don't think that's what happened," said Libby, unsettled.

"You can't mess around with this stuff. There are bad people out there. You gotta guard yourself against them."

"Believe me, I know."

"This has all the earmarks of an Agatha Christie novel. We need to be suspicious."

She needs to be killed before she rats you out to the cops. Get the carving knife.

"I'm not gonna do it," said Libby, hammering the air with her fist.

"Do what?" said Jackie.

"Don't mind me. I'll take care of this."

"I'm telling you the air in here is toxic. It's poisoning your physical and mental health."

"I'm fine."

"I don't think so. You look detached. You're talking to yourself. Your complexion is ghostly. You need vitamin D."

"I have a twenty-four-hour bug or something. Nothing serious."

"Listen to me. You need to tell the cops about that dead woman on your cart so they can't accuse you of being an accessory to murder."

"There was no murder. She killed herself."

Libby refused to kill Jackie, her only friend. But Libby didn't trust herself as long as the demon was harassing her. She had to get Jackie to leave.

"Just because her parents said so?" said Jackie. "That's not good enough for me. This whole thing is as suspicious as hell. Dropping off a dead body at a crematorium and not telling anyone about it? How can that *not* be suspicious?"

"I think you should go. I don't want to get you involved in this," said Libby, taking Jackie's arm and ushering her toward the front door.

"At least talk to a lawyer before you cremate that girl."

"I can't afford a lawyer. I'm barely making ends meet."

"This isn't right."

"What's wrong? Nobody's getting hurt."

"That dead girl might have been killed by her parents."

"And lightning might strike us. But it probably won't. You worry too much."

"The parents could be implicating you in their crime. You need to protect yourself from a charge of accessory to murder."

"How can there be a murder charge after the dead body is cremated? No corpus delicti. I'll show you to the door," said Libby, touching Jackie's arm and making tracks for the front door.

"I'm worried about you," said Jackie, resisting and holding her ground.

"*I'm* worried about *you*," said Libby, fearing Jackie might meet the same fate Carly had met with a carving knife embedded in her throat. "What if the cops come and see you here with the dead body?"

Jackie stopped resisting. "All right. It's your life. If you don't care, I don't care. Are we still on for *The Wicker Man* on Friday night?"

"The restored final cut?"

"That's right."

"The one approved by the director Robin Hardy?"

"Yep."

"I wouldn't miss it for the world."

"I still say you should report that dead woman to the cops," said Jackie, pausing outside the front door. "Disposing of a corpse without getting a death certificate can't be legal."

You have to kill her. Don't let her leave. She saw the dead white-trash stripper here.

"I'll think about it," said Libby, trying to ignore the voice pounding in her head, her temples throbbing.

"I'd tell them myself, but that would get you in trouble for not reporting it."

"I'll take care of it," said Libby, grimacing, trying to prevent her right hand from reaching for the kitchenette.

Get the carving knife. Cut her head off. She's a nosy busybody. She has to die. Cut her throat in half. Gouge her eyeballs out and stuff them down her throat. What business does she have telling you what to do?

"What are you doing?" said Jackie, peering through the doorway at Libby, who was contorting herself.

216

Kill her.

Fighting the demon Libby struggled to close the door with her left hand while her right pulled her in the opposite direction, causing her body to spasm.

"Are you all right?" said Jackie through the gap between the door and the jamb. "You don't look well. You look like you're having convulsions."

"I'm fine. I'll see you Friday night," said Libby, managing to close the door, gasping with the effort of trying to control her paroxysm.

"OK. Take care of yourself. Bye."

Libby leaned her back against the door and breathed deeply, relieved she had saved Jackie's life. But what about the next time Jackie came to visit? Would she be able to save Jackie from the demon again? Libby felt herself becoming weaker and weaker in her attempts to resist the demands of the demon.

The fetid, necrotic air wasn't helping matters any. It was like living in a sewer and a charnel house at the same time. She thought Jackie was right. The noxious air was making her ill.

She heard Jackie's car reverse out of the driveway and peel off.

She cracked the door, saw the driveway was empty, and, fearing she might pass out from the overpowering stench, opened the door to air out the crematorium.

She stepped outside in the sun. It felt better out here, the sunlight bathing her face, the clean air recruiting her lungs. She took a deep breath as a breeze swept past her.

She saw an LAPD Dodge Charger pull into her driveway, and her heart skipped a beat.

She shut the door behind her and approached the squad car warily, a heartbeat away from fainting.

The cops' timing couldn't have been worse. She needed all her wits to figure a way to prevent the two cops from setting foot inside the crematorium.

Chapter 61

"We just stopped by to give you some advice," said Rafa in the driver's seat, sticking his head out the open window as he killed the rumbling Hemi V8 engine.

"About what?" asked Libby, terrified they would want to enter the crematorium.

She hurried over to the squad car to keep Rafa from opening his door and getting out.

"That Brady guy you're seeing," answered Rafa.

"What about him?"

"I remember where I saw him. I hate to tell you this, but the guy's a murderer. He killed his own mother," said Rafa, watching Libby's face.

"Murderer?" said Libby in surprise.

"He didn't tell you that part, did he? Yeah, he killed his mother about eight or ten years ago."

"Why isn't he in jail?"

"He pleaded insanity. He did time in an insane asylum."

"Why did they release him?"

"They must think he's cured."

"He told me he's an occultist."

"That must be his new job. I'd be careful with him if I was you. We thought we should warn you. And I wanted to ask you a couple of questions," said Rafa, preparing to exit the squad car.

Libby didn't move out of the way of the door, blocking him from opening it all the way.

"What questions?" she said.

"Have you heard from Bill the repairman?"

"No."

"What about your father?"

Libby shook her head. "Nothing."

"We're convinced both of them met with foul play. If you hear anything about them, give us a call."

The radio squawked to life on the dash.

"How did you meet this Brady character?" said Rafa.

"I found his website on the Internet."

"Why were you looking for him?"

"I was looking for a medium. His website said he was a medium."

"Why were you looking for a medium?"

Libby had to think of a lie. She didn't want to tell him the truth or he might want to hang around and riddle her with questions.

Rafa tried to open his door and get out of his cruiser again. Libby didn't move out of his way, blocking the door.

"Uh—I'm trying to get in touch with my dead mother's spirit," said Libby. "I thought a medium like Brady could help me."

"Sorry to hear about your mother."

"The dispatcher's calling us," said Anna, listening to the police radio. "We gotta roll."

"Watch yourself with this guy. He's got a criminal record. He can't have much experience as a medium, since he's been locked in an asylum most of his life."

"OK," said Libby, entertaining second thoughts about having hired Brady.

"We also had a murder at a strip joint not far from here. Be on your guard. It could be the work of a homicidal maniac. Keep your door locked."

"Do you know who did it?" said Libby, her palms sweaty, hoping nobody other than Carly had seen her with Chuck.

"We can't divulge that information. This is an active investigation."

Rafa closed his door, changing his mind about leaving his car.

"How can I help?" said Libby.

"You can't. I suggest you stay away from Brady Carney. He's a scammer. I'd lay money on it. For sure he's a murderer, even if the jury did let him off."

Who was Brady Carney? She didn't know any Brady Carney.

Rafa turned on the Charger's siren and flashing light bar and backed out of the driveway, his tires screeching.

Libby angled toward the front door, not eager to return inside the crematorium with its stagnant air redolent of death.

She had no choice. She had to go inside to dispose of Carly's corpse even if the demon was waiting inside to possess her.

Pausing in front of the door she heard a car pull into her driveway. She wheeled around, expecting to see the cops.

It was Brady's red Jeep Gladiator pickup.

Chapter 62

Libby watched Brady park his Gladiator, leap out of the driver's seat, and dash toward her.

"We need to talk," he said.

"You got some explaining to do," said Libby, confronting him, arms akimbo.

"What are you talking about? I have urgent information about your possession."

"The cops were just here. They said your name is Brady Carney. They said you're a murderer. You killed your own mother."

Brady started. His jaw dropped. Thrown off stride, he said nothing.

"Well?" said Libby.

"It's complicated."

"I deserve an explanation."

"It wasn't me."

"Then who was it?"

"It was the demon that possessed me. It killed Mom. This is how I know what you're going through, fighting the demon trying to possess you."

If he was telling the truth about who killed his mother, maybe he *could* understand what she was going through. The demon had forced her to kill. Not just one person but many. But was Brady a scammer like the cops had told her?

"How do I know you're telling the truth?" she said.

"You'll have to take my word for it. I would never have killed my own mother on my own," he said, shaken.

"I would never have hired a medium who's a murderer."

"The demon did it. It used me to kill my mother. You have to understand. This is why your life is in so much danger. A demon is in the act of possessing you. If it succeeds, there's no telling what it will force you to do."

If only he knew the truth. The demon had already forced her to kill. Should she come clean about the murders she had committed? But could she trust him not to tell the cops?

"How do I know you won't kill me?" she said.

"I'm not possessed any more. It's over."

"The cops said you're supposed to be locked up in a lunatic asylum. How do I know you didn't escape?" said Libby, biting her cheek with anxiety.

"They released me. They said I was cured."

Libby threw up her hands in frustration. "I don't know what to believe."

"I'm telling you the truth. That's why I can help you. I know what you're experiencing."

Not all of it. She had withheld the murders from him.

"My life's such a mess," she said, more in anger than in self-pity. "I don't know who to trust."

"You can trust me. I can help you. I found out valuable information from another occultist. That's why I'm here. Let's go inside."

If she let him in, she would have to explain Carly's corpse that was lying out in the open in front of the cremation chamber. If he was telling the truth about his possession, he would be the only person who might understand that she hadn't killed any of her murder victims. It was the demon inside her that was forcing her to commit murders. If she told anyone else, they would think she was mad and accuse her of being a serial killer.

She felt like she had to confide in someone. She couldn't keep going on like this, committing murder after murder and keeping it all to herself. When would it end? She was going to explode with grief and self-hatred.

She agonized over what to do.

If she told him and he didn't believe her, she was opening herself up to multiple murder charges. On the other hand, there were no corpses—except one. Carly's. There was no proof anybody could use to convict her after she cremated Carly. Brady could have her thrown in jail with Carly's murdered corpse as proof Libby had killed her.

Could she trust Brady with her life? She tried to make up her mind, doubts gnawing at her, kneecapping her ability to make a decision.

In the end she had to trust someone. She knew for a certainty that she couldn't fight the demon on her own hook. She needed

222

help. All she had to do was trust a guy who had murdered his mother. What about her? She had murdered her own father. Who was she to cast the first stone?

Chapter 63

"Let's go inside," Libby said quietly. "There's something I have to tell you."

"With what I learned from the occultist Quentin I'm convinced I can exorcise you now," said Brady.

She entered the crematorium, Brady in tow.

The stench of death was overpowering. Even she had a hard time enduring it, and she was used to it.

Kill him. He's not your friend. Don't make the mistake of trusting him. I'm the only one you can trust. Kill him. Kill the murderer. He's a murderer and a rapist and a scammer. Kill him. He's the last person in the world you can trust. Kill him, and we can be together forever. Let me into your heart.

Her friend, the voice.

"I sense the demon's presence," said Brady, sniffing the necrotic air in disgust. His gaze fell on Carly's blood-streaked body sprawled on the cart in front of the oven. "No." He faced Libby, his complexion ashen. "Am I too late?"

"Too late for the cremation? No."

Brady stole toward the cart as if he might wake the corpse if he made too much noise.

"This woman was recently killed," he said, taking in her shredded, blood-smeared throat.

Libby debated about telling him the lie she had told Jackie about who killed Carly.

Kill him. He knows you did it. He'll tell the cops.

She contorted her face, trying to shake the voice out of her head.

"What's wrong?" said Brady. "Is it the entity? I can help you."

He'll help put you in jail. He has seen the girl you killed. He'll snitch to the cops. Cut the liar's throat and cremate him. He raped you. Kill him.

"Who is this woman?" said Brady, indicating Carly.

Don't tell him anything. He'll betray you.

Libby willed herself to fight the demon. This might be her last chance to resist. Its strength was becoming more and more formidable. She could feel her right hand moving toward the kitchenette.

"The demon's here, isn't it?" said Brady. "I believe I know its identity. I can exorcise it now. But I need your help. We need to hold a séance."

Libby clutched her brow in torment.

"I killed Carly," she blurted. *"But it wasn't me.* It was the demon possessing me. I can't resist it."

Brady stared at her.

Libby couldn't read his expression. Was he flabbergasted at her committing murder? Or was he empathizing with her because he too had been possessed and had committed murder and knew what she was going through?

"This is Carly?" he said.

"Yes."

"Why did the demon want her dead?"

"She—she saw me do something last night," she said, not wanting to tell him about what she had done to Chuck.

Brady looked puzzled.

"I don't know why it wants me to kill," said Libby.

She couldn't keep slaughtering people and cremating them to hide the evidence from the cops. Sooner or later the cops would bust her. She was sure they already suspected she had something to do with her father's disappearance as well as with Bill's. It explained why the cops kept coming back to her and pumping her for details about the two missing persons.

But she hadn't killed anyone. It was the demon that possessed her. The demon had forced her to kill. She knew the cops would laugh in her face if she told them the truth.

"The stench in here is becoming more powerful just like the demon," said Brady, gagging on the miasmic odor.

Kill him. He knows you're the murderer. He'll testify against you. You'll spend the rest of your life behind bars. Get the carving knife. Cut the motherfucker up and feed him to your cat. Then we can become one. You'll never be lonely again.

"We need to do the séance," said Brady. "It's your only chance to free yourself. Let's go to the kitchenette and sit down—"

"No," cut in Libby, fearing she might grab the carving knife and kill Brady if they entered the kitchenette.

"We need to sit down and hold hands. It's the only way we can perform the séance."

"Don't we have to smudge the place first?"

"There's no time. I need to summon the demon and exorcise it. I know the demon's identity."

It's a scam. Don't listen to his lies. He wants your money. He doesn't give a damn about you. Kill him. He's a professional scammer. Don't believe a word he says. If you have another séance, he'll rape you again. Kill him now before it's too late. Kill the rapist murderer.

"What's wrong?" said Brady, scrutinizing the conflicted expressions on her face. "Do you hear the demon? Is it talking to you?"

Don't tell him anything. He's a fraud. He'll use your words against you and have you committed to an insane asylum for hearing voices. Kill him. It's the only answer. Then we can be together forever as one.

"Don't listen to it," said Brady. "Demons are masters of deception. They can't possess you completely unless you agree to let them in. Whatever you do don't let the demon in. Once you invite it in, you are doomed forever, and nobody can save you."

Libby believed what Brady said. She continued to wrestle with the demon that was fighting for control of her. Torn between the demands of the demon and of Brady, she tried to make up her mind. She still had some degree of control over her mind despite the demon's increasing power over her.

Rapping on the front door jerked her out of her thoughts.

She gazed at the door, wide-eyed.

Brady glanced at Carly's corpse. "Don't let them in. Pretend you're not here."

Libby didn't answer the door.

"This is the LAPD," said Rafa outside, continuing to knock on the door.

"Crap," said Libby.

"My car's outside," said Brady. "They must know we're in here."

"I can't open the door. They'll see Carly."

"I'll move her somewhere else," said Brady, looking frantically around the crematorium. "How about the oven?"

"It's occupied."

Rafa knocked louder on the door. "We know you're in there."

"I'll roll it into the bedroom," said Brady.

Libby nodded. She didn't know where else to hide the corpse. "Put a sheet over it," she said.

Nodding, Brady rolled Carly into the bedroom as Libby approached the front door.

Brady flung open a louvered closet door inside the bedroom and withdrew a heap of dirty clothes from the half-full hamper that stood on the floor. He tossed the clothes onto the corpse to disguise its shape, found a dirty sheet in the hamper, and draped it over the dirty clothes and the corpse.

Libby waited for him to finish before she answered the door.

Chapter 64

Libby opened the front door.

Rafa and Anna were standing impatiently on the doorstep, their prowl car parked behind Brady's Jeep in the driveway.

"I was in the middle of a job," said Libby.

"We have questions to ask you," said Rafa.

"Is this important?"

"Very."

"Can't you come back another time?"

"No," said Rafa, his voice firm.

"All right," said Libby, seeing no way out of her dilemma. "Come in."

"Is that your Jeep in the driveway?" said Rafa, glancing over his shoulder at the Gladiator.

"No."

As soon as Rafa entered the crematorium he clapped eyes on Brady.

"Look who's here," said Rafa.

"We've been wanting to talk to you, Mr. Carney," said Anna, on Rafa's heels.

"What about?" said Brady.

"Aren't you supposed to be recuperating in an insane asylum after pleading insanity to your mother's murder?"

"They released me."

"Hmm," said Rafa, unimpressed. "That's not why we're here." He turned to Libby. "Where were you last night, Ms. Genet?"

"The smell is revolting in here," said Anna. "It smells even worse than the last time we were here."

"The cremation oven's not working properly."

"Toxic gas could be leaking from that thing," said Rafa.

"It doesn't smell like gas," said Anna. "It smells like something died in here."

"Well?" said Rafa, searching Libby's face.

"Well what? I know it smells in here. This is a crematorium. I'm incinerating a body. What do you expect?"

"That wasn't my question."

"What question?" said Libby, rattled. "You keep bombarding me with questions. I can't keep them straight."

"Answer the question," said Rafa icily. "Where were you last night?"

"I was working."

"At night?"

"I work day and night. I don't have a life."

"Did you know there was a murder committed at the Stacked Deck Strip Club a few miles from here last night?"

"No," said Libby, hoping she was concealing her nervousness, her pulse accelerating.

"Have you been there before?"

"I don't go to strip joints," she said with disdain.

"Were you at the strip club last night?"

"I told you I don't go to strip joints."

"Now that's strange," said Rafa, boring his gaze into Libby's eyes. "One of the strippers said she heard another stripper say she found your AAA card in the parking lot."

Libby's heart stopped beating. Taken aback, she hung her mouth open.

Carly must have told another stripper about the card. On the verge of passing out, Libby steadied herself.

"Are you all right, Ms. Genet?" said Rafa, looking pleased at her agitation.

"That's hearsay," said Brady.

"What are you? Her lawyer?" demanded Rafa, rounding on Brady.

"I know a little about the law."

"Because you were tried for murdering your mother, huh? Well, that doesn't make you a lawyer. There's a little thing called 'passing the bar.'" Rafa turned back to Libby. "Ms. Genet, do you understand the gravity of your situation?"

Libby racked her brains, trying to come up with an answer that wouldn't implicate her.

"Not really," she mumbled.

Rafa fetched a weary sigh. "Let us proceed. Do you know a man called Chuck Mancini?"

"Never heard of him," said Libby, knowing where this was going, her nerves taut.

"Mancini was the man murdered in the Stacked Deck parking lot last night. Eyewitnesses saw a blonde woman running away from his pickup around the time of the murder. Did you see any of this?"

"I told you I wasn't there."

"Then how did your AAA card get there?" said Rafa, gloating, feeling triumphant he had caught her in a trap.

Libby reached into her purse and fished out her wallet, which she opened. She flicked through it and withdrew her AAA card, remembering she had recovered it from the floor where Carly had dropped it when she had dropped dead from a slit throat.

Glancing at the card, she was glad there wasn't any blood on it.

"My AAA card is right here," she said.

Rafa couldn't believe his eyes.

"Is it this year's card?" he said, suspicious.

"Yep. Look at it and see," she said, holding it in front of his face.

He read the card and saw her name and the date of issue.

Libby replaced the card in her wallet and deposited the wallet in her clutch.

"Satisfied, Detective?" said Brady.

"I'm not talking to you, Perry Mason."

"I need to get back to work," said Libby.

"I'm not finished with you," said Rafa. "Do you know Carly Van Noy?"

"No."

"I have questions for her. She's one of the strippers who were working at the Stacked Deck on the night of the murder."

"I don't know any strippers. Are you implying something about me?" said Libby, taking umbrage.

Rafa ignored her question. "She's gone missing, like a lot of folks around here. She's in her twenties with blonde hair and green eyes. The other girls say she's a regular dancer at the joint. Have you seen her?"

Brady showed signs of recognition as Rafa described Carly.

"No," said Libby, picking up on Brady's visage.

"What about you, Perry?" said Rafa.

"I never heard of her," said Brady.

"You looked like maybe you knew her when I described her."

"No—uh—your description reminded me of someone in the asylum."

Rafa snorted. "Carly Van Noy worked at the Stacked Deck Strip Club. Am I getting through to you?" he said, jutting his jaw in Brady's face. "She's gone missing like half the damn town. She's a possible witness to a homicide. Now where is she?"

"How do I know?"

"Let me remind you, Perry. Interfering with a police investigation is against the law."

"Who's interfering?"

"We're trying to find out what's going on," said Anna in an even voice, trying to cool off Rafa, who was getting hot under the collar.

Rafa confronted Libby. "As we understand it Carly Van Noy is the one who found your AAA card at the strip joint last night. Then she ups and disappears. It's suspicious as hell."

"I hope nothing happened to her. I don't know whose AAA card she found, but it wasn't mine," said Libby, patting her clutch which held her Auto Club card.

Put out, Rafa whipped out a notepad from his trouser pocket.

Chapter 65

"This is a list of all of the people who have gone missing in this area," said Rafa, holding forth like a professor. He read the names on his notepad. "Bill Lally the repairman, Dan Genet, Carly Van Noy, and I'm gonna include Chuck Mancini even though he's dead and not missing, because I have the strong feeling all of these unfortunates have met with foul play. Am I getting through to you two?" he said, cutting his eyes back and forth between Libby and Brady.

Libby wished the cop would leave. He was getting under her skin. Plus she had a dead body in her bedroom, none other than Carly Van Noy, who she had murdered. She knew for a fact that the two cops would never believe her if she told them the demon possessing her had cut Carly's jugular. The cops would bust her on the spot.

Kill all of them.

"Oh sure," said Libby, exasperated at having to listen to the bloodthirsty voice once again.

She should have kept her mouth shut, but she couldn't help it. The words were already out. She cringed, wishing she could take them back.

"What?" said Rafa, glowering at her.

"Nothing."

"You sounded like you were being sarcastic. Like you don't believe me about our laundry list of missing persons."

"I—I believe they're all missing like you say. What I don't understand is why you think they were all killed. You have no evidence—"

"I didn't say they were killed. I said I believed they had met with foul play. Why do you say they were killed? Do you know something I don't?"

Libby shook her head. "I haven't seen any of these people. I don't know anything about their whereabouts."

"Then why were you being sarcastic?"

"The police are always jumping to conclusions that people have been killed when there could be an innocent explanation for their disappearances."

"And you're smarter than us?" said Rafa, scowling. "Is that it?"

"I don't know where they are," said Libby, fidgeting.

"Then why are you so nervous?"

"I'm *not* nervous. Why do you keep thinking I have something to do with these missing people?"

"Because they're all connected to you in some way."

"I don't know any Carly whatever and Chuck whatever. How can they be connected to me?"

"Then why did the strippers say your AAA card was found at the strip club?"

"They were mistaken. I showed you my card. I didn't lose it."

"Why would they say it was your card in the parking lot? It makes no sense."

"I'm not a mind reader. How do I know?"

"She's trying to help us," said Anna with sincerity, the good cop. "Aren't you, dear?"

"I'm trying," said Libby.

"I think maybe you're laughing at us on the inside," said Rafa. "That's why you're so edgy. I'm right, aren't I?"

"No."

"You're having trouble keeping from bursting out laughing at us because you think we're stupid cops and can't figure out you killed the people who are missing. Isn't that right?"

"No."

"If you're accusing her of murder, she has the right to a lawyer," said Brady.

"Are you still here, Perry? I'm not accusing anyone of anything. I'm asking questions. That's my job."

Libby's heartbeat picked up speed when she caught sight of Anna begin to wander around the crematorium, idly taking it in, dissembling her interest.

How could she keep Anna from going to the bedroom? Her body taut with nervous tension, Libby felt her palms ooze sweat.

Anna was indeed moseying toward the bedroom as she made her way around the crematorium. When Anna stopped in front of the bedroom doorway, Libby thought she would have a heart attack.

"It smells horrible in here," said Anna. "Aren't you worried about your health?"

"It's part of the job," said Libby. "I deal with a lot of corpses in my line of work. Death is always in the air."

Anna peered inside the bedroom, picking up on the sheet-covered cart. "How do you do your laundry? Didn't you tell us you live here?"

"I do live here."

"How do you do your laundry? I don't see a washing machine or drier anywhere," said Anna, scoping out the crematorium.

"I go to the laundromat."

"How inconvenient. No wonder your laundry piles up. You must not get down there very often."

"I don't have a lot of free time," said Libby, wishing Anna would step away from the bedroom, her heartbeat racing amok the longer Anna remained in the doorway.

As long as Anna didn't inspect the laundry on the cart, Libby would be OK. If, on the other hand, Anna lifted the sheet that covered Carly . . . it would be all over. The cops would bust Libby on the spot.

Do you want to go to jail? Kill the cops before they find the stiff.

The voice. Always the voice.

"No," said Libby in a tight voice.

"No what?" said Anna, turning to face Libby.

"I—I—don't have a lot of free time, I mean."

"Honestly, I don't know how you can stand living here. How can you sleep at night with the awful smell?"

"It's not always in here."

"And no windows. Don't you ever want to look outside?"

"I can open the door for that."

Anna shook her head in disbelief.

Over Anna's shoulder Libby saw the sheet starting to slip off Carly's corpse. Could Carly still be alive? How could it be possible? Could she be moving under the sheet? Was she going to sit up?

Libby struggled to breathe. She forced herself not to pass out.

You're going away for a long time when they see Carly. Kill the cops. It's the only way you stay out of prison.

Libby was thankful Anna was looking away from the bedroom and couldn't see the sheet slipping off Carly. Otherwise, Libby would be lying in a dead faint on the floor. She had to get the cops to leave. She didn't want to have to kill them. They would kill her if she tried. They had guns. All she had was a carving knife. At the thought she felt her right hand reaching toward the kitchenette.

Somehow she managed to breathe.

"Will that be all?" she struggled to say through her dry throat.

"For now," said Rafa, disappointed at his failure to trip up Libby.

Anna met him in the middle of the crematorium.

"Unless you want to confess," he told Libby.

"Confess to what?"

"The murder of Chuck Mancini, for one thing."

"I want a lawyer."

"Lawyering up, huh? It looks like I touched a nerve."

"If you call harassment 'touching a nerve.'"

Libby figured the cops were abusing their authority. They had no evidence against her. No corpus delicti for any of the missing persons they were searching for except for Chuck's corpse.

Libby fought to breathe.

Rafa and Anna retreated to the front door. Unsatisfied, Rafa stood at the door and gazed at her.

"Did you forget something?" said Libby, somehow contriving to speak as she continued to feel like she was suffocating.

Rafa glowered at her in response.

"We'll be back," he said in a threatening tone. "We're not done with you. You may think you got away with it—"

"Got away with what?"

"And you know what's gonna happen to you when we come back with a warrant."

They let themselves out, shutting the door behind them.

Chapter 66

Libby heard Brady talking to her as if from far away. What was he saying?

"You killed Carly?" said Brady.

"The demon made me do it," she said. "I thought you of all people could understand what I'm talking about. It's making me act out of character. It made me strip at the strip joint for Chrissake. I would never dream of doing something like that. I've never even been in a strip joint."

"I understand."

"The demon also wanted me to kill the cops."

"What?"

"The voice in my head told me to kill the cops. It wants me to kill you too."

"We need to exorcise you before you'll be unable to resist its commands. Let's go to the kitchen and hold a séance."

Libby felt dead on her feet from fighting the demon and defending herself from the cops' accusations. And then there was Carly's corpse preying on her mind. Like she didn't have enough to worry about.

Kill the scammer.

And there was the voice forever harassing her.

Brady accompanied Libby to the kitchenette.

Libby clapped eyes on the carving knife inserted in the knife block on the Formica countertop.

Cut the scammer's throat. You can't believe anything the rapist murderer says. Believe in me. I'm the only one you can trust. I'm the only one not giving you a hard time. Save yourself. Invite me in and we'll be one. Why do you keep resisting me when I'm the best thing that ever happened to you?

"Get out of my head," screamed Libby, racked with pangs of distress.

"The demon's here," said Brady. "His presence is strong."

Libby felt her right hand pulling her toward the knife block.

"Sit at the table with me and hold hands," said Brady, killing the overhead fluorescent light.

"Kill," she muttered, baring her teeth.

"I can help you. Now before it's too late. Sit down. How many people have you killed? Carly wasn't your first time, was she?"

"No," she said, continuing to stand, her voice soft.

"I could tell. Its control over you is all but complete. This is the last chance we have of exorcising it. If we fail this time . . ."

"It's telling me to kill you," she said in a barely audible voice.

"Of course, it is. It feels threatened by me. I couldn't exorcise it last time because I misidentified the demon. It's not the serial killer Wayne Bobinsky."

"Who is it?" she croaked through her tense throat.

Kill him before he rapes and kills you.

The voice more urgent now.

"It's the spirit of a living person, not a dead person," said Brady. "That's what had me fooled. I didn't know a living person could send his spirit to possess someone until Quentin told me."

Don't listen to his lies. Kill the phony. Kill the fraudster. Kill the rapist murderer.

Brady sat down at the table. "Sit with me and hold hands."

Libby sat across from him.

He reached his arms across the tabletop toward her.

Libby wavered, fighting the compulsion to reach for the nearby carving knife.

"Hold my hands," exhorted Brady. "We can do this together."

Don't do it. Kill him. Kill the scammer. Kill the rapist murderer. He's your enemy.

Drawing on the last reserve of her strength, Libby reached across the table for Brady's hands.

Brady found her hands with his and clasped them. Shutting his eyes he tilted his head up.

"Leave this woman, Ed Grainger," he intoned. "This is not your body. You don't belong here."

"Grainger," muttered Libby in surprise. "How could . . . ?"

The cabinet doors flung open. Dishes commenced flying through the air, slamming the walls, and smashing into shards.

"Leave this kitchen, Grainger," commanded Brady.

"Who dares speak my name?" said the demon in an ungodly voice.

Glasses hurtled out of the open cabinets through the air and shattered against the walls.

"Grainger's still alive," said Libby, terrified. "How can his spirit haunt me?"

"He practices the dark arts."

Water burst out of the faucet, flooding the aluminum sink.

"No," said the demon. "You're not a believer. You have no power over me."

"I believe in you, demon," said Brady. "You are Ed Grainger. Leave this kitchen. Return to your body where you belong."

The refrigerator door flung open. A grapefruit, carrots, and apples flew through the air, bombarding Libby and Brady. Both of them ducked and cringed at the onslaught. The freezer compartment door swung open. Ice cubes hurled through the air, pelting Libby and Brady.

"Libby rejects you, demon," said Brady, keeping a firm grip on Libby's hands, holding his head down as ice cubes crashed into his skull. "You have no place here. Leave this kitchen, Ed Grainger."

The kitchenette became silent save for the water gushing out of the faucet.

Chapter 67

Continuing to hold hands, Libby and Brady held their heads up.

"Is it gone?" said Libby with a quavering voice, fearing she might have to duck any second to dodge a flying object, her eyes wide.

Brady bolted from his chair and slammed the kitchen door shut.

"I believe it left the kitchen," he said. "But I don't want it to leave the building."

"What are you talking about?"

"I have a plan," said Brady, flicking on the overhead light.

"What do you mean? We have to destroy the demon."

"We can't destroy this particular demon because it's from a living person. If it was a dead person's spirit, we could send it back to the grave. But if we send this demon back to Grainger, he'll send it back to possess you."

"Then what can we do? Are you saying it's hopeless to be rid of it forever?" said Libby, hangdog.

"We need to trick the demon."

"I don't understand."

"We need to lure it for my plan to work."

"Lure it where?"

"To some place where it can't escape."

"Then what?"

"You'll see. But first we have to trap it." Brady thought about it. "Do you have an airtight container?"

"I dunno. Like what? What's airtight? Like a mason jar or something?"

"Too small. It needs to be the size of a human body."

"I don't have any coffins hanging around."

Watching his step, careful not to tread on the glass shards and ice cubes scattered on the linoleum floor, Brady picked his way to the sink and shut off the water gushing out of the faucet.

Libby gazed at all the broken glass covering the floor and shook her head at the mess.

"What about the cremation oven?" said Brady.

"It's being used."

"When will it be done?"

"Very soon."

"We shouldn't delay. We need to trap the demon ASAP."

"Trap it forever, you mean?"

"We can't. Ed Grainger will be able to find it. He'll track it down and release it. That's what I'm counting on. He can't live without his spirit. If he loses connection with it he'll die."

"Then how could he exist if his spirit possessed me?"

"He would've made you his zombie, ordered you to his house, and taken back his disembodied spirit. By then you would be nothing but the empty husk of a human, one of the living dead. He could do whatever he wanted with you."

"You're scaring me," said Libby, dreading the prospect painted by Brady.

"We need to trap the demon."

Libby tried to come up with an idea. She felt like pacing, but she didn't want to step on the glass fragments littering the floor.

"I can't hear the demon's voice in my head," she said.

"I exorcised it. But it's only temporary. The demon will resume possessing you when we leave the kitchen. It knows we can't stay here forever."

"What's keeping it out?"

"My exorcism of it. It's not gonna last. We need to act quickly."

Libby turned over the problem in her mind. "What about the cremulator?"

"What does that do?" said Brady, puzzled.

"It's where I place the bone fragments that don't disintegrate into ash in the cremation chamber. The cremulator grinds the bone into ash, using rotating blades that pulverize it like a blender."

"Is it airtight?"

"I believe so. I think it's lined with lead."

"Perfect. We'll use it. The problem is, how do we lure the demon into the trap? That's where you come in."

"Me?"

"We're gonna have to use you as bait," said Brady, not sure how she would take the suggestion.

"Like how?" said Libby, worried.

"I'm not gonna sugarcoat it. You'll be exposing yourself to danger."

"Isn't there some other way?"

"I wish. We don't have time to think of another plan. I can't keep the demon away from you much longer. The exorcism didn't destroy the demon. I cast the demon out of you for the time being, but I think it's playing with me, making me think I can control it when I can't. It's out there, lurking, waiting for you," said Brady, pointing to the closed kitchenette door.

"What do you want me to do?"

Brady stepped toward her and held her attention with his gaze. "You need to crawl into the cremulator. The demon will follow you. When you crawl out, I'll shut the cremulator door and trap the demon."

"What's to prevent it from coming out of the cremulator with me?"

Brady reached into his trouser pocket and withdrew sage leaves.

"I'll put sage in front of the cremulator door when you crawl out," he said. "The sage will prevent the demon from following you."

"Are you sure this is gonna work?" said Libby, not eager to serve as bait for the demon.

"No."

Libby gaped. She didn't like his answer.

"What if the demon possesses me inside the cremulator?" she said.

"The sage I put in front of the cremulator door should prevent the entity from leaving with you."

"Do you plan on turning on the cremulator to destroy the demon?"

"The whirling blades won't work on a spirit. It's incorporeal."

"Then I don't get it. We leave it locked in the cremulator forever?"

Brady shook his head no. "Ed Grainger can track it and free it. We have to deal with him in order to be rid of the demon forever."

"I hope you know what you're doing."

"I can't be sure of any of this. I've never done it before."

"Wonderful," said Libby, downbeat.

"It's the only chance we've got of exorcising you permanently. I know it's dangerous for you to act as bait, but what other choice do you have? You don't want to be possessed, do you?"

Libby felt ill at the thought. The idea of having the voice back in her head ordering her to commit serial murders filled her with dread. How would she ever live down the guilt from having killed so many people? Even if it was really the demon's fault for commanding her to kill, it was *her* hand that had committed the murders. There was no escaping that dreadful fact. Was she supposed to go on living like nothing had happened? Like she wasn't a serial killer?

She studied the palm of her killing hand. She couldn't face committing another murder.

She weighed her options. What options?

There had to be a better way. But there wasn't. And she knew it.

"OK," she said with a restrained voice. "I'll be your sitting duck."

Chapter 68

"How do we do this?" said Libby.

Brady placed the sage leaves back in his trouser pocket.

"We need to go out there," he said. "After you crawl into the cremulator, I'll close it behind you when you tell me you can hear the demon inside your head."

"I'm gonna be locked in there with that thing inside my head?"

"I know it sounds terrible. But we have to trap the demon before Ed Grainger comes here to retrieve it."

"How will he know?"

"He'll lose contact with the demon if it becomes sealed in an airtight container like the cremulator."

"Then what?" said Libby, trying to understand the flow of events.

"He'll have to come here to retrieve it. He can't lose contact with it for any length of time. It's his spirit possessing you. He needs to be in constant contact with it."

"Or what?"

"He'll die. He can't live being out of contact with his spirit for a long period of time."

"Haven't you forgotten something?"

"What?" said Brady, musing.

"The cremulator is airtight. I'm gonna suffocate if you lock me inside it."

Brady knitted his brow. "I'm hoping Grainger will be here before that happens."

"That's it? That's all you can tell me to cheer me up?"

"If he's out of contact with his spirit for any length of time, he'll die. He's gonna get here, and he's gonna get here fast."

"How will he know the demon's in the cremulator?"

"If he doesn't know, I'll tell him as soon as he steps through that door," said Brady, pointing at the front door.

"Then what?"

"I'll open the cremulator. That's when you crawl out."

Libby heard the cremation chamber wheeze to a halt as it finished its current job.

"The oven's done," she said.

"Would you rather crawl inside there instead of the cremulator?"

Libby shook her head no. "It's too hot. It takes a while for the oven to cool off."

"All right."

At the computer Libby opened the oven door to inspect the brick interior, whose floor was covered with ash and bone fragments.

"It needs to cool off," she explained.

She opened the rear door of the oven and retrieved a wire broom from a nearby closet. She shoved the broom through the front door of the oven and pushed the ash and bone fragments out the rear onto an eight-foot square screen, which lay under a large magnet that would remove any steel medical devices that remained intact.

"You can do that later," said Brady. "You need to get into the cremulator now."

At the computer, the broom in one hand, Libby clicked on the retort rear door logo to close the rear door.

Kill him. It's a trick. He's gonna smother you in the cremulator.

Libby flinched, dropping the broom, her eyes bugging out.

"What's wrong? Is it back in your head?" said Brady.

She stared at him, her eyes agape.

It's a trick. The trick's on you. Kill him before he can smother you. He raped you. He knows you can testify against him. You're the only one who can put him in jail. He has to kill you. He'll smother you in the cremulator.

Brady led her to the door of the cremulator. "Get inside."

He's the enemy. He wants to keep us apart. Get the carving knife and kill him. Kill the rapist murderer.

"What's the matter?" said Brady. "Is it talking to you?"

"Yes."

"Don't listen to it. It's a scammer. It's trying to scam you."

"I can't get it to shut up."

He's the enemy. Kill him before it's too late.

"Hurry into the cremulator," said Brady. "I can feel the demon's power increasing."

Libby fought the demon. She couldn't let down her guard. She told herself to continue resisting. Her heartbeat ramping up, she lay on her back on the conveyor belt in front of the cremulator.

"Ready?" said Brady.

"I guess."

Brady turned on the machine, activating the conveyor belt, which conveyed Libby slowly into the cremulator.

It reminded her of the time she had had an MRI for a back injury, she decided as the cremulator swallowed her body.

She felt snug inside the coffinlike brick- and lead-lined chamber. She could see the plethora of razor-sharp steel blades sprouting out of the cremulator ceiling in concentric circles and gleaming above her in the dim-lit chamber. They would rotate, descend, and chop her to bits at the flick of a switch on the computer. She tried not to think of it as her body entered the claustrophobic compartment of death.

Slide out of here. It's a trick. He's gonna chop you into mincemeat. Slice and dice you. Get out before it's too late.

Could the demon be telling her the truth? Was Brady going to kill her? No. It was the demon that was lying, not Brady. She couldn't let the demon change her mind. She had to lie still as Brady shut the cremulator door behind her. And then she would suffocate. No, she couldn't think like that. Brady was trying to help her. But he had killed his own mother and tried to keep it from her. Why should she trust him?

I'm your friend, your only friend. The only friend you'll ever have in life. Listen to me. He's gonna kill you in this death machine. Get out now before it's too late and kill him. He's gonna take your life and steal all your money. That's what scammers do.

Libby felt her legs sticking out of the cremulator. She still had a ways to go before Brady could close the door behind her. She had to keep going.

Kill him. Kill him. Kill him. He's a rapist and a scammer. Kill him.

Or should she call the whole thing off? She feared she would suffocate in this torture box. She couldn't believe the demon. It had forced her to commit murder many times. She had to trust Brady. He was the only chance she had of getting exorcised.

She felt the conveyor belt grind to a halt. Lying on her back she looked past her feet and saw the cremulator door still open.

"Is it in there with you?" asked Brady, standing outside the cremulator door.

She could see beyond her feet his eyes watching her.

Don't tell him anything. He's gonna kill you. Get out of here and kill him.

"Yes," she answered.

"Are you ready?" said Brady.

She stared up at the myriad high tensile steel knives that pointed down at her prepared to mince her body.

She gasped.

You're helping the scammer rapist kill you. What kind of idiot are you? He's murdered before, and he'll murder again. He murdered his own mother. You're his next victim. Tell him to release you. Then kill him.

Knotting her face she clenched her right fist, trying to resist the demon.

"Are you ready?" repeated Brady.

"How long will it take Grainger to get here?" she said.

"He has to get here quick or he'll die. Should we go ahead?"

"OK," she said with a dry throat.

All she had to do was trust a guy who had murdered his own mother.

Supine, peering past her feet, she watched the cremulator door close.

Silence.

This was either her coffin or her salvation.

Demand to be let out. I'm the only friend you'll ever have in life. You're letting the scammer rapist kill you. Let me inside you, and we'll tell him to open the machine and save your life.

Libby continued to resist the demon's words.

But she didn't know how much longer she could continue to defy him. She was already beginning to feel short of breath, and she had been cooped up in the brick coffin for only a few minutes. Maybe she had claustrophobia. She told herself to relax. She had to keep believing in Brady.

You idiot. This is a trap. Tell the scammer rapist to let you out. You're gonna die in here. Get out and kill him. He's murdered before, and he'll murder again. This time you'll be his victim.

Liar. The demon had to be lying. Everything it said was a lie. She wished she could get the voice out of her head.

Chapter 69

In his Bel Air mansion, flying on magic mushrooms, clad in Tom Ford jeans and a maroon Gucci T, Ed Grainger jackknifed up in bed, his surgically chiseled face a mask of terror. Disoriented, he clutched his full head of black hair in disbelief, cutting his ice blue eyes back and forth across his bedroom.

He had lost contact with his spirit.

Impossible.

And yet he could not summon it. He could not use it to communicate with Libby. It was on its own. He could not control it. He had no idea where it was.

He panicked.

It must be near Libby. It couldn't exist on its own without contact from him. If it was dead, he would be dead. But he wasn't dead. He was sitting here in his bed in his mansion bedroom. Which meant his spirit wasn't dead. It was merely cut off from him somehow.

However, he couldn't go on living without contact with his spirit for any length of time. He had to reunite with it or they would both cease to exist.

He bolted out of bed, pelted down the stairs, and out of his house onto the driveway in the jasmine- and eucalyptus-scented air. He dug out his car keys from his trouser pocket, opened his Ferrari Spider with the key fob, clambered into the driver's seat, and fired the ignition. High on psilocybin, he had trouble concentrating. But he could do it. He could drive when high. He had done it many times. In fact, he thought he drove better when high.

The Ferrari's tires screeching, he backed out of his driveway into the street and tore down the pavement.

At the first traffic light, he noticed people staring at him. Of course, they were. He was driving a Ferrari, the most beautiful and expensive car ever created. They knew the make of the car because they could see the yellow Ferrari logo of a prancing horse on the side of the car. The trained ear could recognize the throbbing rumble of the naturally aspirated 562 hp V8 engine. Everywhere he drove, his car drew stares. He was used to it.

He was a billionaire, a master of the universe. He could do whatever he wanted with his life. The world was his playground. He wasn't about to lose everything because of a stupid arrogant woman who he hated for trying to get him thrown in jail for murdering her mother and sister who were plotting to kill him.

Where was his spirit? He felt his strength ebbing from his body as he drove. He didn't know how long he could live without reconnecting with his spirit. Not long. His shaman had told him he must never lose contact with his spirit. He was running on fumes. Any second could be his last on earth.

He gunned the gas. The Ferrari shot down the street. Looking around, he eased his foot off the accelerator. He had to be wary of cops. It wasn't that he couldn't afford a speeding ticket. He had gotten scores of them. They were trifles. It wasn't the money. It was the time wasted. If he got pulled over, he might not reach his spirit in time to free it from captivity and save his life.

He cruised down palm-lined Rodeo Boulevard in the heart of Beverly Hills, at home among the luxury boutiques that jammed the sidewalks.

He swung west onto Wilshire Boulevard. He could go faster here when it got wider, which it would do after he left Beverly Hills.

He stopped at another traffic light.

Pedestrians crossing the street in the crosswalk in front of him ogled him.

A twentysomething blonde in a tangerine miniskirt flicked her hair at him. She took a deep breath to thrust out her augmented, haltered breasts.

Feast your eyes, idiots, he thought. *You can only dream of owning one of these cars. You need to be exceptional to afford this baby. A superior specimen of the human race. He who dares wins. I dared to make a billion dollars investing in my father's hedge fund, and I won. If you never dare, you can't win. No balls, no way. Get out of my way, you craven, slobbering yokels.*

He caught a middle-aged woman with henna hair sneering at him with her chapped lips as she shambled in front of his Ferrari, her black eyes engulfed in pools of darkness.

Envy. She was jealous of his power. *Scrotum-faced skank. A loser in life's lottery and bitterly resentful of it, wasting her life wallowing in her hatred of winners.*

"Bottom feeder. You are where you belong," he muttered, his face waxing pallid as his energy bled from him.

He had to reach his out-of-touch spirit. What could have happened to it? He drummed his fingers on the steering wheel, waiting for the slowest light in the city.

At last the light turned green.

The Ferrari Spider roared into action. Grainger shot through the intersection, leaving the other cars in his dust as they accelerated in slow motion compared to him. Elated, he laughed with joy.

"Bye-bye, riffraff," he said, glancing in the rearview mirror, enjoying the Ferrari mid-rear engine's throaty rumble that cocooned him. "You can only dream about being me. Do you have any idea how much money I have? You can't even conceive of it."

He clutched his head, suffering shooting pain in his temple. Where was his spirit? He might black out any minute. He had to reconnect with his spirit.

"You're gonna die in agony for doing this to me, Libby, you bitch from hell. You don't know what hate is till you suffer my wrath."

Another pang slammed his temple, which throbbed mercilessly. He narrowed his eyes as pain racked his head.

"Never mess with a billionaire. You hear me, bitch? I'm coming for you."

He shot through an amber light turning red, his Ferrari growling in contempt.

"There's no place on earth you can hide from me."

He reached for the glove compartment, flipped open its door, and, gloating, withdrew a loaded SIG Sauer P226. Right where he had put it. He inserted it back into the glove compartment so he could concentrate on his driving.

He would be prepared for whatever awaited him. Some meddlesome psychic must be helping Libby. It was the only explanation. Libby by herself was helpless against the implacable supernatural power he wielded.

Chapter 70

Brady wished he knew how long Libby could continue breathing in the sealed cremulator. He had no idea. It didn't look much bigger than a coffin. If she was having trouble breathing, he hoped she would knock on one of the cremulator's walls to let him know he should open its door.

Brady knew Grainger lived in Bel Air. It shouldn't take him too much longer to get here, decided Brady, glancing at his wristwatch, if indeed Grainger had lost contact with his spirit and was suffering as a result. Brady was depending on Quentin's information that Grainger couldn't exist cut off from his spirit. If Quentin was bullshitting, Grainger would never show up at the crematorium. Brady didn't want to go there.

He stared at the front door. Grainger would be knocking on it soon.

The question was, what was he going to do when Grainger arrived? Convince Grainger to stop trying to possess Libby? Brady doubted Grainger would listen to him. The guy was a billionaire who bore Libby a grudge. He didn't take orders from anyone. He did as he pleased.

Brady hadn't thought out his plan to the end. What was he going to do to Grainger when the guy walked through the door? And he *would* walk through the door soon, because he wanted to reconnect with his spirit. He *had* to reconnect with his spirit or he would die if Quentin was to be believed.

Brady didn't see many options. To prevent Grainger from completing his possession of Libby, Brady would have to kill him. Otherwise, Grainger would reconnect with his spirit and sic it on Libby again, and this time it would complete its possession of her, zombifying her.

The trouble was Brady didn't have a gun.

He cast around the crematorium for something he could use as a weapon.

He continued his search, entering the kitchenette, stepping on fragments of dishes and glasses that the demon had hurled out of the cupboards. He picked up on the carving knife inserted in the knife block resting on the Formica countertop, which was also littered with glass fragments.

He withdrew the carving knife from the block. He detected a drop of dried blood on the blade. He wondered how blood had gotten on it. When the demon had possessed her, Libby must have used the carving knife to kill Carly at the demon's behest.

Brady wondered how well Libby was holding up inside the cremulator, imprisoned with the demon. Brady had to get her out of there ASAP. He didn't think she could resist the demon much longer. Brady could feel its power increasing despite its lack of connection with Grainger. In any case, Libby would suffocate if Brady didn't open the cremulator soon. He wished he knew how much air she had left. He had no way of finding out. He would have to listen for her signal indicating she couldn't breathe.

Knife in hand, Brady entered the main room. He peered inside the empty cremation chamber. He could feel heat emanating from it as it cooled down from its recent use.

He didn't want to kill Grainger, but what else could he do? Where was the guy? What was taking him so long?

Knife in hand, Brady paced around the room, burning off nervous energy. He realized he should conceal the knife. Grainger wouldn't enter the crematorium if Brady answered the door with a knife in his hand. Brady wedged the knife under his waistband at the small of his back. He would have to remember to keep facing Grainger to make sure the guy never glimpsed the knife.

Brady couldn't stop thinking about Libby's running out of air in the cremulator. Locked up with the demon, would she be able to continue to resist it? Maybe it couldn't possess her, since it was out of contact with Grainger. But Grainger would be here in no time, demanding to reunite with it.

Haunted by the image of Libby smothering to death, Brady willed Grainger to get here quicker even though he knew it didn't do any good. The idea of Libby smothering because of him terrified him. He didn't want to be responsible for another death of someone he cared about. Killing his mother was bad enough.

He considered calling the whole thing off and letting Libby out of the cremulator. But then the demon would escape and finish its possession of her. And Grainger wouldn't show up, because he had no call to, since he could reestablish contact with his spirit.

Brady had no choice. He had to wait for Grainger. He had to leave Libby inside the cremulator.

Tense with anxiety, Brady waited.

He almost jumped out of his skin when he heard knocking on the front door.

"He's here," Brady called out to Libby, hoping she could hear him, but somehow he doubted it if the cremulator was airtight.

Chapter 71

Time to beard the lion.

Brady felt for the carving knife wedged inside his waistband and proceeded toward the door, jacked up and primed for attack.

He twisted the doorknob and opened—

The two detectives Rafa and Anna stood at the door. Rafa looked particularly surly.

Shit. Brady hung his empty hands at his sides.

Rafa looked surprised to see Brady. "What are *you* doing here?"

"Visiting," said Brady, trying to figure out how he could get rid of them before Grainger pulled into the driveway, where they had parked their black-and-white.

"We're here to question Libby."

"She—can't come to the door."

"Why not? This is important. We're conducting an active murder investigation."

"She's busy," said Brady, breaking into a cold sweat, fearing Grainger would drive up when the cops were here and skedaddle when he spotted them.

Libby's supply of air was running out.

"Which part of 'active murder investigation' don't you understand?" said Rafa.

"Maybe *I* can help you."

"Let us in. We're not giving you a choice," said Rafa, his voice edged.

"What do you mean?"

"We have a warrant."

Rafa reached inside his blazer's interior breast pocket and produced a sheet of paper.

Brady didn't have a choice. He let the two detectives in.

"Now what's going on here?" said Rafa, casting around the crematorium.

"Nothing," said Brady. "What's the warrant for?"

"We have a warrant to search this place. Evidence at the scene of the murder at the Stacked Deck implicates Libby Genet in the murder. We're looking for the murder weapon and any other incriminating evidence located here."

Brady heard a car engine and saw through the open front door Grainger's Ferrari pull into the driveway and halt behind the LAPD patrol car. Rafa and Anna were gazing in the opposite direction, their eyes intent on Brady's face. Brady was careful not to show any emotion as he spotted Grainger's Ferrari.

Brady hoped Grainger didn't drive away on account of the cops' presence. Brady tried to think of a way to prevent Grainger from scramming, but he drew a blank.

"I don't know anything about any weapons," said Brady.

Over Rafa's shoulder Brady saw a figure climb out of the Ferrari driver's seat. Grainger must know he was running out of time and had to reunite with his spirit or he would succumb.

Grainger strode past the black-and-white and made for the front door.

"How are you involved in this?" said Rafa, scrutinizing Brady's face. "That's what I want to know."

Grainger entered the front door, gun in hand, his face drawn.

"Where is it?" he asked Brady.

Rafa wheeled around at the sound of Grainger's voice. "Put that gun down."

Grainger trained his SIG on Rafa.

"This is important," said Grainger. "I have no time to waste."

"You're gonna do time for assaulting a police officer. Put that gun down," said Rafa, reaching for his service revolver holstered in his shoulder rig.

Grainger shot Rafa twice in the chest. "I don't have time for this."

Fumbling his grip on his gun, Rafa crumpled to the floor, gasping.

Anna whipped out her FN 509 pistol.

Grainger pumped her chest full of lead.

Coughing blood, she collapsed on the floor.

Brady threw up his hands, his eyes wide.

Enervated, Grainger pulled a face and trained his SIG on Brady. Grainger staggered forward.

Brady thought Grainger was going to fall. Brady circumspectly lowered his hands.

"Start talking," said Grainger, managing to keep his balance, brandishing his SIG in front of him, his face drained of blood.

"I don't—"

"Bullshit. You know what I want. Where is it?" said Grainger, drawing a bead on Brady's head with the SIG even as he struggled to keep upright.

"If you shoot me, you'll never find out," said Brady.

"I could kneecap you, moron," said Grainger, aiming at Brady's knee. "You wanna be a cripple for the rest of your life?"

"I'll tell you," said Brady, careful to continue facing Grainger, keeping the knife snugged in his waistband out of sight.

His face beaded with sweat, Brady edged toward the cremulator. He knew Grainger was desperate. Nobody but a guy unhinged by desperation would shoot two cops. Grainger would go to jail for the rest of his life if anybody fingered him. Brady could finger him, having witnessed the two murders. Brady figured Grainger would kill him whether he opened the cremulator or not. But Grainger didn't know how to open the cremulator. He would have to keep Brady alive to open it before killing him.

Brady edged toward the cremulator computer, sneaking his hand behind his back.

"I don't have all day," said Grainger, shaking his head, trying to clear it and prevent himself from falling, his SIG leveled at Brady.

Brady flinched when he heard knocking inside the cremulator. Libby must be running out of air.

"What was that?" said Grainger, lowering his SIG a fraction as he scoped out the cremulator.

Brady watched Grainger's knees begin to buckle.

Brady snagged the carving knife from his waistband and plunged the blade into Grainger's side.

Caught off guard, groaning, dropping his SIG, Grainger reeled backward and fell onto the conveyor belt in front of the cremation chamber, writhing in pain.

Brady pricked up his ears when he heard more thumping inside the cremulator. This time the thumps sounded feebler. Libby was losing energy as her supply of air ran out. He turned on the conveyor belt with Grainger moaning on it. The belt carried Grainger into the oven.

Brady pressed the computer button to open the cremulator and pelted to the machine's door, which was sliding open. He whipped out the sage in his trouser pocket to prevent the demon from leaving with Libby.

Her face blue, lying on her back, Libby gasped for breath as the conveyor belt transported her out of the cremulator.

Brady waved the sage leaves in front of the opening cremulator.

Chapter 72

Libby glimpsed the crematorium ceiling with relief, realizing she was outside the suffocating confines of the cremulator.

I'm the only one that cares for you. Open your arms to me. Let me in. You can't trust anyone else. I'm the only one you can trust.

"I can still hear that voice inside my head," she said, seeing Brady standing over her as the conveyor belt conveyed her supine body toward him.

"Grainger's here," said Brady, holding out the sage leaves, trying to prevent the demon from leaving the cremulator.

"Where?" said Libby, sitting up on the conveyor belt and looking around the crematorium, fear in her eyes.

"In the oven."

Libby leapt off the belt and with shock in her eyes took in the dead cops sprawled on the floor.

"What happened?" she said. "Why did you kill the cops?"

"It wasn't me. It was Grainger."

"Why did you let the cops in?"

"They had a warrant to search the place. They suspected you killed the guy at the strip joint last night."

Libby looked at Grainger writhing and grimacing in the cremation oven.

"What do we do with him?" said Libby.

Brady waved the sage in front of the cremulator's open door, trying to fend off the demon.

"Is the demon still trying to possess you?" he said.

Kill the scammer rapist Brady. You can't trust him. Trust me. Kill him now.

"He's still here," said Libby. "He's still in my head."

"The sage isn't keeping the demon trapped. It's gonna reunite with Grainger and empower him. He's got one foot in the grave as long as he's separated from his spirit. He's gonna recover quickly if we don't do something to prevent them from reuniting."

Libby dashed to the computer and turned on the retort.

The flames in the oven roared to life, engulfing Grainger.

Grainger released an ungodly scream that shredded Libby's nerves.

"I can't close the oven door," said Libby, pressing a button on the computer with no effect.

The nauseating reek of burning hair and flesh wafted into the crematorium.

Grainger screamed in horror as yellow tongues of fire consumed him. Flipping onto his belly, he tried to squirm out of the oven.

Libby heard the agonized, desperate voice in her head.

Turn it off. Turn it off.

Libby latched onto the wire broom and shoved it into the oven into Grainger's face, preventing him from crawling out.

"Help," he cried. "Help me."

Libby saw melting flesh drip from Grainger's howling face. She couldn't stand it. She turned her face away, but she kept the broom in place, blocking his exit.

Nodding at her actions, Brady watched her. "It's the only way."

Libby firmed her resolve.

"Get out of my head, you bastard," she hollered into the retort.

"The demon will die with Grainger," said Brady.

"I'm gonna be sick," said Libby, breathing the necrotic air, continuing to shove the broom against Grainger to prevent him from crawling out of the oven.

"Does that hurt?" she cried at Grainger.

"Bitch," he screamed in anguish, the flesh on his face blazing and melting, his eyeballs boiling. "Turn the oven off."

She stared in revulsion at him.

"I've figured out why evil exists," said Brady, his face gaunt.

"What?" she said.

"When I was in the asylum, I had a lot of time to think. I kept wondering why evil exists. I believe I know the answer."

"I don't care why. I just want it gone."

"Do you?" said Brady, eying her. He paused. "I believe it exists because we *want* it to exist."

"We want grief and misery in our lives?" said Libby in disbelief. "Because that's what evil brings."

"We don't want the grief and misery part. But we want evil to exist."

"Why?"

"Because—because it's exciting."

"That makes no sense."

"Does anything about life make sense?"

Sneering at Grainger, Libby heard his final yelps of horror as he burned to death.

"How are we gonna explain this?" said Libby, realizing her and Brady's peril.

She put down the broom.

Brady mulled it over. "Grainger killed the cops and fell into the oven after the cops shot him."

He retrieved Anna's pistol from the floor and shot Grainger, who had ceased shrieking and weltering. Brady fired another slug into Grainger's chest for good measure.

Brady used his handkerchief to wipe his prints off the pistol grip and placed the pistol in Anna's motionless hand.

"I can't believe that godforsaken demon voice is out of my head," said Libby. "Do you know how many people it made me kill?"

She wanted to confess to the cops to get it off her chest. On the other hand, she knew they would never believe a demon had made her murder her victims. The cops would cart her off to jail, where she would rot for the rest of her life. She couldn't tell anyone. Nobody could understand but Brady. She would have to carry her burden of guilt to the grave without telling another soul if she wanted to remain free. The murders she had committed were her and Brady's secret.

"I hope it doesn't come back," said Brady.

Libby did a double take, her apprehension rising. "I thought you said it died with Grainger."

"Evil always comes back in one form or another," said Brady, brooding, feeling too old for his years.

"Then we're damned to suffer at its hands forever."

"And to fight it forever."

Tandy scampered into the room, meowed, and rubbed his head against Libby's leg.

Smiling, Libby looked down affectionately at him.

Tandy's glittering lime eyes stared up at her, mesmerizing her.
Kill him. I'm your only friend. Get the carving knife and kill the rapist murderer. Cut off his face and feed it to me.

ABOUT THE AUTHOR

Multi-award-winning author Bryan Cassiday writes horror fiction and thrillers. His postapocalyptic horror thriller *Horde (Zombie Apocalypse: The Chad Halverson Series Book 6)* won both the Independent Press Award for Best Horror Novel 2022 and the American Fiction Award for Best Horror Novel 2021. His Scott Brody thriller *Threads* won the Independent Press Award for Best Thriller Novel 2023 and the American Fiction Award for Best Hard-Boiled Crime Novel 2022. He lives in Southern California.